PARTY FAVOURS

PARTY FAVOURS

A NOVEL

JEAN DOE

A Phyllis Bruce Book
HarperCollins*PublishersLtd*

This is a work of fiction. While some people referred to are real individuals, the events and conversations in this novel are completely imaginary. The political world created, while it may appear to be real, is, in fact, an invention on the part of the novelist.

http://www.harpercollins.com/canada

First edition

Canadian Cataloguing in Publication Data

Doe, Jean
Party favours : a novel

"A Phyllis Bruce book".
ISBN 0-00-224562-0

I. Title.

PS8557.0229P37 1997   C813'.54   C97-931650-2
PR9199.3.D529P37   1997

97 98 99 ❖ HC 10 9 8 7 6 5 4 3 2

Printed and bound in the United States

R.L.: To me ma an' all o' dem who live down by de sea.

"The job of satire is to frighten and enlighten."
— Richard Condon

"Politics is for abnormal people."
— Lech Walesa

CHAPTER ONE

Bullshit.

As I stood there with my colleagues in the press corps, separated from the political types by velvet ropes and Rideau Hall's watchful aides-de-camp, I was hit — not for long, mind you, but long enough for me to remember it now — by a bit of nausea. *Boom*. Just like that — like biting into a piece of mouldy cheese.

Most of the time, I made a conscious effort not to succumb to that sort of thing. To me, post-Watergate reporters were far too cynical about politics, and the people who practised it. But on this one occasion, as the new government of Robert Laurier was about to take office, and as I waited to record the brief swearing-in ceremony for the news service that employed me, I was momentarily aware that, everywhere I looked in Rideau Hall's crowded ballroom, bullshit was in ample evidence.

Ministers-to-be preened themselves in their chairs, family bibles in hand, ready to take the oath of office from the Clerk of the Privy Council, silently repeating *bons mots* they had rehearsed to deliver at a hoped-for press scrum. A few rows behind them, looking tired, was a gaggle of senior people from Laurier's personal political staff at the Prime Minister's Office, flush with an exaggerated self-importance, and pretending to be bored. A dozen or so political assistants-to-be buzzed around the periphery of the room, trying to catch the eyes of the PMO staff or the big hitters in the mob of Press Gallery types, wishing they had scored a ticket for one of the seats reserved for the newly minted ministers and their families. And, pressed up against the south wall, there was me, Canadian Press newcomer Christopher O'Reilly, and a swarm of the ink-stained men and women who made up the Parliamentary Press Gallery — the ones who, a lot of the time, were the biggest bullshitters of all: the ones who laboured under the misapprehension that what they wrote or broadcast could consign entire governments to the ashes of history. Or, if they were properly seduced, raise governments from the ashes, too.

"Bullshit theatre" Robert Laurier's predecessor as Liberal Party leader had called these staged encounters between the patricians of the political class and the grasping media horde, and he was right. There hadn't been much to distinguish the leadership of Jack Gibson, the deconstructed jock and booze-hound who had briefly secured the Grit leadership through good looks and not much else. But occasionally Gibson would loosen the grip of Johnnie Walker long enough to surprise us all with some pithy bit of wisdom, like the "bullshit theatre" line. And if there was ever an instance of "bullshit theatre," this was it. Laurier had invited Gibson along with every other living Liberal Party leader to the swearing-in — and there he sat, no longer as robust or handsome as he once was, grinning and waving at whoever came too close. I had no doubt that, had Gibson somehow conjured up an electoral win, he wouldn't have bothered to invite his archrival Robert Laurier to the swearing-in. But Laurier had made sure to invite Gibson, and I found that encouraging, somehow. Maybe Laurier wouldn't be such a bad Prime Minister after all.

I looked up to the front of the ballroom, where Laurier was standing awkwardly beside the Governor General and his wife, waiting for the singing of the national anthem and the beginning of the ceremony.

He was, and always had been, a funny-looking fellow, with oversized ears and a lopsided grin. He was an Albertan, unlike his illustrious predecessor of the identical surname, Sir Wilfrid, which made him a true Ottawa outsider. He was a franco-Albertan, he never tired of reminding us, from a farm up north of Edmonton, and he had made his outsider status work for him. As he stood there in his ill-fitting blue suit, I was struck — for about the millionth time — by how readily I could picture him as someone's favourite uncle Bobby, serving burgers by the barbecue, telling bad jokes to the kids. The mantle of Prime Minister did not hang easily, yet, on his broad shoulders. The jury was still out, for me.

Robert Laurier — they called him "Bobby" — had been the compromise candidate, the one the party delegates had turned to, three years earlier, with a lot of hope, but not much apparent enthusiasm. During his tenure as Opposition leader, he had seemed distracted and uninterested in his job, like some Off-Broadway actor waiting for the call to the big time. He appeared to be content with watching the Tories' poll numbers disintegrate, playing golf and doing a lot of fundraising dinners. But — to give him his due — when the writ was finally dropped, he campaigned like a pro, rushing from church basement to bus stop to podium, looking as if he was having the time of his life. Because he had known my dad, he had granted me two or three lengthy year-end interviews, which was a bit of a coup for a media newcomer to Ottawa, as I was. In each interview, he had told me — off the record, of course — what he would do to reverse the Grits' decade of crushing defeats.

"In any election, Chris," he said, his accent thick, "you have two buttons to push. You got hope, an' you got fear. I'm going to win dis ting wit' hope. And I'll let de other guys talk about fear. It's simple."

It hadn't seemed all that simple to me, to be honest, but when the election rolled around, I finally saw what Laurier had meant. The country was weary of almost ten years of slavish devotion to parsimony and mean-spiritedness masquerading as government policy; it was fed up with the politics of fear. The Conservative government was not interested in dissenting voices. But in every province, including the right-wing ones like Alberta and British Columbia, people were angered and frustrated by supper-time newscasts featuring stories about homeless children — and by televised images of block-long lineups at food banks. Even among the debt-and-deficit purists, the country seemed to be sliding, perceptibly, towards some sort of American-style social Darwinism, where nobody gave a damn about anybody else.

I remembered one campaign stop outside of Prince Albert, where Laurier climbed up onto a farmer's tractor — his sleeves rolled, his tie loosened, his jacket long-discarded — and gave one of the best political performances any of us had ever seen. The Saskatchewan sun was beating down, hard, and the sky seemed to go on forever. It was a beautiful spot, and the TV guys were in love with the visuals, but the print gang was cranky: there hadn't been any real news since the televised debates, about a week earlier, and the Grits were cruising with a lead of about twenty points. As a result, most of the press were looking for something to criticize about Laurier and his campaign, which had turned into the classic "low-bridging" exercise — lots of photo-ops, little in the way of content. At that point in the election, Laurier pretty much had it in the bag, and nothing short of an Act of God was going to change that. So Laurier had decided to ditch the stump speech.

He pointed down at one of the farmers, an older guy who had retreated from the halo of microphones that surrounded his tractor.

"Dat man, dere, is a friend of mine," said Laurier, his voice hoarse, but loud enough to be heard without any amplification. "Before today, I hadn't met him face to face. His name is John Oczkowski. A few weeks before the campaign began, he wrote me a letter." He pulled a piece of paper out of his shirt pocket. "Dis letter." *Click click click*: the press photographers recorded the gesture, as they are wont to do whenever a politician flings his or her arms about.

"When you are Leader of the Opposition, you get a lot of letters. Last year, my staff tell me I got more dan a hundred thousand. When you get dat many letters, you don't have enough time to read dem all. But sometimes my staff come in to my office and show me de good ones. And dis is a good one."

He started to read it, occasionally stumbling over a few words, as he usually did when he was obliged to read something (especially in English). But after a little while, I don't think many of us were noticing.

"Dear Mr. Laurier," he read. "My name is John Oczkowski. I am a farmer from near Albertville, Saskatchewan. My wife's name is Debbie, and I have three sons. My grandparents came to Canada from Ukraine almost one hundred years ago, because they believed they could find freedom and food for their children. We have lived near Albertville for almost all of that time. And we are proud Canadians. We pay our taxes, and we obey the laws, and we send our children to school."

Laurier paused, and looked up to see if we were listening. We all were, frankly, because we didn't know where he was going with John Oczkowski's letter. He read on. "For the past eight years or so, the grain prices have been bad. We have been getting deeper and deeper into debt. My two oldest boys quit college, and came home to help me out. Our youngest, Peter, was in junior high school in Albertville. He would help after school, and on the weekends. He got worried because we were worried. I tried to talk to the bankers about refinancing, but they told me there wasn't very much that they could do. They seemed as if they wanted to help. But they said we would lose our family's farm if things didn't pick up. They said I should try to get some help from the FEB." This was the Farmer's Equity Board, a controversial Conservative government innovation that answered to the Agriculture minister, Prentice Johnston, Saskatchewan's sole representative at the cabinet table. Johnston was a legend in Ottawa — always at the centre of various sleazy kickback allegations, but always seeming to be one step ahead of the RCMP. And always getting re-elected.

Laurier continued reading the letter. "I went to one of Mr. Johnston's political meetings with my brother and my three sons, so I could ask him for help. There were a lot of Conservative people there. There was a big barbecue before, and I think a lot of them had been drinking. Mr. Johnston gave his speech, and then I stood in line to ask my question. I wanted to know why his party had forgotten about people like us. So I asked him, and Mr. Johnston got mad. He said a lot of things about competition, and how government couldn't 'coddle' people like me anymore. I got mad, too, because my sons were there, and I have never been coddled by anyone in my life. I told him his government didn't give a damn about the farmers. Someone tried to push me away from the microphone, and I pushed back. There was a bit of a scuffle, and one of Mr. Johnston's fellows punched me in front of my boys. It was nothing serious. But my youngest boy, Peter, was very upset. He is a sensitive boy. He cried all the way home. For a week after that, he wouldn't talk."

Laurier lowered his voice to a whisper, and his face reddened. At first, he seemed to be angry. Then, from where I was standing near the campaign bus, his eyes seemed to be getting teary. "Two days ago, Mr. Laurier, we buried Peter in our family's plot. He did not leave a note, so Debbie and I do not know why he took his life. He got up one night while the rest of us were sleeping, and he ran a hose from the exhaust of the pickup into the cab. His mother found him the next morning."

Laurier had tears streaming down his face at this point, and his voice was quavering. I looked over at John Oczkowski, who was also crying, his face turned away from the cameras, some of which were now pointing his way. I shot a quick look at some of my colleagues — and a few of *them* were sniffling, too. This was the rarest of times in a political campaign: a moment of genuine emotion. Laurier continued: "It may have been the pressure from losing the farm, or it may have been something inside him. We don't know. I am writing to you, Mr. Laurier, because you come from a farm family in Alberta, and because I admire you. If you win this election, I want you to promise that, in a country like Canada, a man will not be punched in front of his sons because he has an opinion."

Laurier looked up from the letter and said nothing. This was one of those things that could go two ways, politically. It could blow up in Laurier's face, with lots of columnists pounding him for raising a child's death in an election campaign. Or it could go another way. Laurier waited; there was silence. No cell phones, no whispering aides. Not a sound. "John Oczkowski," he finally said, so quiet the audio guys had to move their microphones closer. "John, I promise you. I make dat promise, an' I make it to everybody who can hear me right now. Dis is de greatest country in the world. An' I have served it for tirty years. An', if I am elected, you will be heard. *You will be heard.* You will be heard by me, and by my government. We work for you — not de other way 'round. Dat is all I have to say."

And with that, he stepped off the tractor into a circle of farmers, all of them slapping his back and shaking his hand, some of them still weeping. They were quickly ringed by television cameras. It was, by unanimous decision, a massive political home run. With a single letter, Bobby Laurier — and John Oczkowski — had dispatched old Prentice Johnston to political oblivion, and delivered every Saskatchewan seat to the Liberals. *Bang.* Just like that — right out of the ballpark. Even though I had been covering national politics for the Canadian Press for only three years, I knew I had seen something remarkable. On election night, the pundits would call it the letter that wiped out the Tories for good.

And now I was standing in Rideau Hall's historic ballroom. Sure enough, there at the back was John Oczkowski and his wife, looking nervous and thrilled at the same time.

Bobby Laurier had invited them to the swearing-in, too.

*　　　*　　　*

The strains of the national anthem faded away, and the ceremony finally began. After the first two or three ministerial swearing-ins, it got pretty boring. For me, there weren't many surprises. I looked around the ballroom, which was as beautiful as the rest of Rideau Hall. Sitting on an estate south of the Ottawa River, the place was about 150 years old and, unlike many other official residences, was still in one piece. Those of us in the Press Gallery generally only got to see the viceregal villa whenever a new cabinet was sworn in. I suppose it would have been possible to view the place more often, such as when Orders of Canada are handed out, or when a new ambassador presents his or her credentials to the Governor General. But, to me, that would be about as exciting as listening to Robert Laurier's election stump speech again. Which is to say, pretty dull.

"Hey, O'Reilly, you young twerp," someone whispered, to my left. I looked over. It was Joey Myers, my buddy from Southam News.

He edged over, squeezing his sizable belly past the CBC technician running the pool camera. Joey was the archetypal print guy: thinning hair, a beard that looked as if it had never been groomed, shiny little eyes that didn't miss a trick.

With his girth, and his perpetual jolliness, it was no surprise that he was pressed into dressing up as Santa Claus, every year, at the Christmas party the Press Gallery executive threw for reporters' kids. Because he was Jewish, the Santa Claus role amused him tremendously. "Imagine me, a good Jew, being asked to be Santa Claus, the very symbol of Christian capitalism. Tut tut," he'd say, then laugh.

"You twerp, O'Reilly," he repeated, this time loud enough for one of the aides-de-camp to shoot us a warning look. "See this?"

I looked down at his tattered, coffee-stained Hilroy notepad, which was filled with his impenetrable scrawl. The page he was pointing to had been filled about a week earlier; I had given him my predictions for who would get what portfolio in Laurier's cabinet. Halfway through the ceremony, it appeared that I was ten-for-ten. Joey's own predictions had been spectacularly wrong. Apart from the Prime Minister, he hadn't gotten one right. Even old journalistic hacks can get things wrong, I guess.

Joey squinted at me and wagged a finger. "So who is it? Who are you screwing at PMO? Who's your source, you awful man?"

"Well, if the truth must be told," I said, "I'm sleeping with your good friend Flash Feiffer. He's real sexy. And he sings like a canary."

At this, Joey started giggling uncontrollably, and loudly enough for the severe young aide-de-camp to tell us to shut up, or else. Joey ignored him and continued to snort quietly. Both of us looked towards the front of the ballroom, where Bernie Feiffer — or, as he was sometimes called, Flash — sat sprawled in a seat, his skinny frame swallowed up in an ancient polyester suit. Flash Feiffer was Bobby Laurier's political fixer, the guy who got unpleasant things done. He was even less attractive than his boss, with a handshake that was limper than a noodle, and eyeglasses thicker than the bottom of a Coke bottle. But Flash was a legend in Ottawa political circles, for his smarts and his ability to always keep Laurier focused on the big picture. He was also, I had learned on the day I first met Joey Myers, legendary for something else: his penis.

On that memorable day three years earlier, Joey and I had both taken one of the tiny green Parliament Hill buses up to Kingsmere, the estate used by the Speaker of the House of Commons. The Speaker was throwing his annual garden party, and — being new in town, and a little lonely — I figured it would be a good place to meet some people.

So I climbed onto the bus, and was minding my own business, when a huge, sweaty figure lumbered up the steps and crashed into the empty seat beside me. He eyed me for a moment, then reached across his belly to extend me his hand.

"I'm Joey Myers, Southam hack," he said. He had a bit of a Brit accent. "You must be the boy wonder CP hired, right?"

I shook his hand and winced a little. Because of my age (I was in my mid-twenties at the time) and because of my recent history (I had won a National Newspaper Award for an investigative piece I did for CP, when covering the B.C. legislature), my arrival in Ottawa had been the subject of a lot of Press Gallery carping and criticism. Many of my colleagues, I guessed, were annoyed that I had leapfrogged over some older veterans to get the coveted national bureau job. Joey confirmed this.

"Listen, young man, some folks say you got this gig because you had connections," he commented, as the bus bumped across the bridge into Hull. "But I read that stuff you did on those wackos out in B.C. Nice work. Ottawa's a lot different from Victoria, though, and you need to know what to watch out for."

And with that, Joey launched into a three-hour dissertation about who was who in Ottawa, and who is a good guy, and who isn't. Because Bobby Laurier had just won the Liberal Party's leadership convention in Calgary, much of Joey's commentary — interrupted only long enough to inhale some of the Speaker's peeled shrimp, or ogle young female Tory political staffers — concerned what he considered to be the most interesting member of Laurier's entourage. Or, to be precise, the member *belonging* to a member of Laurier's entourage — Flash Feiffer's appendage. "You should see it, O'Reilly," said Joey, his arms extended wide, narrowly missing a waiter and a cheese tray. "The guy's penis is so huge, it looks as if he's carrying a bag of groceries in his pants."

The rest of the evening continued in a similarly juvenile fashion: Joey dreaming up newer and more colourful analogies relating to the size of Flash Feiffer's penis, and me trying to stop laughing. We became instant friends.

＊　　　＊　　　＊

Standing there in the august surroundings of Rideau Hall, remembering, we both grinned as we stared at Flash. He caught us looking and gave a little wave. Joey started to giggle again.

The swearing-in continued without much fanfare for another few minutes. It was stupendously boring. Some reporters and guests started whispering to each other. For the most part, Laurier hadn't taken any chances: every region was represented with either a full or junior cabinet post. The members of Parliament who had been big Laurier supporters during the Jack Gibson years were in the majority, which was no big surprise. Some of these loyalists, however, were not what you could call towering intellects. The Saskatchewan choice was a long-time Grit hack who had run, unsuccessfully, for every elected position extant until being swept to office on the Bobby Laurier tide. The Alberta pick was a woman who was known to have slept with every Liberal Party leader since the early 1960s. One of the Quebec ministers was a tiny fellow called "Papa Smurf" because, well, he looked like one. Apart from John Derbyshire, a long-time source, the Atlantic picks were notable for little. And so on. The whispering continued.

Everything became very quiet again, however, when Jean Rioux rose from his seat. The various blow-dried TV types assembled behind us immediately started to tell the pool cameraman not to miss anything. Press photogs craned for a better shot. Oblivious to all this, Rioux stepped out into the centre aisle, pausing for a moment to pat Jack Gibson on the shoulder. Rioux — called "One-Eyed Johnny" by Joey, because he wore an eyepatch — had been the runner-up to Laurier at the Liberal leadership. It was widely believed that Gibson, who loathed Laurier, had done everything he could short of an open endorsement, which would have been a scandal, to ensure that Rioux won the leader's post.

Although Rioux was Montreal-born, and Gibson was older and from Toronto, the two men had a lot in common. Both were wealthy blue-chip lawyers, and both travelled easily in corporate boardrooms. Both were telegenic, and had been born to old money and Big Liberal families. To most observers, Rioux seemed to have more political smarts than Gibson. Like Gibson, he was rumoured to consider Laurier an intellectual lightweight, but, when the leadership race ended, he seemed to behave himself. Rioux had been considered a shoo-in for the Finance minister's post, if he wanted it, and he did. After the Prime Minister, it was the most powerful position in cabinet.

Rioux walked slowly down the aisle towards the Clerk of the Privy Council. With his tailored suits, and his excellent posture — and the eyepatch, which became a necessity after a decades-old encounter with a friend's tennis racket — Rioux certainly looked impressive. But Joey scowled.

"What's the matter, Joey? You still hate One-Eyed Johnny?"

"There's something about the guy, don't ask me what it is," Joey said. "I just don't trust him. He's too bloody slick by half, the pirate. Did you see the stunt he pulled in today's *Citizen*?"

I shook my head. Joey told me that Rioux had let it be known that he would never use his ministerial Buick — that he would drive himself, or take cabs. The *Citizen* had run a fawning story about it. Joey called it "suck-hole politics." For a millionaire like Rioux, he said, it was a meaningless gesture, calculated to grab a few cheap headlines and make the rest of cabinet look like big spenders.

"I think you're reading too much into it," I responded. "I don't think Rioux is so bad."

Jean Rioux took the oath of office in French, then stepped a few paces to his left to shake Bobby Laurier's hand. Rioux was all smiles and *bonhomie*, seemingly unwilling to let go. Laurier looked as if he didn't know how to get his hand back.

"Doesn't seem to be any bad blood there," I said to Joey, who was still scowling at Rioux.

"Don't be such a sap, O'Reilly," he retorted. "Rioux knows every fucking camera in Central Canada is pointed his way. He's pouring it on to avoid a repeat performance of that night in Calgary."

Joey was referring to a minor incident that, in my view, had been grossly overanalysed. More often than not, I found that some of my more jaundiced Press Gallery colleagues attached more significance to minor political slip-ups — fumbled footballs, lost luggage, you name it — than they did to things like a politician's voting record, his or her speeches, or the platform he or she had endorsed. The minor slip-up in question came on the final night of the Liberal leadership campaign, following the voting. All of the losing candidates — Jean Rioux, an anti-abortion lunatic, and Annie Frosini, the only woman who had bothered to contest the leadership — stepped onto the Saddledome stage to greet Laurier and his wife, Michelle.

Emerging from the biggest and craziest scrum I had ever seen in my life, Laurier clambered on stage, waving to the delegates, who were giving him a noisy ovation. Sweat gleaming on his face, Laurier shook the hand of the anti-abortion nut. He was hugged by Annie Frosini, who seemed genuinely happy. And then he turned to find Rioux — but Rioux had moved to the far side of the stage. There he stood, on the very edge of the platform, waving to the crowd, clapping, dancing a little in his Gucci loafers. About twenty thousand pairs of eyes watched Laurier to see what he would do. Was it a simple gaffe or a deliberate snub? Would Laurier go over to Rioux, or vice versa?

Looking more embarrassed than annoyed, Laurier made his way over to shake the hand of the millionaire he had whipped — despite his money, despite his good looks, despite his media skills — on one ballot, in record time. After a fashion, Rioux shook Laurier's hand. From where I was standing — on the convention floor, near the feet of Annie Frosini and the anti-abortion nitwit — it looked fine. But to many of the grey-beards in the gallery, Rioux's handshake looked forced. To Joey Myers, it was and remained an Olympic-sized *faux pas*.

Now, as the swearing-in continued, Jean Rioux glided away. But, judging from the reaction of the media and the political staffers — and even a few of the other ministers — it was clear that Rioux had already been designated "The Man to Watch." He returned to his seat, stopping for a moment to whisper in the ear of an undersized man wearing an earring and a flashy suit. It was Mike Mahoney, Rioux's frenetic political right arm. He didn't look like much, but I knew he was an impressive media manipulator. Most of the Press Gallery considered him to be the smartest assistant on the Hill.

Mahoney caught me watching the exchange with Rioux and turned on a high-watt smile. He held up an imaginary phone to his ear and pointed at me. He was mouthing some words.

"What is he trying to say?" I asked Joey.

"He's probably intending to bed you, like he has most of the Liberal caucus in the Senate," answered Joey, who tends to be a homophobe. "That way, you'll write nice stories about nice Jean Rioux."

I turned to Joey, surprised despite myself. "He sleeps with people to get good stories?"

Joey laughed. "You are ever the innocent, O'Reilly. In this town, *everyone* sleeps with people to get good stories." In Ottawa, it seems, everything is up for grabs, including your sexuality.

＊　　＊　　＊

Back at the Wellington Street rabbit warren that Canadian Press called its national bureau, I sat on my desk and scrolled through my voice-mail messages. There were quite a few. One from the CP Ottawa bureau chief, Kevin Ritchie, reminding me about my assigned news analysis of who were the movers and shakers in the new Laurier cabinet. One from the guy at Sam the Record Man, to tell me the Jimi Hendrix bootleg I'd been looking for was in. One from Joey, recorded before the swearing-in, reminding me to meet him for a beer at the Press Club after I'd filed for the day. And one from my mother, Maureen.

"Christopher, it's your mother," she began, as if I wouldn't know. "Christopher, I've been watching the ceremony for the new cabinet on the TV, and I think Mr. Laurier has made some good choices, don't you? I particularly like the fact that he put that charming Annie Frosini in there, although he probably could have appointed a few more women. Anyway . . . the reason I called is to tell you that I picked up a copy of UBC's new law-faculty brochure, and I thought you should take a look at it. You need to think about your future, Christopher. It's what your father would have wanted. That's all for now, dear. I send my love, and God bless. Bye-bye."

That was the end of my voice mail, except for a breathless, chatty message from Mike Mahoney, asking me to give him a call "ASAP."

I replayed my mother's message and sighed. I was almost thirty years old, I had been a reporter for almost six years, I had won multiple journalistic awards, and my mother still hoped that my chosen career was a phase — like skateboarding, or wearing an earring, both of which I had done. My deceased father, Howard O'Reilly, had gone to law school at the University of British Columbia and had practised law in Victoria for most of his life. He had wanted me to go to law school, too, I think, but had never said as much. He left the lobbying effort to my mother, who never seemed to take no for an answer.

I stirred and picked up the phone to call Mike Mahoney at Jean Rioux's office. After I made my way through a couple of secretaries who sounded harried, Mahoney came on the line.

"Christopher O'Reilly," he said, oozing charm. "We need to talk and we need to talk fast. Whaddaya say to lunch, so I can try out my new Finance minister's office credit card?"

And so it all began.

CHAPTER TWO

From the air, from the window of an Air Canada 767 afternoon flight from Vancouver, Ottawa seemed — to me, at least — to be unusually fond of outdoor, in-ground swimming pools. As I squinted through the window, I lost count of the tiny, turquoise ovals arrayed on the ground below. Hundreds of them. Thousands, maybe.

It was a Friday in early July 1990. I was on my way to Ottawa to start my new job with the national bureau of the Canadian Press. As the plane continued its descent, I looked out over my new home, wondering what awaited me below.

It was not my first flight to Ottawa, of course. During the four-year period in which my father laboured as a backbench Liberal member of Parliament in the 1970s, I had been to the nation's capital many times in the company of my mother and my sister, Sheila. We travelled there making use of the fifty or so free air-travel passes MPs are given every year by Canada's major airlines, mainly during the summer, or at Easter. Thinking back, I could not recall seeing so many swimming pools.

The pools conjured up an image of the classical Ottawa bureaucrat: an overweight white male killing time as an information systems analyst somewhere deep in the shadowed recesses of Statistics Canada, let's say, scrambling home at 3:30 P.M. every July afternoon to slouch by his pool. He carried a briefcase, purchased at the Bay, that almost always contained little more than his lunch and the Ottawa *Sun*. He drove to and from work in a dented three-year-old Pontiac sedan. He voted Liberal. He earned much more than I did. And he had a swimming pool nestled alongside his suburban split-level, where he and his wife and their offspring congregated in the muggy Ottawa summer.

Although I did not know it at the time, this little bit of airborne stereotyping would turn out to be eerily realistic. Ottawa, I would soon learn, is like everything you have heard about it. But worse.

At the Ottawa "international" airport's single terminal building — a structure whose architecture was not unlike a well-upholstered, and large, mobile home — I looked around. A small billboard welcomed travellers to the city on behalf of a lobbying firm. Young men in expensive suits, probably Tory ministerial aides, muttered into cellular phones by the door to the VIP lounge. And, at the luggage carousel, waiting for my two huge hockey bags of belongings to be disgorged, I spied a couple of B.C.'s veteran New Democrat members of Parliament. I stood near them, eavesdropping.

Despite the rigours of the five-hour flight, the pair looked rested and unrumpled. They had a practised, *political* air to them: tanned, trim, good teeth, excellent postures. This sort of political species was new to me. They were certainly unlike the variant I was used to, in the wilds of British Columbia's legislature, where politicians did not seem to spend a lot of their disposable income on clothes or haircuts. Or personal hygiene.

The two MPs chatted about a successful town hall meeting one had sponsored a few days earlier. Finally, one of them — a fellow I recognized as Nils Andersen, the NDP's long-time House leader — turned my way and made a few good-natured remarks about Ottawa's infamous summertime humidity. Andersen was a good-looking guy in his forties, with a squared jaw and hair that was as blond and as shellacked as Malibu Ken's. There looked to be enough hair spray on his head to have punched a couple of substantial holes in the ozone layer. Andersen had the reputation of being a genial, middle-of-the-road New Democrat who had friends in every party. Years before, in fact, Jack Gibson had apparently come close to enticing Andersen into crossing the floor to the Liberals, to bolster the Grits' near-total lack of representation west of the Lakehead. But Andersen, sensing a Liberal rout in the offing, politely declined Gibson's offer. Smart move.

Andersen, clearly, was a pro. In just a few minutes, he had deftly extracted from me my name, my home town, my hotel destination, and — most significantly to him — my chosen career.

"I'm a reporter," I said.

Andersen's blue eyes brightened, and his eyebrows arched. He moved a lot closer, and I became the focus of all of his attentions. This was my first personal involvement with the Ottawa MP–reporter mating ritual; it would not be my last. Typically, it involved an MP making a reporter feel that he or she was the very centre of the known universe. Andersen grinned. "That so?" he said. "Who with?"

"Canadian Press," I said. "I've been transferred to the national bureau. Start next week."

Andersen's eyes were fixed on me like Krazy Glue. He seemed to be frantically scanning his internal Rolodex for my byline. To most politicians, and Andersen was one of them, forgetting a constituent's name was punishable by a lengthy prison term. Forgetting a reporter's name, particularly one from one's own province, was a capital offence.

"So you'll be working for Kevin Ritchie, Chris?" Andersen asked.

"Yeah. He recruited me. He hasn't told me what my beat will be yet, though."

"And, uh, where were you before?" He looked traumatized that he didn't already know. "You were working in, uh, B.C.?"

"I was at the legislature," I told him. "I was there for a couple of years."

"*Now* I remember!" Andersen boomed, loud enough to make a few people look our way. His NDP colleague was collecting her bags —

Louis Vuitton, no less. Some socialist. "You're the guy who did the Socred stories! The scandal stuff, right?"

"That's me."

"Listen, Chris," Andersen said, breathless. He whipped out one of his business cards. Scribbling a number on it, he handed the card to me. "Here's my business card, and that's my home number. When you get all settled in, let's have lunch, okay?"

"Sure," I replied, trying to act blasé, even though I was reluctantly impressed. Barely off the plane, and already politicians were trying to curry favour with me. Ottawa was *very* different. "I'll give you a call."

Andersen grabbed his suit bag off the carousel. Not a Louis Vuitton, but a pretty nice all-leather number. He winked and strode towards the exit doors, giving me a final wave as he went. I looked down at his business card. It had his name and photo and the Canadian coat-of-arms, stamped in the trademark House of Commons green ink, on one side. On the other, there was a quote from Robert Frost: "The middle of the road is where the white line is — and that's the worst place to drive."

I smiled. Any guy who quotes Robert Frost on his business card can't be all bad.

*   *   *

The self-doubts came flooding into my room with the daylight on Saturday morning, as I lay on the bed at the Hotel Claret, in unlovely downtown Hull, Quebec.

I'll make a confession: I may have been born a newspaperman, but I have never been very self-confident. I don't know why. I do know one of the reasons I love journalism is the vicarious thrill — the ego boost — that comes with seeing my byline in print. That probably sounds childish, but it's true. Part of my reluctance to try lawyering comes from my conviction that any successes I've experienced are largely due to luck or chance or instinct, but not anything resembling the sort of ability, intelligence and talent I saw in a lawyer like my father.

It's the same on the personal front. I've dated enough attractive and bright women, for example, but I always made certain to keep an eye trained on the exit door, just in case things got too serious. If they got serious, *ipso facto*, I would get dumped, or screw something up. I "arrived," as one perceptive former girlfriend told me, but I "never unpacked." She was right (and if she had ever seen my bedroom, she would have discovered she was literally right, too). Success, in whatever form it took, was a difficult concept for me to grasp. Most of the time, I considered it to be as attainable as a mint copy of the first British release of the first Jimi Hendrix album. Which is to say, not very.

Let me give you an example, one that concerns a career "success." While my friends, family and colleagues had applauded me for my National Newspaper Award, I remained utterly convinced that the whole thing was a fluke, a case of mistaken identity. At the awards banquet in Toronto a few months before my arrival in Ottawa, I sat at a table with some of the Canadian Press's Toronto bosses. They looked thrilled to death. I, meanwhile, felt as uncomfortable in my rented tuxedo as I did being there.

If I won, I told myself, it would be the result of media-industry politics — the need for one of the winners to be from the West, or the fact that the Canadian Press hadn't won a major reporting prize in two years. Anything, but not me or my stories. Even after I won — after posing for the obligatory photograph with CP management and the chairman of the awards ceremony, after getting my back slapped a dozen times, after seeing my name in fine print among the list of winners in the next morning's *Globe* — I remained disbelieving. It was a big joke. It had to be.

Over the years, I had received no end of lectures about all of this from my parents and my sister. They greatly disapproved of my museum-sized inferiority complex. My mother got genuinely upset about it more than once. "Christopher, you are a handsome young man, you are bright, you have so many friends," she had said at dinner one night, during a long weekend in my final undergraduate year at the University of British Columbia. She looked exasperated. "Why do you persist in running yourself down?"

"Yeah, Chris, why?" Sheila echoed. I scowled at her.

My mother had somehow learned that I had been nominated by two of my profs for a graduate scholarship at UBC — but she had learned about it from a friend who was a professor there. I hadn't told her, or my father. Why bother, I had figured; I wasn't going to win, anyway.

I glanced to my right, where my father was watching me. He looked bewildered and faintly annoyed all at once. A successful lawyer, a former MP, a likely choice to be a judge if the Liberals ever figured out a way to get back into power: Dad did not suffer from a lack of confidence. I knew he'd never understand. My beloved older sister, Sheila, was no help, either. She was engaged to a great guy, she had great marks in her final year of law school, she always looked great. I turned back to my mother.

"Mom, it's something I can't explain, okay? Let's just talk about something else."

"No, Christopher," she said, "we won't just talk about something else. Your father and I want to know why, after you were nominated for this very prestigious scholarship, you never said a word to any of us. And why, when we ask you if it is true, you react as if you hate the very thought of being recognized for your achievements."

"I don't know," I responded, playing with the remains of my spaghetti. "I just think that awards are a lot of bullshit, that's all."

"Christopher, I'll thank you not to use that kind of language," my mother huffed. My father gave her a go-easy look.

"It's all right, Maureen," he said. "Chris must have his reasons for not telling us."

Ouch. I would have preferred that he hit me instead.

*   *   *

I know many a son has believed that his parents didn't understand him. But mine, living a charmed life as they did in idyllic Victoria, largely didn't. They had come from back east in the late 1950s, before

Sheila and I had come along. My father, Howard O'Reilly, had been a Montrealer, from Notre-Dame-de-Grâce. He had come from a big Irish family, made up of about a dozen kids — I had aunts, uncles and cousins in every port, it seemed — and various hangers-on. They were poor, of course, but not as poor as most. With both my grandfather and my grandmother working at Bell Canada — my grandmother as an operator, my grandfather as a labourer — they were able to save enough money to send Howard, the brightest of the lot, to McGill. He got a B.A. in history, and then he applied to the university's law school. Back in those days, they didn't have anything like the Law School Admission Test, but they did have a quota system, in which a finite number of Jews, Catholics and so on were admitted. He was one of the three stipulated Catholics accepted by the law school, and he excelled. The law energized him; he loved it. He spent his spare time in court, watching the lawyers at work. And he participated in a lot of moot courts which, from what I've been told, are fake trials that law schools put on.

It was at one such moot court, at the University of Toronto, that he met my mother, Maureen Hall, a part-time secretary at the law school. When her father died, she had abandoned her own plans to pursue a degree in English at U of T, and was working to help her mother pay the bills. She was an only child. As my father told it, he and his McGill buddies were waiting in a hallway for the moot to begin, when my mother walked by. "That was it," my father said. "I couldn't concentrate much after that. We lost the moot, but I got your mother's address." They didn't give out phone numbers in those days, I guess.

They corresponded after that, and — when he could afford it, which wasn't often — my father would travel to Toronto by bus to see my mother, staying with an aunt and uncle who lived there. The romance culminated in marriage a couple of years following my father's call to Quebec's bar. Their honeymoon involved — is this hyper-Canadian or what? — riding the rails across the country in a tiny sleeper car. When they arrived in Vancouver, they fell in love with the place. After another year or so in Quebec, they saved up enough to move to B.C. Victoria was chosen because my father had heard they needed generalist lawyers there, which they did. He made a comfortable living, enough for my mother to stay home.

My sister was the first to arrive. Sheila, named after my dad's mother, was your typical first-born: bossy, autocratic, overbearing, self-confident. Like Dad, she excelled at school, winning scholarships and awards and essay contests. If she hadn't been my sister, I probably would have hated her.

I came along a couple years after Sheila. By then, my parents owned a small house on Beach Drive, towards Cordova Bay. I went to Our Lady of Lourdes Elementary School and, as near as I can recall, my early years were not distinguished by much of note. Except that I was in love with newspapers.

* * *

I was, and will always be, a newspaper guy. I still remember when I was eight or nine, sprawled on the floor of my father's den, the *Times-Colonist* spread out on the floor in front of me. It smelled good — it really did. I loved the smell of the ink on the newsprint. I loved the feel of the paper, and the look of it. As young as I was, I could imagine nothing as exciting as being a war correspondent or a sports writer, chasing after a breaking story, afraid of no one.

I mentioned this to my father, Howard, who was sitting at his desk, smoking his pipe. He was a handsome man, with Gaelic features that made him look merry even when he wasn't. He was tall, about six-four, and he had big hands. His hair was black with splashes of grey in it. As a recently elected Liberal member of Parliament, he was already not too big on the journalistic community, but he indulged me.

"And what's so great about being a reporter, Chris?" he asked.

"They get to see everything before everyone else does," I told him. "And then they get to tell everyone about it."

He laughed.

For many years, he would retell this story to friends and family, and he would laugh, a big, throaty, man's laugh, and look at me. I had always been the kid who would tear to the end of the driveway whenever I heard the wail of an ambulance or a fire truck — to see where it was going, to see if something heroic was about to happen. Then I would dash back to the house to tell my father — if he was back from Ottawa, or if the House wasn't sitting — what I had seen. The way I figure it, my veins are filled with printer's ink.

I was always the first in the family to read the *Times-Colonist*; I collected papers from our occasional family vacations in Seattle or Portland. I hoarded my father's copies of *Time*, which actually published a bona fide Canadian edition in those days; I watched CBC's *The National* religiously. Knowlton Nash was godlike, to me. Using an old Smith-Corona my mother had picked up at a garage sale on Shelbourne, I wrote up articles for a newspaper I titled, appropriately enough, the *O'Reilly News*. It was filled with stories about our family. My mother kept all six issues, and still has them hidden away somewhere in the house. She and Sheila will doubtlessly haul them out to embarrass me if I ever succumb to marriage.

What hooked me for life, ironically, happened at a newspaper that I had never even read. When I was still a kid, the *Times-Colonist*, and just about every other newspaper on the planet, ran stories by Bob Woodward and Carl Bernstein of the *Washington Post* about the break-in at the Watergate complex in Washington, and all of the revelations that followed it. Even though I had barely graduated from episodes of *Scooby-Doo*, I was transfixed by the Watergate scandal. To me, the political players were incidental: what was incredible was that two lowly journalists — a cop reporter and a court reporter, no less — were able to write things that would shake the most powerful nation on Earth, and knock off a President along the way. My father was drawn to the story for different reasons. As he later explained to me, he had been growing a little tired of the law, and had started to dabble in Liberal Party politics locally. The Watergate stories shook him to the core. "Sociologists like to say the North American public started to become cynical about politics after JFK was shot, or when the Vietnam War turned unpopular," my father told me much later. "But I trace it all back to Watergate. Before Watergate, people had some degree of confidence in public institutions. After that, they started to hate politicians. Just blind, irrational hate. And they still do." Why he decided to run for politics, despite that cynicism, was no great mystery: my father was unabashedly in love with Canada.

*   *   *

I reminisced about Bob Woodward and Carl Bernstein, and how glorious it would be to achieve only one-tenth of what they did, as I sprawled across the lumpy surface the Hotel Claret calls a bed. I had not slept well. The bed had been so slanted to one side, I had jammed a couple of cushions under the mattress in a vain effort to even it out. On top of that, the air conditioning had apparently broken down, and the humidity had hit me like a door swinging open in a sweaty locker room. As a Westerner, I did not have a lot of experience with the kind of climate Ottawans seem to accept as their lot in life.

My insecurity, magnified by fatigue, started to blossom into paranoia. The crumminess of the room, I started to suspect, was CP's way of telling me that I was not a valued member of the team. The fact that nobody from CP had greeted me at the airport — or even left a message for me at the hotel's reception desk — was the new agency's way of indicating, I figured, that my move to the national bureau was still controversial among my colleagues. And so on. I was probably going crazy.

The phone rang. It was my mother.

"Mom! What are you doing, calling so early?" It was about nine in the morning — meaning it was barely 6:00 A.M., Victoria time. Maureen O'Reilly was, among other things, an early riser. She had called at precisely the right moment. Just like a mother.

"I wanted to see how you are doing, dear," she said. "Did they put you up in a nice hotel?"

I looked around the room. A cockroach jogged under a peeling length of wallpaper, near the door. "It's great, Mom. Very nice. Nice place."

"Well, you should see if they can get you a room at the Château Laurier," she replied. Can't fool old Maureen. "That's where we usually stayed when your father was an MP, you know."

"I remember," I said. "By the way, thanks for the hockey bags, Mom. I couldn't have gotten all of my things here without them." Including my mini-stereo, and my prized collection of 124 Hendrix tapes, most of them bootlegs.

"Well, Christopher, I knew that if I had left it to you, you would have been travelling with your belongings stuffed into one hundred garbage bags." She was correct, of course. "When do you think you will get an apartment?"

"I'm going out to look for one this morning," I said, not relishing the prospect of apartment-hunting in the suffocating heat. "Once I buy a newspaper and something to eat."

"Well, if I might make a suggestion, you should take a guided tour around Ottawa, to see which neighbourhoods look nice. I remember Sandy Hill and the Glebe being nice areas for young people, but it's been a few years since any of us were in Ottawa. You should look around."

I took my mother's advice. After picking at my "continental" breakfast — a thimbleful of orange Tang, syrupy coffee and a croissant hard enough to play rugby with — I picked up Saturday's *Ottawa Citizen*. It was not an impressive newspaper. Like most Southam dailies, the paper had gone through a series of costly — and fruitless — design makeovers to recapture readership that was watching television, picking up one of the *Sun* tabloids or otherwise staying away in droves. It was a thick paper, with a respectable amount of advertising, but it didn't offer much in the way of groundbreaking Parliament Hill coverage. Most of its national stories, in fact, were scalped from the Canadian Press wire. I turned to the classifieds.

Because it was July, I supposed, the students of Ottawa's major post-secondary institutions — the University of Ottawa, Carleton

University and Algonquin College — had mostly fled town for summer jobs, or unemployment, back home. There were plenty of apartments available in my price range, although most seemed to be in the Centretown area, and not Sandy Hill or the Glebe. I circled a few promising prospects, and made my way down to rue Laurier, which ran parallel to the Ottawa River.

Hull was, without a doubt, a blight on the nation's landscape. No politician would ever say so publicly, of course, fearing being tagged anti-Quebec. But even Quebecers, as I would eventually learn, were prepared to offer the city as a nuclear test site.

A jumble of rundown convenience stores and strip joints, grimy three-storey apartment complexes and — at the entrance to the city, across from the Portage Bridge — a monstrosity of concrete and steel where a quarter of Ottawa's bureaucrats laboured: that was Hull. It was not much to look at. Two hundred years earlier, Hull had been settled by a group of New England farmers — before Ottawa itself was developed, in fact. Eventually, both towns were devoting themselves to sawing logs for the American market, and jobs were abundant. For more than a century, the rank odour of pulp drifted over the toniest neighbourhoods, and Parliament Hill itself. By the 1970s, all of that had changed, of course. Ottawa's exponential government-fed growth — coupled with Quebec's own discriminatory language policies in the same decade, and its separatist referendum in 1980 — had driven away lumber businesses and investors from places like Hull. From my hotel-room window, the area resembled postwar Berlin: prosperity, shiny new buildings and greenery on one side, the Ottawa side; and chronic unemployment, abandoned storefronts and cracked asphalt on the other side, the Hull side.

To alleviate Hull's undeniable economic hardships, successive federal governments had dumped truckloads of money into the place. They had built Place du Portage and Place de la Chaudière, the sprawling office complexes where thousands of federal bureaucrats passed the hours. These two collections of buildings, which were generally considered unsafe and unhealthy by the people who worked in them, had been erected by a couple of high-rolling contractors — with impressive Tory or Grit connections, naturally — who paid their workers in cash out of stacks of bills jammed into the trunks of their Lincoln Continentals. Among the departments located there were Public Works, Employment and Immigration, Labour, International Development and the Secretary of State.

Hull also played host to the new Museum of Civilization, on the riverbank facing Parliament Hill. The museum looked nice enough from the outside. But it, too, had a somewhat sordid history. Various Eastern Quebec Conservative MPs had been prosecuted for establishing a clumsy kickback scheme there. The participants included various contractors who had passed along enough cheques to the Tories to win one of the museum's fat contracts. If that wasn't bad enough, cheap materials had been used to erect the museum: water leaked all over various priceless artifacts whenever it rained, and some of the bricks were actually "exploding" from moisture that had found its way into the mortar.

No shortage of federal largesse had made its way north across the river into Hull. But however well intentioned, the pork barrel hadn't worked. Hull remained the national capital region's unsightly blemish. Its pimple.

*   *   *

I waved down a cab after a few tries. In some kind of a metaphor of Canada itself, Hull cabbies are not permitted to pick up fares in Ottawa, and Ottawa drivers are prohibited from doing likewise in Hull. I'm sure someone has a good reason for this arrangement, but I can't think what it might be. I headed across the Portage Bridge towards Parliament Hill. I had decided to check out the city in a guided tour. On an air-conditioned bus of some description, I hoped.

At the point where the deserted Sparks Street Mall met Elgin Street, beside the War Memorial, a whole raft of guided-tour operators was already working at enticing Japanese and American tourists to board. I found a bus that looked reputable and boasted air conditioning, and climbed in.

The tour was clearly a popular one. In a matter of minutes, quite a few tourists had filled the seats around me. The bus driver, a tall skinny guy in a uniform, jumped up the steps and greeted us.

"My name is Danny," he said. "Welcome to Confederation Boulevard Tours. We'll be visiting all sorts of interesting locations this morning, and you'll get a chance to get out and take pictures. If you have any questions, don't hesitate to let me know."

Danny slid into the driver's seat and pulled on a microphone headset. The bus moved away from the curb and turned west, then north. We were on Metcalfe Street, facing Parliament Hill. At the red light, Danny pointed left at a tidy white stone building facing north. This, he explained, was the American embassy. On cue, a snippet of "The Star-Spangled Banner" could be heard on the sound system. Everyone laughed. Danny pointed right, at a dark, dirty old building squatting at the corner of Metcalfe and Wellington streets. This, he said, was the Langevin Building, where the offices of the Prime Minister and his bureaucrats, the Privy Council Office, were located. To me, it didn't have the sort of visual appeal of a White House; it was grimy and looked unoccupied. A tinny segment of "O Canada" could be heard through the speakers. The fact that the U.S. embassy was physically closer to the House of Commons than the PMO building — and the fact that it was much nicer to look at — was, I recalled, an accident of history that had been commented upon by the likes of Pierre Berton or Peter C. Newman. If it hadn't been, it should be.

The bus moved through the green light and up onto Parliament Hill and turned right. Even though it was still somewhat early on a Saturday morning, tourists clutching cameras were milling all over the green lawn framed by the Centre Block, West Block and East Block. Bored-looking RCMP officers kept watch over them, occasionally shooing away a car that had lingered too long. Up ahead of us, Danny said, was the East Block. Built in the mid-1850s in a Gothic Revival style, Danny explained, the East Block was slightly more posh than its cousin across the way. It was the home to the offices of various ministers, veteran MPs and senators. Outside the building, three older men in blazers were talking animatedly. "It's early on Saturday morning, so there's no chance those three guys could be senators," Danny said in a stage whisper. I was the only person on the bus to laugh. I suspected he was a university student — his comments were more perceptive than your average tour guide.

The bus ground to a halt as Danny told us that, because it was a Saturday, no one would mind if we hopped out to take a few pictures for a minute or two. I didn't have a camera, but I joined a group of Japanese tourists in Nike runners on the sidewalk, where the humidity and heat had suddenly become a lot worse.

I edged towards the elderly trio Danny had pointed out. Although I did not know their names at the time — I do now — the three men were obviously all senators. Danny had been wrong. I listened for a minute or two. One of them, whom the others called Giovanni, was describing in elaborate detail the novel he was writing — presumably at taxpayers' expense. His balding pate shining in the sun, he related how he intended to include many sex scenes. The second senator, a gangly francophone with drooping eyelids and impressive eyebrows, related how he, too, planned to write a novel one day about the unholy influence exercised — and I am quoting him here — "by those goddamned Jews." This fellow, I later learned, was an enthusiastic supporter of the Arab side in the endless Middle East conflict because, as Joey Myers observed, their leaders "provided him with young males to sodomize during his frequent junkets in the region." The third senator said little, but the other two treated him with obvious deference. He was, I would discover, formerly a senior member of successive cabinets of Maurice Johnson Bechard in the 1960s and 70s, was once the most powerful New Brunswicker in the history of the province — and, Joey swore, was "another charter member of the Senate bum-blasters club." According to Joey, there was a large number of bum-blasters, quote unquote, in the Red Chamber. Joey is a bit of a homophobe, as I mentioned earlier, but that's another story.

At Danny's signal, we climbed back onto the tour bus. Because of an unpleasant incident a few years earlier — in which an emotional, and armed, Lebanese fellow had been permitted to highjack a crowded Voyageur bus in Montreal, drive it to Ottawa and onto Parliament Hill, and engage in a brief shoot-out with a few RCMP officers — we were not allowed to stop in front of the Centre Block, Danny explained. We slowed down long enough to get a close look at the place, however, and I was surprised by what I saw. Brick and mortar were cracked and splintered; in some cases, protective fences had been erected to keep a largish stone from falling on a litigious American tourist's head. Danny picked up the narrative.

"This building is the Centre Block, folks, where the Prime Minister works with a small staff on the third floor — in the corner there, on the west side — and where the Leader of the Opposition works in the same corner, but one floor up. The House of Commons is in the middle of the west wing, and the Senate Chamber is in the middle of the east wing. This building dates back to 1917, the year after a huge fire destroyed all but the Library of Parliament, which is at the back. But as you can see, the fire of 1916 was only slightly worse than what the politicians have done to it. They have been so desperate to look like penny-pinchers, they have skimped on the most basic maintenance."

It was. My father, who had loved being an MP, used to call Centre Block "the church of government." To him — and, I'd say, most Canadians — this building, in particular, was the property of the people, not of the politicians. And it deserved to be cherished, and treated with a certain reverence. But two decades of Liberal and Conservative governments had let it fall into serious disrepair. Welcome to the nineties, in which politicians get elected by boasting about spending *no* tax dollars — even in those rare instances when tax dollars need to be spent.

We moved on. The West Block was also in fairly bad shape; Danny mentioned that asbestos in the walls had rendered its tenancy almost an illegal occupation. It was home, he said, to the offices of a large number of junior members of Parliament, a few cabinet ministers and a taxpayer-subsidized cafeteria. The bus turned right and stopped in front of the entrance to the West Block. Danny pointed south, across Wellington Street. "That's the National Press Building," he said, and a taped snippet of typewriter keys could be heard clacking away. I grinned to myself, trying to remember the last time I had *seen* a typewriter, let alone used one.

My mind wandered a bit as the tour continued. The sound of the typewriter keys was oddly reassuring to me; they reminded me — along with looking for an apartment, which I needed to do fast — why I was in Ottawa on this sweltering Saturday morning. I was here to be a *reporter* — an honest-to-God, big-wheel national news reporter. It was exciting and somewhat terrifying at the same time. Did I have what it took? Was I up to the job? I certainly had my doubts. While I had received no shortage of plaudits for my work at the legislature in B.C., I also knew, in my heart of hearts, that I wasn't quite as lily-white as many of my editors seemed to think. While chasing the Social Credit corruption story, I had strayed a little close to the ethical line more than once. There had been times when I had wondered whether I was placing the pursuit of The Big Story above everything else. And, in my case, that had meant consciously burning a source (using material that had led to her identification) and massaging a few quotes (meaning that I had twisted someone else's words to suit my purposes).

I looked out the window of the bus as the tour continued. I was in Ottawa to get some Big Stories. But I hoped I didn't get so single-minded again that I would come so close to breaching the journalistic rules of ethics. I wondered what my father would make of all this. Somehow, things seemed simpler for that generation.

Danny's voice broke through my thoughts. "There's the Wellington Building, where the staff of the Leader of the Opposition work," he said. There was also a fully equipped, taxpayer-subsidized gymnasium in there, he added, for members of Parliament and senators.

Danny pulled the bus to the side of the road in front of the West Block and offered us another picture-taking opportunity. Most of the tourists rolled out and walked towards the Centennial flame. I remained near the entrance to the West Block, chatting with Danny. The doors to the place were open, and a commissionaire chatted with two women, who were smoking. A couple of large, navy blue Buicks were parked out front. Another pulled up.

The Buick's driver jumped out to open the rear curbside door while Danny and I watched. A Gucci loafer was followed by a pair of Valentino slacks and an Aquascutum blazer — politicians in Ottawa seem to think "dressing down" is donning a blazer, I guess — and the cheerful grin of Hubert Jolicoeur, the Conservative Minister of Revenue, and Nova Scotia's senior cabinet representative. Jolicoeur was balding and slightly cross-eyed. He was carrying a large green House of Commons–issue briefing book under one arm. After assuring himself that Danny, the commissionaire, the two secretaries and I were all watching, he turned to offer his free hand to a woman inside the car.

Sliding across the seat, her microscopic leather miniskirt obscuring little, was Jolicoeur's infamous friend Bibi de la Chèvres, a bleached-blonde stripper from his hometown. The stripper — who towered a full head above Jolicoeur, but he didn't seem to mind — was decked out in five-inch spike heels, a clingy blouse, the leather miniskirt and not much else. Some time before, Jolicoeur had been briefly removed from the Tory cabinet, following a celebrated incident in which he had become polluted in a Nova Scotia strip joint — Bibi's former work-place, I think — and punched out a big bouncer whose father was a provincial Liberal MLA. Once he was charged with assault, Jolicoeur had been obliged to tender his ministerial resignation forthwith. His constituents had loved the incident, however, and, after the nation saw just how much bigger the bouncer had been than Jolicoeur, many guys I knew became fond of him, too. (The charges were later dropped.) He was a little scrapper, and Atlantic Canadians love scrappers. Despite the bar-room brawl, and despite swirling and unconfirmed rumours of Jolicoeur's penchant for exotic dancers, the little Nova Scotian was soon back in cabinet.

Jolicoeur bounced over to us to shake our hands. The commission-aire and the two secretaries were greeted in French, but he used accented English on Danny and me. We looked like anglos, I guess.

Then, with a flourish, Jolicoeur introduced his female companion to Danny and me. "Dis, gennlemen, is Mademoiselle de la Chèvres, who is a well-known dancer and actress."

Danny and I mutely shook her hand — she had fake red fingernails as long as golf tees — and she swivelled away in her spike heels to present herself to the commissionaire and the two women, who looked shocked. Jolicoeur watched her go, then winked at us. "Pretty nice, eh, fellas?" he said, then laughed and moved on. We laughed too. Jolicoeur and Bibi disappeared into the West Block, and the tourists started walking back from the Centennial flame.

As Danny was helping people onto his tour bus, another Buick pulled up. This time the door was opened by the sole passenger in the back seat himself, the Secretary of State for External Affairs, the Right Honourable Pat Stanton. Stanton stepped out onto the side-walk. He was wearing an argyle sweater — it was really hot, remember — and a pair of jeans that actually appeared to have been ironed. Where Hubert Jolicoeur had been flamboyant, upbeat and loud, Stanton looked the opposite: awkward, timorous, uncertain. He barely made it out of the Buick without bopping his immense skull on the door frame. A Northern Ontarian, and — for a year or so when I was still in high school, Prime Minister — Stanton was a walking example of politics' intolerance for the commonplace. The commissionaire and the two secretaries barely noticed him. "Uh, hello," he mumbled, in a deep voice, as he walked past me to the West Block's entrance. His hands flopped at his sides like apron strings.

Stanton wasn't as banal as he looked. Like the vast majority of his male colleagues on the Hill, the bumbling former Tory leader apparently had an eye for the women. He had certainly told his fair share of bold-faced whoppers to the public. And — contrary to popular opinion — he had inflicted as many knife wounds on putative political allies as he had received. He was very much a subscriber to the British parliamentary model: dull as proverbial dishwater on the outside; a libidinous plotter on the inside.

Much later, Joey would tell me that Pat Stanton was living, breathing proof that television ensured that only beautiful people ever excel at public life. But he was wrong, of course. Three years later, Bobby Laurier — who was no male model — would demonstrate that Canadians don't always embrace American-style pretty-boy politics.

Back on the bus, we rolled down the Hill, heading west. We passed another haunt of ministers and MPs, the Confederation Building. Next, on the right, were the offices of the Department of Justice. Across the way, Danny informed us, were the East and West Memorial buildings, where various departments — among them Canada's spy agency, the Canadian Security Intelligence Service — could be found. The windows at CSIS were obscured by some kind of reflective material, and cameras could be seen sprouting out of the exterior walls like roots on an old potato. Concrete barricades, like the ones we saw outside the U.S. embassy, had been positioned to prevent anyone from parking out front. But, in the centre of all this security — presumably designed to prevent foreign nations from learning the true identities of our own spies, among other things — a half-dozen employees lounged at the building's entrance. Danny seemed to read my mind. "If you want to find out who our spies are, just sit across the street with a camera and shoot away," Danny said. "All of our spies who smoke hang out at the front there, because they can't smoke inside." That got a few laughs, especially from the American tourists, who seemed amazed by this fairly obvious flaw in our security measures.

Farther west, at the edge of the area pretentiously labelled "the Parliamentary precinct," stood the Supreme Court of Canada. This building was beautiful and, compared with others we had seen, in good shape. The copper roof had recently been replaced, so it had not turned the distinctive green shade seen on the Centre Block and its two twin structures. Danny related the court's history, and a few tourists got out to snap photographs. I stayed inside, where the air was cool. My mother's wishes notwithstanding, courthouses were not my bag. When all were back on board, the bus turned around and headed eastbound on Wellington Street, past the Château Laurier, north to the Mint, and towards the moneyed lawns of Rockcliffe. I wouldn't be renting an apartment there — subdividing your house was a social gaffe of major proportions.

On our way, we passed a number of office towers where various federal departments were located. On the top floor of each of these buildings, Danny explained, were usually the responsible ministers' offices. Each minister — if he or she didn't work out of a smaller suite somewhere on Parliament Hill — would normally employ an entourage of twenty or so, including a driver, a press secretary or two, a chief of staff, a personal secretary and approximately a dozen special assistants assigned to certain files, or certain geographic regions. These assistants were paid about $60,000 a year, while the chiefs of staff earned about $100,000, Danny said, a revelation that produced a bout of disapproving head-shaking from the Canadian tourists on the bus.

Danny's bus cruised past the External Affairs building, where a few self-important young foreign-service officers were marching to and fro. Didn't these people know it was Saturday morning? With the number of federal employees or politicians I had seen in or near their places of work on a Saturday, I was already reassessing my view that nobody worked in Ottawa. Some, clearly, worked very hard. Or at least worked hard at giving everyone the *impression* that they worked very hard.

We passed the French embassy, and then we pulled off Sussex Drive, near the entrance to Rideau Hall. After some chitchat about the Governor General, and his role as Canada's head of state, Danny pointed across the street. There, Danny announced, was none other than 24 Sussex, the residence of the Prime Minister. He advised caution in crossing the road, which had a lot of Volvos (residents) and Mercedeses with red licence plates (diplomats) whizzing by. Everyone piled off, cameras in hand. With the rest of the group, I peered through the black iron fencing, and the trees, towards the Prime Minister's house. My father had taken me to see the house on one or two occasions when he was an MP. Back then, it had seemed very big and very important. Not this time.

The home was still occupied, at this point, by Ross Hamilton, the reviled Conservative Prime Minister. Hamilton was widely expected to be retiring soon enough to allow his Tories to elect a new leader who would — they hoped — lead them to electoral victory. Hamilton, the author of two spectacularly unsuccessful attempts to amend the Constitution, had led his party to two successive majority governments. Two big wins, two big losses, which is a pretty good political batting average. But something about the guy — maybe his $3,000 suits, or his toadying to the Americans, or his genetically perfect family — now irritated the hell out of the Canadian public. Personally, I thought he had been an okay Prime Minister, but I knew not many people agreed with me about that. Even people I usually associated with sober judgment — people like my late father, for example — could work themselves into paroxysms of fury about the guy. One night after a couple of glasses of port, my father had called him "an unctuous, strutting peacock in a fifteen-piece suit." I hadn't agreed with him, but I had laughed upon hearing such a colourful string of discourtesies emanating from someone as courteous as my dad.

The bus moved on. We cruised past various embassies. Periodically, one of the white Rhodesians who live in Rockcliffe's stately mansions would look up at the bus and pointedly frown at us. Tour buses were controversial among the people who lived in Rockcliffe, Danny explained, and he soon expected them to be banned altogether. Sounded unconstitutional to me.

We rolled along Acacia towards Stornoway, the official residence of the Leader of Her Majesty's Loyal Opposition. It wasn't all that fancy, really: two storeys, stucco exterior, about eighty years old. A row of hedges surrounded the place, but from our elevated positions on the bus it wasn't difficult to see over it. And there, by the side of the house, in a pair of slacks and a red golf shirt, was Robert "Bobby" Laurier, newly elected Leader of the Liberal Party of Canada, future Prime Minister of Canada — putting. He was crouched over a dozen golf balls and squinting at a beer mug lying on its side about twenty feet away. He was oblivious to us, putting away on the closely cropped lawn.

Danny, our faithful driver, was not one to miss an opportunity like this. He punched a button, and his voice suddenly boomed out of speakers on the exterior of the bus. "HEY, MR. LAURIER!" he bellowed. "HEY, MR. LAURIER! ANY HOLES-IN-ONE TODAY?"

*   *   *

The first thing that writers of profiles inevitably mentioned about Bobby Laurier was his extraordinary face.

It was not the sort of face you saw on the likes of Nils Andersen, the NDP veteran I had met at the Ottawa airport, which was a masterpiece of right angles and flawless skin. It was, instead, the face of a farmer, or a logger, or a fisherman — the face of a guy who worked out-of-doors all day: reddish, lined, ordinary. He had, for instance, oversized ears. He had a nose that looked as if it had been broken. His hair seemed to resist all attempts at combing and, unless he had recently had it cut, a lock of hair was always sticking out at some unusual angle. His face was remarkable, I suppose, because in politics just about everybody else looked like Nils Andersen, or Jack Gibson, or Jean Rioux: you know, handsome, noble, well bred, that sort of thing. Bobby Laurier's face was uncommon because, anywhere beyond Parliament Hill, it would be the reverse — it would be decidedly common. He was the anti-politician, right there on his face.

For a long time, the Liberals didn't understand that. Seven years earlier, Laurier had fought Gibson for the party leadership and lost. After the leadership convention, my father, who had been a Laurier delegate, recalled with anger how the Gibson delegates (who in due course became Jean Rioux delegates) had ridiculed Laurier's face and speech. They had mistakenly believed, I guess, that Gibson would win back the country primarily on the basis of his looks — despite the fact that he lacked an operating brain. Or liver.

The Tories didn't understand that political imperative either. They had become so used to Ross Hamilton, with his Hermès ties and his *haut monde* politics, they imagined the voters thought the way they did. They had started to *believe* that Canadians admired guys like Hamilton, because he wore expensive suits and shirts with cuffs, or Missoni sweaters when he was feeling casual. So, during the election that would see Laurier win a majority Liberal government, the Conservative brain trust — among them a pretentious new-age poll-ster and a blue-blood lawyer who ran their doomed campaign —

decided to make an issue out of Laurier's face. They threw together some quickie commercials of the Liberal leader giving speeches, during which his features are as twisted as a pretzel because of facial paralysis, and topped them off with some voice-overs by "average" Canadians making less-than-subtle remarks about his looks. Spin legend has it that the spots were run past a few focus groups without any difficulty, but I doubt that. Unless it was done at a maximum-security prison somewhere in Kingston.

Lots of people believed the Liberals had been hoping for the now-infamous "face" ads. But I was travelling on Laurier's bus through Northern Ontario at the time, and I can report, solemnly and truthfully, that Laurier's advisers — Flash Feiffer in particular — had been absolutely shocked that the Conservatives would do such a thing. Especially considering that they were already down the toilet. One Liberal junior press aide told me, with awe in her voice, that Feiffer had actually cried when he saw the spots on TV in a Sudbury hotel room. Later on, lots of reporters would write analysis pieces saying the ads had been the factor that resulted in the Tories winning only a half-dozen seats. They were wrong. At that point in the race, Laurier was already going to win big with his "give 'em hope" platform. The significance of the "face" ads, to me, was that, during their long tenure in power, the Tories had forgotten the irresistible magnetism of the commonplace. They had forgotten — or never knew — that Laurier never looked phony, or snobby, *because* of his face.

Under his off-the-rack suits, he was deceptively powerful. Although he was in his late fifties, he could bound up the Centre Block steps three at a time, leaving the press horde gasping far behind. When he shook your hand, his grip was firm and strong. You could tell that he could squeeze a lot harder if he wanted to.

Not that it matters, but Laurier's was not the toughest grip. That dubious distinction belonged, of course, to Jack Gibson. When Gibson worked a crowd, he would turn his trademark laser-beam stare on a voter, and then squeeze the living daylights out of the digits of old ladies and grown men alike — as if he were some steroid-crazed high school wrestling team coach. Gibson was definitely in the Political Handshake Pantheon.

     ❋   ❋   ❋

Laurier had indeed grown up on a farm, as he never tired of remind-ing everyone. Born to a farmer and a farmer's wife in a little place called Bon Accord, north of Edmonton, he had been raised in a community of francophones, and he hadn't spoken English before his teens. (Some said he still didn't speak English, but some unique idiom all his own.) His parents, despite their relative poverty, had encour-aged him and a couple of his brothers to pursue higher education. At first, Laurier considered agricultural science at the University of Alberta in Edmonton. That, he told me in the first of our year-end Canadian Press interviews, had seemed to make sense.

But in his final high-school year, during a field trip to Edmonton, he had heard a speech by Louis St. Laurent, Canada's twelfth Prime Minister. Like Laurier, St. Laurent had come from a poor family and — most notably, to young Bobby Laurier — he was only the second francophone Prime Minister in the country's history to that point. St. Laurent's speech to the Edmonton-area high-school students had not been a remarkable piece of oratory, but the simple fact of Louis St. Laurent's existence had a powerful impact on Laurier. "He was dis French guy, from dis poor family in Compton, Quebec," Laurier told me, in one of our year-end interviews. "An' he was de Prime Minister of Canada! Until dat day, all I ever tought I would be was a farmer. Dat changed when I saw St. Laurent."

Rocketing through his undergraduate arts degree at the U of A as quickly as the curriculum would allow, Laurier — despite his uncertain command of the English language, and despite his family's precarious finances — was granted a coveted spot in the university's law school, the only such school in the entire province. According to some of his class-mates, a few of whom I had interviewed for a profile the year I moved to Ottawa, Laurier was consistently underestimated by his professors and many students. In moot-court competitions, they told me, Laurier would stand there in borrowed robes, big hands gripping the podium, ears sticking out, squinting at those present — and, to those who didn't know him well enough, he was thought to be as stupid as he looked. But, by making use of an impressive knowledge of case and statutory law, simplistic and convincing arguments, and armfuls of self-deprecating humour, he would often win. One of the guys he beat, oddly enough, was Howard Thomas O'Reilly, of McGill University. My father.

The two of them went head to head in a moot on international law at the U of A. It had been a big deal for my father's team to be flown out west from Montreal, so — as he later told me — it had been essential that they win. They had studied and practised for weeks. When my father walked into the courtroom and saw Laurier, with his farmer's face and dazed expression, a couple of his pals had quietly chuckled. "Look at this rube," they said. "This won't take long." For his part, when he spotted the McGill team, Laurier jumped up to shake their hands, and confessed that he was nervous. "Jesus," he told them, smiling, "youse guys are going to kick my ass, aren't you? Well, don't be too tough on me, hokay?"

"And, over the course of the next few hours," my father remembered, "asses were kicked, all right — *our* asses. He had this aw-shucks routine down to an art. My McGill friends and I were so serious, and so intent on the technicalities of our arguments, we had forgotten that courtroom advocacy is all about convincing another person — the judge or jury — to go along with your argument. Laurier, I think, had spent as much time researching the judges of the moot competition as he had spent researching the law."

My father and Laurier had kept in touch after that, exchanging letters a couple of times a year about articling positions, law-firm gossip, that sort of thing. "I was probably the one who kept the correspondence going," my father said. "I could tell that this guy was going to go places one day. From his letters, I figured it would be politics. He told me he was spending more and more time helping out Liberals in municipal and provincial campaigns. It was only a matter of time before he made the big leap."

Along the way, Laurier married Michelle Chiquette, a Quebec City girl whose father was a rail engineer and had moved his family west to Edmonton, where Canadian National had a lot of employees. She had met Laurier while he was going door to door, polling a riding during someone's political campaign. "From what I know," my father said, "Bobby had never really dated anyone else. Law school and politics had kept him busy. But Michelle was a catch: she was French, she was a Westerner, and she didn't mind politics. He sent me a picture of the two of them on their honeymoon, which was a weekend in Banff."

After marrying Michelle, and after about three years in private practice as an associate in a small firm in St. Albert — where he had a sizable francophone clientele — Laurier sought the nomination in a mainly rural riding north of Edmonton. Because he had won so many markers with his efforts on behalf of other Liberals, the nomination had been a cinch. But few gave him much chance of winning against the Alberta Conservative machine even though his Tory opponent could speak no French and was a wealthy WASP.

My mother and father were living in Victoria by that time. During a two-week holiday — I hadn't come along yet, but Sheila had — the O'Reillys drove their Rambler station wagon to Calgary, then up to Edmonton. Bobby Laurier found room for them at a motel owned by one of his contributors, and my dad, who was bilingual, went door to door with him for a couple of days.

"It was his first campaign, and he was only in his early thirties," my father would recall. "But he was already a real pro. He could make people laugh, and he could make them listen even when they didn't want to. He may not have been a matinee idol, but he had a wonderful way of making people feel at ease, of making them come over to his way of thinking. So when he called me about fifteen years later, and asked me to run for the Liberals in Victoria, I couldn't say no. It's hard to say no to Bobby Laurier."

As I was to find out in the first few months of the new Liberal government.

CHAPTER THREE

The National Press Building, where most of the Press Gallery make their home, is also where Joey and I had made plans to meet for dinner, after filing our swearing-in stories. It is an attractive old grey stone structure, a dozen or so storeys high, and sandwiched between a Bank of Montreal branch and the Wellington Block, where the staff offices of the leader of Her Majesty's Loyal Opposition are located. The press building's main-floor entrance opens onto Wellington Street and the Parliament Buildings. Connecting to the minuscule lobby is the theatre, where most Prime Ministers hold their encounters with the gentlemen and ladies of the media — when they are still talking to us, that is. Global News has a couple of offices on either side of the lobby. And in the middle of the lobby, there is a tiny desk belonging to a pal of mine, Raymond Aquin.

Ray Aquin is a member of the Canadian Corps of Commissionaires, the group that supplies the elderly security guards — retired Canadian Armed Forces folks, mainly — found in government offices all around Ottawa. Ray is a former Royal Canadian Air Force lieutenant, a pilot.

He flew with the 417 Squadron in North Africa, and later in Italy. "I knew all the great ones," he told me shortly after we met, three years ago. "Black Mike McEwen and Buzz Beurling. Knew 'em all."

My father had also been a member of the RCAF during the last year of the Second World War. He never saw any action, having spent most of 1945 at Training Command in Trenton. But because my father had been RCAF, and because — from what I could see — I was one of the few reporters who would stop long enough to talk to Ray, we established an easy rapport. He was a nice old guy. And, I learned, he was a great source of information.

"It's amazing, those reporters and political guys waiting for the elevators beside my desk," Ray would say. "They forget I'm here. And they talk a lot. So I listen a little bit, and I learn a few things."

He was being too modest. Ray Aquin knew a lot more than "a few things." He was a veritable gusher of gossip about the couple of thousand people who make their daily living on Parliament Hill. Whenever I was in the press building, I'd sit on the corner of Ray's desk and chat with him, and he'd have some hot rumour for me. A couple of times in the summer, we'd go for hot dogs on the Sparks Street Mall, and he would fill my ear with off-the-record "bits," as he called them.

I stepped through the press building doors. "Hey, Ray! How's it going?"

Ray looked up from his crossword puzzle and winked. "Hey there, Chris," he said. "Busy day around here, eh?"

"Sure is," I replied. We talked for a little while about the new cabinet. Being a franco-Ontarian, Ray had a great affinity for Bobby Laurier; to Ray, there was no minority as significant as the French-speaking minority found outside the province of Quebec. He told me that Laurier's cabinet looked pretty good, and that he expected a long honeymoon for the new government. When the lobby cleared of people, he looked around and waved me closer. He had a "bit" for me, he said, winking again behind his horn-rims.

"Listen, Chris, there were a couple guys around here at lunch time, going up to the restaurant. I've seen them before," he said. "I think they work for the Registrar General. They were talking about a company called Prince or something and laughing. They said that Bobby Laurier may have sworn in his new cabinet, but that this Prince thing was going to be the *real* cabinet. What the hell do you think they were talking about?"

The Office of the Deputy Registrar General was the group of bureaucrats charged with registering all individuals and companies lobbying public-office holders in Ottawa. There were maybe a few hundred lobbyists in Ottawa, most of whom had conducted their business with little or no scrutiny for much of the Conservatives' two terms in power. Towards the end of their mandate, when lots of stories were being written about lobbyists selling access to cabinet ministers, the Tories had hastily drafted some legislation requiring lobbyists to disclose their names — and their clients' names — to the Deputy Registrar General. The legislation had been denounced by the Liberals as toothless, but I didn't know much more than that. And I knew nothing about a company called Prince.

"Beats me, Ray. I've never heard of a company called Prince. Did these guys say anything else?"

"Something about a cabinet minister, but I didn't catch which one it was," he responded. "That's it."

"Well, I'll check it out," I said. "I'll let you know what I find out."

"Okay, Chris." He waved me on. "Your crazy friend Joey is already upstairs."

The elevator creaked its way upwards to the second floor of the National Press Building, where, according to Joey Myers, the Government of Canada is run. It is there, in the Press Gallery bar, or towards the back of the building, in the restaurant, that governments are made or broken, Joey has informed me more than once. Over drinks, or over the restaurant's execrable beef dip, reporters decide which politician is entitled to support, or which ones are deserving of a Press Gallery summary execution. Using the weapons at their command — stories choked with quotes from anonymous sources, editorials based on imaginary facts, and puerile tattletale columns — a determined group of reporters can lay waste to a budding parliamentary career. Or so Joey believes.

* * *

When I arrived at CP Ottawa from the comparatively naive confines of the Press Gallery at the Legislative Building in Victoria, I wasn't a believer. In B.C., where kookiness is a state religion, reporters are usually too disputatious to agree on who pays for lunch, let alone which politician they should collectively kneecap. The two big media outlets there, for example, are the paper where I started out, the *Vancouver Sun*, which is generally supportive of Social Credit or "free enterprise" alternatives, and BCTV, which is essentially the communications arm of the provincial New Democrats.

Joey was right about one thing: Ottawa's Press Gallery *was* different. While I had never seen any proof that a group of reporters or editors possessed enough clout to "topple governments," as Joey put it, there was a great deal to support his argument that Pack Journalism was widely practised in the nation's capital. After my first few Question Periods, I had seen groups of reporters walking from the Centre Block back to the National Press Building, carefully comparing notes or sharing quotes. At first, I had believed this exercise to be a polite way of assisting one's colleagues. After reading these reporters' stories, however, I changed my opinion: in reality, they were ensuring that they all wrote the same thing. I asked Joey about this.

"Welcome to the big city, young fellow," he said, greatly amused by my innocence, annoying me in the process. He did that a lot. "They are ensuring they all write the same thing to protect themselves. That way, nobody back in head office can give them shit for what a colleague got, and what they didn't. Pack Journalism doesn't produce many investigative stars, but it results in careers that last longer."

This, to me, was perfectly absurd. "Well, what if someone does get a scoop? Do they share that with everybody else, too?" I asked him.

"Christopher, my boy," he said, rolling his eyes. "This is Her Majesty's Press Gallery. Scoops are frowned upon here. First, few media organizations have enough money to support investigative work anymore. And, second, scoops jeopardize job security. A reporter who gets too investigative can lose most of his political and bureaucratic sources in a weekend." He regarded me solemnly. "And, quite frankly, that is one reason why so many of your beloved colleagues didn't greet you with open arms, when you made your debut in Ottawa. You had carved out a reputation as an *investigative* reporter, and they were worried you would make them look bad."

To my regret, my three years on Parliament Hill hadn't been distinguished by many "scoops" at all. In B.C., I had been seen as a veritable West Coast Woodward and Bernstein rolled into one, churning out loads of award-winners about the then-Socred government. That, I was told, was how I was selected by head office in Toronto to join CP's national capital bureau. But in Ottawa, it seemed that it was Bobby Laurier's Opposition Liberals who had been best at digging up dirt on the Conservatives, a fact that had nothing to do with their investigative skills. Instead, I attributed the Liberals' successes to leaks from public servants eager to curry favour with the Conservatives' likely successors. The leaks seemed to grow in direct proportion to the Grits' popularity in the public-opinion polls: when Laurier's numbers grew, so did the leaks.

The other problem was time, or a lack of it. More often than not, I had more than enough on my hands chasing down my assigned beat — the Liberals, Finance, Treasury Board and the Privy Council Office. My editor, Kevin Ritchie, certainly encouraged me to do investigative work. But Ritchie had cut back on the number of bodies in our bureau by a third, and the work load grew proportionately. I never seemed to have enough hours in the day.

With this new government, I had resolved, I would find the time to do some investigative stories. At the moment, I was assisted by the complete absence of a social life. I had severed ties with my last female "friend," an attractive but loudly self-absorbed CTV reporter who shall remain nameless. (She had been posted to one of CTV's Far East bureaus, where — she complained — her hair dryer never worked.) Apart from Joey and a few guys I played soccer with, I didn't get out much. My new priority would be some investigative work. It was time to topple governments.

*   *   *

I wasn't off to a good start. The first day of the new Laurier regime, and there I was, stepping off the elevator and into the second-floor Press Gallery bar, and straight into the beer-soaked lair of The Olde Journalism.

The Olde Journalism was practised by precisely the types I saw slumped in chairs and couches, like beached beluga, here and there throughout the lounge: bloated, malodorous men in their fifties, with features turned a reddish hue from too many cigarettes and far too many beers. They were the sort who had worked for various failing newspapers for three decades or so, and they were suspicious of anyone who got into "the business," as they called it, with a university degree. (Like me.) The only other reporters they trusted, or deigned to speak to, were those who had started off as copy boys at the *Ottawa Journal* or the Toronto *Telegram*, as they did, back in primeval times. They prided themselves on their sartorial tastes (wearing the same Tip Top Tailors jacket every day for a year) and on their unhealthy lifestyle (booze, butts and lots of poutine on the Sparks Street Mall).

The Svengali of this sad crew was a former CTV reporter from the Prairies, a hard-drinking bingo-caller named Mac Lee. Lee was still in mourning over the Tories' loss — but his weekly syndicated program, *The Insider,* produced a ratings bonanza at his new home, the CBC. It featured the kind of "reporting" that drove me crazy — lots of chummy interviews with the politicians Lee liked, lots of snide and unattributed shots at those he didn't. The fact that he was occasionally willing to overlook a politico's screw-ups didn't improve my opinion of him. Joey, predictably, thought he was great. Joey was a charter member of The Olde Journalism club and, at the moment, was standing at the bar, deep in conference with Mac Lee and Patrick Stone.

Patrick Stone was the anchor of the CBC's late-night news program, *The Nation*. He was also, without much doubt, the most powerful person in the Canadian journalistic establishment. His ratings and his connections had made him a survivor in the internecine world of broad-cast journalism. If he wanted to interview a Prime Minister, he did. If he wanted to play golf with the Governor General, he did. Stone wasn't exactly The Olde Journalism, but he wasn't The New Journalism, either. He dressed well, as you would expect anyone with a taxpayer-subsidized clothing allowance to do. He had a reserved, cultivated manner about him, as if he was used to shopping for Hermès ties at Holt's with Ontario's Lieutenant-Governor. But, on the half-dozen or so occasions he had jetted up from Toronto to cover big stories — election nights, leadership conventions, that kind of thing — I always spotted him hang-ing out with the likes of Mac Lee. Maybe he was slumming.

I stepped over to Joey's side. "Gentlemen," I said, hoping this would not take long.

"Chris O'Reilly!" Mac Lee bellowed, slapping me on the back, pushing his face up towards mine. He gave off an odour of sour beer and perspiration. "Nice call on the new ministers, kiddo! Got every one right! Who're ya sleepin' with at the PMO?"

Joey laughed. "That's what I said to him, that's what I said to him! And you know what he said?"

Oh, terrific, I thought.

"Flash Feiffer!"

Joey and Lee shrieked with laughter, while Patrick Stone gazed around the bar, smiling tightly. He looked bored.

I stood there for a few more minutes, while Mac Lee and Joey exchanged data about Flash Feiffer's penis. While I waited for Joey, I coaxed a few words from Stone. He wasn't a matinee idol — he had his share of wrinkles, his hair was going grey, and his jaw line was no longer likened to granite — but he was possessed of the most remark-able voice I had ever heard. It was deep, resonant, mellifluous: his voice actually made him *look* handsome. Following the CBC's special news coverage on the first cabinet meeting of the new Laurier government, he sniffed, he planned to spend the weekend at his cottage in the Gatineau Hills. "I bought it a few years ago," he intoned, in his remark-able voice. "It isn't much, but it's a nice place ... Mike! How are you?"

Stone was looking past me. I turned to see Mike Mahoney, hands on his hips, chest thrust out, beaming at Patrick Stone. He looked as if he wanted to throw his arms around the news anchor. "Patrick! How *are* you? I was *worried* I wouldn't get a chance to see you!" Beside Mahoney was Donna Curtis, an apparently unemployed lawyer and another long-time Rioux minion. Most of the time, Mahoney and Curtis were inseparable. As unpleasant as Curtis was, she had a terrific body. Amazing, in fact.

Mac Lee, having grown weary of Joey's bottomless supply of Flash Feiffer penis analogies, brightened when he saw Curtis. He readied himself to plant an unsolicited, and wet, kiss on Curtis's cheek, then did so with a lascivious look. "Donna Curtis," he wheezed, totally ignoring Mike Mahoney. "You are one hot fucking broad."

There are three sexist realms with which I am personally familiar: my father's former vocation, law, which is overwhelmingly domi-nated by men; journalism, where management is also overwhelmingly dominated by men; and, most of all, politics. Politicians are the most sexist because of their piety about being the *reverse*: they loudly proclaim their support for more female MPs in the House of Commons, for example, while ensuring that women candidates are tied to unwinnable ridings at election time. But even so, in most of Ottawa, these days, calling a woman a "hot fucking broad" to her face — or behind her back, come to think of it — would have been met with lots of disapproval, if not a pop in the nose. It was decidedly inappropriate in the extreme — The Olde Journalism at its very worst. Coming from Mac Lee, I wasn't surprised to hear it. But I watched Curtis to see how she would react.

Before she could say a word, Mike Mahoney giggled loudly. "Oh, Mac, you're such a fucking *charmer*," he said, as Donna Curtis eyed Patrick Stone. Mahoney seemed to speak in italics. "Don't you *know* we don't say 'broad' in politically correct Ottawa? You should say Donna is a 'hot fucking *person*,' don't you know?"

Mac Lee and Patrick Stone chortled at this. Joey, who apparently disliked Mike Mahoney as much as he disliked Jean Rioux, looked at his watch. Not missing a beat, Mike Mahoney turned to me. "Chris! Long time no *talk*!"

"Hi, Mike," I said. I had wanted to see someone tell Mac Lee to fuck off, and was disappointed nobody had. Mike seemed to sense this immediately and pointed at me.

"Now, this fine young man, Mac, *this* is a real *gentleman*. And a fabulous reporter, too," he said, swishy as hell. "He'd *never* call anyone a broad."

Mahoney, Lee and Stone laughed. Joey and I listened to Mahoney do some low-level spinning about Jean Rioux for a few minutes; Stone and Curtis exchanged smouldering looks. Then we excused ourselves, pleading hunger. As I stepped away, Mahoney slid a manicured hand onto my arm, and reminded me of our meeting in his office tomorrow. He reeked of cheap cologne. "I won't forget," I said.

Down in the restaurant, I ate a salad while Joey tore into some over-done roast beef. Despite our many differences — in age, in size, in the way we looked at our jobs — he was probably my best friend in Ottawa. He was much admired by many of the political oldtimers because they knew he could be trusted. When someone said something was off the record, Joey would immediately put his notepad away. Unlike a lot of the new, younger reporters, who confused ambition with talent, Joey was not interested in destroying anybody's career for a ticket to a National Newspaper Award banquet, notwithstanding all of his jokes about "toppling governments." He genuinely believed that politicians were, generally, well-meaning people who worked hard. He was willing to give most of them the benefit of the doubt, thus ensuring that many of them would talk to Joey before they would talk to anyone else. This, he told me, was why Southam News had never rotated him out of Ottawa and into an editorial post in Hamilton or Windsor, where he had worked after he and his wife, Judy, emigrated to Canada. He could always be counted on to produce good, solid stories; he didn't regard politicians as evil personified. But it also made his dislike of Jean Rioux so unusual.

"Hey, big guy," I said. "Why didn't you say anything to Mike? Isn't it you who always says that we shouldn't be so hard-assed about those who work in politics?"

"Yes, young Christopher, that is true." He tapped his nose with a stubby forefinger. "But this device in the middle of my face enables me to sniff out bullshit. And I smell a great deal of it whenever I see Jean Rioux or your knob-gobbling pal Mike Mahoney."

"He's not my friend," I said. "He's the chief of staff to the new Minister of Finance, and Finance is one of my beats. And I need to have at least a civil relationship with him. That's my job."

"Well, don't get sucked in by that crowd," he responded, smearing butter over his second baked potato. "They're a bunch of satanists."

I laughed. "Don't worry, none of them appeal to me. Not even Donna Curtis."

"Bullshit, my boy. Didn't you see those massive breasts?"

"I did," I said, then remembered Ray Aquin. "Listen, Joey, have you ever heard of something called the Prince company?"

Joey looked up at me with surprise. "Where did you hear about the Prince Group? You impress me."

"Someone told me the Prince Group, or whatever it's called, was going to be more powerful than the new cabinet."

Joey nodded at this and returned to his potato. "Your someone may well be right. Nothing surprises me in this town anymore."

*   *   *

Here begins Joey Myers's lesson on the Ottawa Liberal feeding chain.

"I have covered many Grit governments before your time, Master O'Reilly. And you should know, at the outset, that the Liberal feeding chain is the product of many decades of back-stabbings and political ritual sacrifice," Joey told me, a couple of weeks after the election, but before the swearing-in of the new Liberal government. It was a beautiful Indian summer day in late October, and we were sitting on a bench across Wellington Street from the Centre Block, where the old Rideau Club was located before it burned down. "Many have attempted to disturb the imperatives of the Ottawa feeding chain, but none have emerged victorious. As a reporter begins his perilous journey, notepad and *stylo* at the ready, he must remember that he should never attempt to reverse nature's delicate political checks and balances. Or he will be" — and here he paused to raise his hands above his head — "*crushed* like a grape."

"You know, Joey, I've known you for three years, but you never cease to amaze me with your weirdness," I said.

"Quiet, you insolent pup, and listen." So I listened.

According to Joey, at the top of the Ottawa Liberal feeding chain, as he called it, was the Prime Minister. While there were plenty of reporters, and even more cabinet ministers, who would suggest this was not the case, Joey assured me that the PM was indisputably the boss. He — or, just once and very briefly, she — was the person who decided who was in cabinet, who got what major patronage appointment, and so on. While it wasn't unusual for a Prime Minister to be unaware of some of the finer points of his or her government's comings and goings, the PM was still in charge. The only time a PM was not in charge, he said, was when a leadership race had been called to replace that PM. At that point, a Prime Minister became yesterday's bagels.

"Who would be next in line, do you think?" he asked me, looking confident that I would not answer correctly.

I didn't disappoint him. "Well, the cabinet, of course," I said.

"Pshaw," he retorted, delighted. "It is the PMO, my boy, the PMO. The cabinet is a few ornaments on the Christmas tree, nothing more."

The Prime Minister's Office, Joey informed me, was mostly made up of a hundred middle managers, most of them doing little more than shepherding correspondence through the system, or writing press releases no one ever read, or organizing unimportant trips across the Great White North. To Joey, these PMO staff were worse than useless — they were powerless. Only three PMO employees, he said, typically possessed enough influence to short-circuit any bureaucrat, minister or group of ministers: the chief of staff, the principal secretary and the director of communications. "Those three are the *real* PMO," he said.

The chief of staff was the one who ran the Prime Minister's Office. This person, Joey explained, could make or break a Prime Minister. Spouses notwithstanding, he or she was the last one a Prime Minister spoke to before bedtime, and the first one to chat with the PM at sun-up. The chief of staff, if he or she acted according to Ottawa's ordinances, worked tirelessly to isolate a Prime Minister from cabinet, the press and (of course) the great unwashed, thus ensuring that the PM ultimately would come to subscribe to only one world view — the chief of staff's. In Ottawa, controlling someone's schedule was everything.

Bobby Laurier's chief of staff was Charles Lafontaine, a former mayor of North Hatley, a small hamlet in Quebec's Eastern Townships. The two men had become friends in their law school days, when Lafontaine met Laurier — as had been the case with my father — during a moot court contest at the Université de Montréal. Lafontaine slipped into the Office of the Leader of the Opposition about a year after Bobby Laurier won the Liberal leadership, and after the House had shut down for the summer. He was hired to run the OLO primarily because Flash Feiffer had made such a spectacular mess of the place. Following his arrival, a few Liberal staffers started referring to Lafontaine as "Charlie" — as in the late 1970s American television show *Charlie's Angels*. Like the Charlie in that historically bad piece of popular culture, Lafontaine was known to all but a few as a friendly, accented voice on the other end of a telephone. He was rarely seen in public. Before coming to Ottawa as a federal Liberal, in fact, he had been a Quebec provincial Liberal, which meant that he had been a federal Tory. It was all very complicated, Joey said, but so were Quebec's nativist politics.

After jettisoning a few pieces of deadwood in the Office of the Leader of the Opposition — mainly chronic political losers left over from the Jack Gibson days — Charlie Lafontaine used his charm and telephone manner to soothe the competing egos and agendas of senators, members of Parliament and senior political staff. In Opposition, there are no ministerial Buicks, patronage appointments or regional-development grants to fight for. All such things are the prerogative of government, Joey declared. "So all that is left to disagree about is policy," he said. "That, and who gets to ask what in Question Period. Big deal." Charlie Lafontaine kept focused on management, and he kept his nose out of policy. So he survived.

Policy was left, instead, to the next vertebrate in the political feeding chain, the principal secretary. In the office of Bobby Laurier — both before and after the election — the principal secretary was, and always had been, Bernie "Flash" Feiffer. As near as anybody could tell, Flash had been with Bobby Laurier since the dawn of time. He had come aboard as a lowly special assistant to Laurier some twenty years before, when the Liberal leader-to-be had been Treasury Board president, in one of the first cabinets of Maurice Johnson Bechard. Feiffer was designated as "Flash" by one of his friends, CBC-TV reporter Ralph Nearing, on account of his obvious brilliance. A University of Toronto law school gold-medallist, the lanky Feiffer never combed his hair, and he always wore his ancient Dacron suits buttoned up, even when he sat down.

But he was smart — probably smarter than any political assistant the Hill had ever seen. He could debate constitutional minutiae with Supreme Court justices, and win. He knew more about social programs than the bureaucrats who drafted the enabling legislation — or the Maritimers who used the dole the most. He was, by popular consensus, Bobby Laurier's disembodied brain. In the Press Gallery, most of us assumed that Flash Feiffer ran the government while Bobby Laurier worked on his slice at the Royal Ottawa Golf Club.

Feiffer probably resented the fact that Charles Lafontaine had been brought in to fix the problems he had created at the OLO, in the year he had been permitted to run it. "But he's too smart to let his resentment show," said Joey. "He sticks to the big policy files and keeps his nose out of staff matters, appointments, scheduling, stuff like that. And, the moment Lafontaine stumbles, and opinion is turning against him, just you watch. Flash will jam a pound of stainless steel between poor old Lafontaine's shoulder blades. It will be ugly."

The last member of the PMO triumvirate was the director of communications, the one we in the Press Gallery were obliged to deal with the most. In the first few chaotic months in the Opposition leader's office, Laurier had gone through three different press secretaries. The first had been a nice but chronically slow fellow who was shuffled off to a member's office. The next had been a former railway communications director who was capable in every respect, except one: he could barely speak English. *Bonsoir*. The third was the one who would go on to serve as communications guru in Bobby Laurier's PMO, Walter Hume.

Walt, as he insisted on being called, had been recruited to the OLO job by Flash Feiffer, just around the time Lafontaine was about to make his debut. Hume was a London real estate agent with a long involvement in Liberal politics. His father had been a wealthy venture capitalist, and he had sent his son to a string of posh private schools. Thin, dishevelled and always grinning, Hume was clearly intelligent. You could always count on him to be ready with a quick quotable quip or a bit of self-congratulatory spin. But to Joey — and to me, too, frankly — he was too glib, too superficial by half. In short, a perfect press secretary.

Hume was also ideally suited to the OLO press secretary's job — and, I had been told, got the job — because of his connections to the Jean Rioux crowd. For much of the Liberal leadership race, Hume and his family had been on an extended vacation in Asia, ostensibly visiting relatives. He was Mike Mahoney's closest friend, but he knew that Rioux could not hope to win the leadership race to succeed Jack Gibson, said Joey. So he stayed away in Asia, returning only when Bobby Laurier had been crowned as leader. "His selection as press secretary happened for two reasons," Joey declared. "First, he could string sentences together in both official languages, which is more than could be said for his predecessors. And, second — and this is the real reason, if you ask me — his selection was an attempt to throw a bone to the Rioux crowd, who were at that time agitating against Laurier in the Liberal caucus."

"Okay, okay," I said. "So that's the PMO. What about the cabinet? Or do the janitors have more power than cabinet ministers?"

"I'm surprised by your cynicism, young Christopher," he chided, all accent and arched eyebrows. "You, an investigative reporter, discounting the importance of the men and women who clean out the wastepaper baskets of our nation's highest offices?"

"Okay, you're right," I said, and he was. "But don't any cabinet ministers count?"

"Some, but not all," he replied, continuing the lecture.

According to Joey, governments could usually be divided into two factions: the "ideas" group, and the "bucks" group. In the latter camp were the ministers controlling the government's purse strings — the ministers in charge of Finance, Revenue, Industry, Energy, Employment and the Treasury Board. This faction, now led by Jean Rioux, was the one that literally controlled the economy, influencing interest rates, investment and income supplements like UI. In the former camp, the ideas camp, there were the softer portfolios like Justice, Health and the Secretary of State. As far as Joey was concerned, and as far as the bulk of the Press Gallery was concerned, the economic portfolios were the ones that mattered most. But I wasn't so sure.

I thought back a few months. During the course of 1992's off-the-record chat, when the Conservative leadership race to replace Ross Hamilton was about to kick into high gear, I asked Bobby Laurier which cabinet portfolios work against a man or woman seeking the leadership.

"Finance," he said, without missing a beat.

"But, Mr. Laurier, you held Finance," I said to him. "Does that mean you won't become Prime Minister?"

"I'll be de first," he said, sounding supremely confident. "And I only survived Finance 'cause I got in dere fast, I did as little as I could, an' I got out as soon as I could. Anybody who tinks Finance is a steppin' stone is crazy. It's de kiss of death."

I thought of Laurier's words as Joey continued his "feeding chain" discourse — after cabinet, he was saying, came certain ministerial chiefs of staff, then their press secretaries, and a handful of MPs, but, under the Tories, some lobbyists had more power than most of cabinet, and every chief of staff and MP, et cetera, et cetera — but I didn't tell him I disagreed. I just kept quiet, and looked at the maples turning red and orange, in the spot between the West Block and the Centre Block. It was very pretty. It wasn't Victoria, but it was pretty.

❊   ❊   ❊

Mike Mahoney swept out of the door beside the receptionist's desk in precisely the manner of something aquatic. A shark, maybe.

I was in the waiting area of the office of the Minister of Finance, the Honourable Jean Rioux, PC, MP, and his chief of staff was suddenly upon me, a swirl of racy cologne, rapid movement and teeth that were unnaturally white. I was about to be devoured.

He looked as if he wanted to kiss me. You know, on both cheeks, the little peck-peck thing that Western Canadians never understand or do. He didn't, but I was momentarily speechless, just the same.

"*Chris*," he said, emphasizing the last consonant. "It's so *good* to see you again! Come on in and see our new digs!"

Still mute, I followed him past the receptionist, who buzzed us in, and into a huge corner office that offered a magnificent view of the Gatineau Hills on two sides. It was as big as half the entire Canadian Press national bureau, a fact I mentioned to him.

He frowned quickly, probably making a mental note not to show any reporters his office in the future. Being smart, Mahoney understood one of Ottawa's immutable rules: those who lord power and its trappings over reporters are not going to stay in power very long. He smiled: "Well, the *Tories* looked after themselves," he said. "We moved in here, and we couldn't *believe* how opulent the offices were. And we haven't spent a *cent* on furnishings or renovations, you know." This, despite the fact that the departing Conservatives had seemingly removed every stick of furniture, and every fax machine and computer. He motioned me to sit down.

"Mike, don't worry," I responded, sitting on a leather-covered couch. He sat on a smaller matching chair, perpendicular to the couch. "I'm not here to do a chequebook-journalism piece. I'm just here to get an idea of what you and your boss have planned."

In meetings with political assistants, I had learned, it was always a good idea to suggest that the assistant, as well as the minister — or even instead of the minister — ran a particular department. It was meaningless flattery, but, nine times out of ten, it worked.

It worked with Mike Mahoney. "Well, you know, *Chris*, we have so many plans, I don't know *where* to start," he told me. "Jean considers himself so *lucky* to have been chosen as Finance minister."

"I've heard he lobbied hard for the post," I said.

He sized me up for a minute, still smiling. "We're off the record here, aren't we? No quotes, no nothing, *right*?" he asked.

"Of course. I don't even have my notepad with me."

"Well," he said in a conspiratorial tone, leaning close enough that his knee touched mine. "Well, *Chris*, the fact is that Jean could have had *any* post he wanted in cabinet. *Including* Finance. He didn't have to lobby for *anything*."

"So he and Laurier have patched up their differences?"

He tittered, but it sounded forced, like PeeWee Herman's laugh. "*What* differences? Bobby Laurier and Jean Rioux are old friends, they go *way* back. And the Prime Minister is such a *nice* man." He said "nice man" in such a way that it didn't quite sound like a compliment. It sounded like the way someone describes a doddering old fool.

That had been one of the nasty spin lines the Rioux people had used during the leadership race: that Bobby Laurier was "yesterday's man," that he was so old he was barely competent. One or two of them had apparently suggested that his deficiencies with the English language were due to the onset of Alzheimer's. After he became leader, word leaked out that Laurier had been rushed to the Canadian Armed Forces Hospital complaining of chest pains. Some Liberal assistants — all of them Rioux loyalists — had hinted that Laurier was too sick to continue, and that Rioux was about to be called in as interim leader. But Laurier's chest pains turned out to be nothing more serious than a hiatus hernia. The rumour, like all the others, was shown to be baseless.

As I listened to Mike Mahoney effortlessly bat back my questions, pausing only periodically to light cigarettes — he was a chain-smoker, and not about to be deterred in his habit by the government's strict no-smoking policy in federal buildings — it became evident to me that I had underestimated him. Slowly, surely, imperceptibly, he was taking control of the discussion. Listening to him, I started to wonder whether the Liberal Party had made the right choice at its leadership convention. Mahoney had an impressive grasp of economic policy, of how government worked, of what he and Rioux planned to do. He was campy and as outrageous as a drag queen, but he was no dummy. If only a few of Rioux's people were like him, they would be running the entire government in no time.

Rousing myself, I decided to throw him a curve ball. "Listen, Mike, what is Mr. Rioux's connection to the Prince Group?"

Mike Mahoney's cigarette momentarily froze in midair, halfway between the ashtray and his mouth. For the briefest of moments, he paused, and the smile slipped.

"I did a corporate search this morning, but all I came up with was the name and address of a lawyer in Montreal, some guy named Roger Fournier," I said. "When I called his office, I got a recording saying the number was out of service. Do you know who he is?"

He laughed the PeeWee laugh again. "Chris, *wherever* did you hear that Jean was connected to the Prince Group? That's *silly*," he responded. "I can tell you what I know about the Prince Group, but it isn't much ..."

And then, as if on cue, the door to his office opened and Jean Rioux stepped into the room. Even with his suit jacket off, he looked very much the part of Finance minister. He was wearing a tailored shirt with his monogram on one of the French cuffs. His shoes looked like Ferragamos. And he had a bit of a tan, although I suspected it may have been artificially induced. With the eyepatch, he looked not unlike that guy in the shirt ads. Rioux smiled when he saw me.

"Chris, how are you," Rioux asked, crossing the room to shake my hand. "Is Mike spinning you too hard?"

"No, Mr. Rioux, not at all," I answered. "We were just talking about this and that."

We chatted for a while. Although I am now reluctant to admit it, the guy was charming as hell. He had an easygoing manner about him, one that was certainly unique among politicians. For a francophone, his English was flawless. It was better than mine, in fact. The only disconcerting feature, I suppose, was his famous eyepatch. I found my gaze lingering on it once or twice, and then I would look away, fearing I was being rude. Rioux didn't seem to notice. We started to talk about his new portfolio when Mahoney abruptly snatched a file off his desk. He gave Rioux a look and nodded towards the door. "Oh no," Rioux said, "I'm in trouble. Will you excuse us for a minute?"

"Sure," I replied, a little flabbergasted. I hadn't planned to say anything to him about the Prince Group, but Mahoney seemingly thought I was. Maybe I was just imagining things. They walked out.

I looked around Mahoney's office. Apart from its size, there was nothing in it to distinguish it from a thousand other offices around Parliament Hill. All of the art carried federal Art Bank tags; the furniture was obviously not new. A few cardboard boxes were stacked in one corner, still unpacked. I strolled over near Mahoney's desk, which was crowded with magazines, paper and cigarette packages. I looked towards the door through which Mahoney and Rioux had disappeared. Nothing.

At UBC, one of my journalism profs had once suggested to my second-year reporting class, only half-jokingly, that reading documents upside down is a valuable skill for any reporter to acquire. I had taken his words to heart, and actually spent a few weeks learning how to do it. Once I got the hang of it, so to speak, it turned out to be easier than I had thought it would be. Three years later, when I got around to practising journalism at the B.C. legislature, I had used the technique on a couple of Socred ministers, to great personal benefit. They don't tell messy people to clean their desks for nothing.

So I read what was on Mike Mahoney's desk. A lot of pink telephone message slips, a couple marked "URGENT" from a "Mr. McMillan." And a couple of memoranda, sitting side by side.

One memo was on Office of the Minister of Finance letterhead; typos had been highlighted in red ink. It was a memo from Mahoney to John Keitel, the Assistant Deputy Minister of Corporate Services at Finance, and was marked "PROTECTED." Keitel was the bureaucrat who did all of the spending for the Department of Finance, buying everything from paper clips to opinion polls.

"The Minister has directed," the memo read, "that the department undertake an immediate review of all procurement policy in the Department of Finance. Specifically, the Minister requires a listing of all personal-services contracts that have been carried over from the previous government. The listing should contain the names and addresses of the contractors, as well as the amounts contracted, and for what duration."

Nothing unusual there, I thought. The Grits are trying to find out which Tories are still on the payroll. Pretty standard.

There was also a letter from someone at Nicol Press, a publishing house in Toronto. I couldn't read all of it, but it appeared to be an embarrassingly flattering letter to Rioux, asking him to consider an authorized biography. I couldn't see who had sent the letter.

I heard some voices and moved away from Mahoney's desk, turning to look out the windows just as he and his boss returned. Mahoney's eyes flickered from his desk to me, but he kept smiling. Rioux was smiling, too.

"Chris," he said, "we have a proposition to make to you."

I stood there, not quite sure what he meant. "A proposition?"

"How would you like to come and work for us?"

CHAPTER FOUR

Jean Rioux had it all. Of that, there could be no doubt.

He had come to Ottawa from a Montreal corporate boardroom a few years earlier, midway between the beginning and the end of Jack Gibson's doomed tenure as Leader of the Liberal Party of Canada. After a few years of service as co-chair of various Grit policy committees, during which he feigned interest in what grassroots Liberals had to say, Rioux was asked by Gibson, his mentor, to run in a by-election in St. Henri–Westmount, one of the three wealthiest ridings in the country. The St. Henri part, which was quite poor, drove down the per-capita income statistics somewhat — but not enough to push the riding below Vancouver's Quadra or Toronto's Rosedale.

For Rioux, it was a natural fit. Although he and his wife, Bunny — real name Beatrice — lived in the biggest mansion in Outremont, on the other side of Mount Royal, he was well suited to Westmount's rarefied air. Bounded by multimillion-dollar estates farther up the mountain, and upscale shops down below where bored trophy wives of industrialists, doctors and lawyers dropped thousands without batting an eye, the riding was the very epicentre of privilege and wealth in anglo Quebec. It had gone Liberal since Confederation. Even during the FLQ crisis in the late 1960s and early 1970s, when Maurice Johnson Bechard's Liberals were still in power — and seemingly doing nothing about separatist bombs going off in Westmount mail boxes every second day — the loyal Grits of the riding dutifully returned Liberal candidates to Parliament with massive majorities.

For most of two decades, the area had been the personal fiefdom of Toby Robertson, the ultra-rich descendant of a brokerage-firm empire. Robertson's parliamentary career had been untouched by either cabinet post or achievement. After he was felled by a heart attack — dramatically, and fittingly, near the roast beef on the buffet table at the Parliamentary Restaurant — Jack Gibson telephoned Jean Rioux. A deal was struck.

Rioux, about a decade younger than Gibson, was a handsome man, with one pale blue eye and a regal profile. His hair, which was disappearing near the top of his head, was always combed forward across his bald spot. It was not quite as comical as the sort of bizarre follicle gymnastics favoured by the late René Lévesque, whom Rioux had known, and secretly admired for his Quebec nationalism, but it was getting there. To some, it hinted at Rioux's vanity.

And Jean Rioux, above all else, was vain — vainer, even, than most of his colleagues in Parliament, where the twin monarchs Narcissism and Ego had reigned forever. He was unabashedly in love with himself. He was in love with his looks — although he could have lived without the patch, some days — and his effortless bilingualism. He was in love with his business acumen and his wealth, and the status it brought.

But he was bored. The mansion, the estate in the Townships, the garage filled with Jaguars, his suite at the Ritz-Carlton — none brought him the sort of contentment Rioux believed to be his entitlement. He wanted more. Having become one of Canada's richest men, he would become its Prime Minister, too. Canadians, he knew, needed him.

So he threw himself into a whirlwind of parties and fundraisers, trying to decide which party was most deserving of his membership. The Tories courted him mightily, believing that the Rioux name could boost their diminishing electoral fortunes. For his part, Rioux liked the Tories' plans to "devolve" huge amounts of power to the provinces, particularly Quebec. But he suspected that the Conservatives were unlikely to win a third majority in the House of Commons. So when Jack Gibson called, Rioux was ready.

Rioux met Gibson while articling at Pepper, Goosebaum and Maltais, one of Montreal's most prosperous law firms. Gibson had gone to Pepper's to improve his French and stayed for a few years. Rioux — whose law-school marks had been anything but stellar — had gone there because his father golfed with the managing partner. With their shared interests in tennis, sailing and exaggerated accounts of sexual conquests, the two men — despite the age and cultural differences — struck up a friendship that endured.

When the Tories finally called the by-election to fill Toby Robertson's vacant seat, Gibson telephoned Rioux. "One condition, Johnny," Gibson growled, using the name that Rioux favoured while courting Liberals in English Canada. "You support me, and I'll support you when your time comes. But no running for my fucking job until I'm gone, okay?"

So Jean Rioux ran. He loved it. He loved seeing his name on the red lawn signs, and his picture in the *Gazette*. He loved it when the paid campaign workers chanted his name. He loved the fact that he was convincingly concerned when people told him about their worries. He loved it all.

Along with his vanity, he also possessed another major personality handicap — a legendary vindictiveness. Apart from Bunny, and a couple of employees, not many knew about it. His ability to remember insignificant slights and perceived criticisms was, however, indisputable. In part, he saw the prime-ministerial post as an excellent opportunity to settle some scores.

But he was clever enough to know that self-absorption and a spiteful nature were not likable traits, particularly to voters. So he largely held his vanity and temper in check. During the by-election, held in January, he took to wearing a down-filled jacket as he moved door to door in poorer St. Henri. He spoke convincing *joual*, making his French as colloquial as he was able. He made certain to be photographed eating poutine — a mixture of french fries, cheese curds and gravy adored by French Canadians — pretending to love it, when he felt like upchucking. He was always careful not to berate staff and family — particularly Bunny — when any reporters were within earshot.

Among his many passions — one of them involved something about nurses' uniforms, Joey swears, but I told him I was not interested in the sordid details — was a hatred of Bobby Laurier that was as long and as deep as the St. Lawrence. Long after the Liberal leadership convention had faded from memory for every other sane person, Rioux remained bewildered and astonished that the party's delegates had selected a monkey-faced moron like Bobby Laurier over him. Periodically, his rage over this cruel twist of fate would result in towering, red-faced rages, wherein he would fling papers, pens, books and whatever was within reach. During these episodes, Mike Mahoney would quietly shut the doors to his office and send away staff who were within earshot. It was better that way.

*   *   *

Bobby Laurier's time as Leader of the Opposition had been anything but stellar. He seemed strangely uninterested in the duties of the job, as I have mentioned before. But Rioux's minions — chief among them Mahoney — didn't make things any easier for their party's elected leader.

Not only did the Rioux forces regularly leak damaging stories about Laurier's health and mental fitness, they pushed for only pro-Rioux members of Parliament for the coveted spots on the daily Question Period list; and, above all, they conducted clandestine meetings of the 829 Club, as it was called.

The club was a group of MPs, political staffers and prominent Liberals who had been among the final 829 delegates — thus the name — to vote for Rioux on the convention's single round of balloting. Like most of the delegates who had supported Rioux — with the notable exception of a group of Indo-Canadians from B.C. and Ontario whose support had been quite literally bought by various ethnic power brokers — the 829 Club's regulars seemed to be cut from the same pricey cloth. For the most part, they were the sons and daughters of privilege, having grown up in the well-to-do families of diplomats, bureaucrats, bankers and former cabinet ministers. Unlike Bobby Laurier's scruffy crew — who were largely the descendants of barbers, cab drivers and immigrants — Rioux's 829 Club members were impeccably educated, bilingual and thoroughly snobby. They were, I eventually decided, Conservatives who were Liberals only to the extent that they believed it would assist them in achieving power. They were also lousy political organizers, which may be explained by the fact that a lot of them seemed to have been educated in private schools in Switzerland and places like that, where stacking delegate-selection meetings is not a required course.

Bobby Laurier, in an off-the-record aside, had another theory. "My people were closer to de ground," he told me with a sly grin. "Rioux's guys, dey aren't so close to de ground." I had to think about it for a while before I understood what he meant.

Petulant and sulking following their loss to a man they all regarded as a lumpen-class simpleton who was better equipped for janitorial duties than leading what was rightfully *their* party, the members of the club would gather in an office somewhere deep in the bowels of Parliament Hill every Tuesday evening, the day prior to the Grits' weekly caucus meetings. There, they would plot what to say in caucus that would destabilize Laurier's leadership.

The members would be called to the meetings by one of Rioux's trusted circle of advisers. These included Mike Mahoney, Dick Thorsell, Mark Petryk and Donna Curtis. Thorsell was a portly former Jack Gibson aide with a talent for self-promotion and little else; he claimed to have been a banker once, but most of his time was spent as a lobbyist for companies with which Rioux had links. Petryk — bearded, brainy, big — was also a lobbyist, for dozens of assorted industrial polluters and union-busters, but at least he was honest enough to admit he was an influence-pedlar, which Thorsell would not. Petryk was best known as a former Olympic pole-vaulter. He had also been one of Rioux's leadership campaign bosses, and was a masterful media spinner. Curtis, meanwhile, was a serpentine political organizer who selected which leadership candidate to support, whenever Grit conventions rolled around, on the basis of pocketbook size. She would always pick the richest. When it was convenient, Curtis would service an 829 Club member who needed to be placated.

Mahoney, Thorsell, Petryk and Curtis, when making the rounds, would swear the 829 Club's members to strict secrecy, and solicit pledges of undying loyalty to Rioux and his Tory-in-disguise economic policy (sell off government, characterize the poor as a bunch of whiners, etc.). The meetings were regularly attended by various Quebec MPs and staff people who despised Laurier for his patriotism, and who — like Rioux — favoured a radically decentralized federation; Ontario members of Parliament and senators who had ties to, or who sat on the boards of, various banks, tobacco companies and multinationals; and, from across the country, multi-degreed academics who simply thought they were *smarter* than Bobby Laurier and his ilk. This was Jean Rioux's palace guard: the ultra-rich, the crypto-separatists and the eggheads. The 829 Club.

Rioux himself would rarely attend the meetings of the group, so as to ensure he maintained what indicted American far-right politician Oliver North had called "plausible deniability" during the Iran-Contra scandal. That is, if anyone ever asked about the club, Rioux could plausibly deny having participated in its deliberations. Or so he thought.

Most of the time, the club's members would pass an hour or two bitching about what they saw as Laurier's intellectual inferiority — or Flash Feiffer's lack of respect for them, or Charles Lafontaine's lack of interest in either them or their leader. Occasionally, the group would ask Mahoney to pass along some embarrassing tidbit about Laurier or his loyalists to one of the many reporters he had flattered. Or they would seek to block the nomination of a Laurier follower to some party executive somewhere. Or, when the Great Man himself was present, they would try to talk him out of quitting.

Jean Rioux talked about quitting a lot. He chafed mightily under the ignominy of Laurier's leadership, pathologically unable to accept the legitimacy of the delegates' decision three years earlier. He saw virtually every decision made by the Liberal boss as a personal affront. He would fling objects around his office and — if this didn't make him feel any better — he would castigate Mike Mahoney, Dick Thorsell or Mark Petryk. His features a deep crimson, he would call them all sorts of names, curse their parentage and declare them incompetent. And, if none of that improved his mood, he would dial up some of the 829 Club's members and inform them, his voice choked with indignation and melodrama, that he was going to quit. Again.

The members of the 829 Club would then go into high gear, apostle-like, tearing themselves away from meetings of boards of directors, golf games at WASP-only country clubs and fundraisers for causes favoured by blue-haired millionaire widows in Westmount or Point Grey. They would plead with Rioux to remain, swearing that Bobby Laurier's leadership was but a temporary setback before Rioux attained his rightful place in history. They would tell him that only *he* possessed the political pedigree required for the job. They would tell him that he was brighter, shrewder and better-looking than Bobby Laurier. And, every time, Jean Rioux would allow himself to be persuaded by the 829 Club, his ego stroked enough to assure his presence for another couple of months, until the next perceived humiliation.

Bobby Laurier, I learned much later, saw Rioux as a crybaby — the one-eyed Richie Rich of Canadian politics. But, as the leader of a group of at least 829 rich malcontents who admired him, Jean Rioux had a power base, and Bobby Laurier needed to be careful about how he treated the millionaire Montrealer. The Liberal Party of Canada is, as my father once remarked, "a big tent — there is room for everybody, because there has to be." The country was already too divided by language, geography and relative degrees of affluence for the Grits to be too doctrinaire, he told me. To fashion a government, they needed to fashion an alliance between the centre-left populists, like Bobby Laurier, and the pro-business right-wingers, like Jean Rioux, if they were ever to assume power.

Now, as I stood there in Rioux's posh office, his offer of employment still hanging in the air like the stink of one of Mike Mahoney's endless string of European cigarettes, I puzzled over all of this. I had heard about most of these things, but I had never given them much serious thought. In my three years on the Hill, I had picked up rumours about the shadowy group of Rioux supporters who met periodically. But that was hardly news — every politician I knew harboured ambitions for higher office and the greater power that went with it. So, too, the stories about his supposed vanity and vindictiveness. Most of the politicians I had run across were also prone to fits of pique and most believed, sincerely, "that their shit doesn't smell," as Joey succinctly put it.

The surprise of Rioux's offer — plus my abiding sense of insecurity, which left me feeling strangely flattered by the new Finance minister's offer — caused me to forget all about the Prince Group, or even why I had come to see Mike Mahoney in the first place. Rioux explained that they were looking for a press secretary, one who knew the Hill as well as Finance issues, and that I "fit the bill." I stammered, stupidly, that I didn't know what to say. Mike Mahoney gave a thin smile, as if he had anticipated my reaction.

"Uh, I'll have to get back to you on that, Mr. Rioux," I muttered, embarrassed by my complete inability to say anything intelligent. Glancing at my watch, I lied and said that I was late in filing a story, and would have to go. Mahoney escorted me to the elevator.

"*Bye*, Chris," he said. "We'll talk again *soon*, right?"

Yeah, right.

*   *   *

Like most things that are pious, stuffy and just generally humourless, The New Journalism was born and raised in the dainty environs of academe. Insidious at first, its exponents started to slip out of university classrooms and into news rooms in the early to mid-1970s, filling vacancies on editorial boards, foreign news bureaus and newspaper business departments.

These serious young men and women — and, significantly, there was an historically high number of the latter in The New Journalism wave — had been drawn to reporting by the Bernstein and Woodward–inspired notion that journalism could correct most social and political ills. The New Journalism's adherents, me included, were shockingly naive to believe anything of the sort. But the Watergate stories — and the tantalizing image of Richard Nixon's political corpse, felled by a thousand tiny media pinpricks — were excellent sources of recruitment. Many other New Journalists were drawn to the "profession" — I'm using quotation marks because it may be a practice, or a craft, or even an obsession, but it sure ain't a profession — by a strongly pro-capitalist mindset. Having been alienated by Watergate and other seemingly bottomless revelations of political sleaze, they found a home in the one sector that was (then, at least) unsullied by scandal: big business.

Believing in their rightness and the power of ten column inches a day, these young women and men flocked, like geese, into journalism schools across the country, at places like Ryerson, Carleton or — my *alma mater* — UBC. Many had already obtained undergraduate degrees in other fields, most often political science. This, along with the increased numbers of women in news rooms, represented the most dramatic departure from what we saw as the discredited ways of The Olde Journalism. In the old days, women were hired to fetch coffee, or staff the rewrite desk — not do real reporting. Men who sought university degrees, meanwhile, were sissies.

Apart from Joey Myers, who is hard to dislike, I must confess that I do not admire the followers of The Olde Journalism. On Parliament Hill, theirs is a lazy, boorish, booze-addled lot. In my view, they are too friendly with those in power, and they are too willing to write stories that are choked with bias.

That said, I will admit that they generally seem to be enjoying themselves a lot more than the rest of us. They laugh. They talk baseball or hockey with members of Parliament in the West Block cafeteria without feeling guilty about it. They enjoy off-colour jokes at the annual Parliamentary Press Gallery dinner. They have — and I guess this is their most attractive point — a more forgiving nature about those who choose public life.

There's the rub. The New Journalists, and I am certainly among their number, hold politicians to an impossibly high standard. To them, to us, no indiscretion — of the flesh, of the pocketbook, of *anything* — is permissible. Do No Wrong — ever — is The New Journalism's credo.

✻   ✻   ✻

Stanley Silversides was one of the movers and shakers in The New Journalism crusade. A somewhat shy — but intelligent — Toronto native with a stutter, Stanley had worked his way up through various business beat assignments at the *Star*, the *Financial Times*, and the *Globe*. At the moment, he was reportedly planning to co-author a book describing the Liberals' first term in power; if it read anything like his news-analysis pieces, it would probably sound like a call for Jean Rioux's beatification. Stan loved Jean Rioux, as did many of my colleagues.

Stan was well liked by The New Journalism crowd, and intensely despised by the Olde school. Joey Myers, for instance, was not a fan. "When you go to someone's home, you secretly try to check out their bookcases or record collection, to see what they are like, right? That's how you learn what kind of person they are," said Joey of Stan. "Now look at the politicians Stanley Silversides pays homage to, day in and day out, in those pedantic thumb-suckers he writes for the *Globe*. To all you new guys, you ... what do you always call it?"

"The New Journalism," I replied.

"Yeah, that's it, The *New* Journalism," Joey sniffed, "you love millionaires. You adore them. And you fall all over yourselves to congratulate the likes of Rioux for their pathetic and meaningless public bleatings about returning ethics to public life, dispensing with patronage, and the rest of that bilge. And Stanley Silversides is the worst of the lot."

Stan, however, was a friend of mine. Unlike The Olde Journalism cabal — who attached themselves, barnacle-like, to their sweaty perches in the Press Gallery bar — he and I would gather, every once in a while, with various other proponents of The New Journalism in trendy restaurants around Parliament Hill where potted plants and ferns were in abundance. Also in attendance at these earnest get-togethers were Kurt Tasse, one of the up-and-comers at Southam News; Sherry Bickle, the *Financial Post*'s chain-smoking constitutional expert; John Moore, the perpetually stodgy national columnist at the *Globe*; Avie Fleischmann, from Global television news, and another Rioux acolyte; Roxanne Perry, the *Toronto Star*'s monotone-voiced bureau chief; and George Cunningham, the *Financial Times* columnist and chief reporter. And assorted others.

These encounters would make for a good play, one of those favoured by those wordy, self-affected troupes found in university drama clubs. You know:

ACT ONE: THE NEW JOURNALISTS
CONSIDER MR. LAURIER'S
CABINET OVER LUNCHEON
AT THE CHÂTEAU

We gathered in Wilfrid's, the restaurant located on the lobby level of the Château Laurier. It's a nice place, and frequented by senior bureaucrats on expense accounts. We had found ourselves a spot under a large set of windows on the west side of the restaurant, around two tables that had been pushed together. The linen tablecloths were covered with the detritus of our lunches — salads and low-fat meals ordered off the specials menu — and a few discarded newspapers (but none of the *Sun* tabloids, of course). Around the table, deep in conversation, were Stanley Silversides, Sherry Bickle, John Moore, George Cunningham, Avie Fleischmann and me. As usually is the case, I was scribbling doodles of Jimi Hendrix in my notepad, listening to my colleagues and saying little.

Sherry was all right, I suppose, but she had a tendency to be a bit too much of a journalistic cheerleader for those politicians she favoured at any given moment. George wrote like a bureaucrat. For the longest time, I had thought of John as one of the most screamingly dull people I had ever met — until the day he surprised me. He was one of those people you least expect to know something about counter-culture — but he did. I learned of this appealing feature of his character on a day I was talking to a colleague about Jimi Hendrix and drug use. John had been nearby, eavesdropping, and he had interjected a few comments about Jimi's December 1969 drug arrest in Toronto. It turned out he had covered the incident, and had even interviewed Hendrix. That impressed the hell out of me.

Stan Silversides was, as I mentioned, my friend. I admired his intelligence, and his writing skill. While he was the *Globe*'s bureau chief, he wrote as much — or more — than any other of the reporters he edited daily. At our spot at Wilfrid's, Stan was seated at the head of one of the tables, speaking excitedly, which often has the effect of magnifying his speech impediment.

"I am c-c-c-convinced! Laurier's new government h-h-has n-n-no choice but to reopen the c-c-constitutional file!" Stan said. "I d-d-don't care if he c-c-campaigned against c-c-constitutional change!"

Sherry, the cynical one, snorted loudly. "Get real, Stan. People are sick to death of the Constitution. Take my word for it — my last book on the subject flopped like a wet turd." She paused. "Do you think I could smoke in here?"

John Moore waved a finger in the air; he was about to give one of his lectures. "I'm afraid Sherry is correct, Stanley. It is rather doubtful that the Laurier Liberals could be persuaded to do such a thing. Given the yawning gap between Laurier's views on the subject, and current opinion in Quebec, it is akin to asking ... it is like ..." He trailed off.

"Q-q-quick, someone!" Stan said, laughing. "G-g-give John a sports analogy. It m-makes him f-f-feel he is c-c-closer to the unwashed."

George Cunningham, who was a smart guy, grinned knowingly. "John, it sounds to me as if you're quoting from tomorrow's column."

John Moore looked completely chastened. Cunningham, being a columnist himself, understood that columnists quote from their own columns all the time, barely realizing that they are doing so. Everyone laughed.

John Moore was undeterred. "I predict, and I have predicted before, and will again, that Mr. Laurier will regret not agreeing to the constitutionalization of Quebec's distinctiveness," he declared. "He is sadly out of step with popular opinion in Quebec City. Does anyone have a cigarette?"

Sherry perked up. "Does anyone know if we can smoke here?"

"Avie, y-y-you're the guru of the superficial q-q-quick analysis, being from TV and all," Stan said. Avie grimaced. "Who in the Laurier c-c-cabinet possesses any c-c-credibility on the C-c-constitution?"

Avie didn't hesitate. "Well, Rioux, obviously. He's the only one who possesses any credibility on most issues, frankly. And he's the only one with any media smarts."

By this, of course, Avie meant that Rioux was the only new cabinet minister who could be reliably counted upon to leak gossip and spin facts against his cabinet colleagues, most of whom shared Bobby Laurier's aversion to leaks to the media about fellow Grits. George Cunningham stirred, his deep voice sounding odd coming from one possessing such a reedy frame: "Avie, aren't you being too harsh? There are a few good ministers with experience in the cabinet — Rodney Linden in International Trade, or Tom Aspinall in Employment." George squirmed in his seat a bit. "I think Aspinall will be one of the stars in this cabinet."

"Linden is a stuffy old fart in tweed underwear, although he's on the right side of the free-trade file," Avie said, shrugging. "And Aspinall — he's just so ... so ..."

"*Left,*" Sherry Bickle said, almost spitting out the word. "He's too left-wing. He's a relic from another age. He'll bankrupt the country. But Rioux won't let him get away with all of that ridiculous social spending." She paused and wrinkled her substantial nose. "Do you guys think I can smoke in here?"

"D-d-don't be ridiculous, Sherry," Stan said. "Th-th-this is Ottawa. You c-c-can't s-s-smoke anywhere in Ottawa anymore. Christopher, what do you think? You're being t-t-too quiet, as usual."

I continued to doodle in my Canadian Press Hilroy notepad, saying nothing. I felt uncomfortable discussing Rioux, having just come from Mike Mahoney's office at L'Esplanade Laurier. I didn't look up at my colleagues, most of whom — I think — respect my judgments, despite my age. "Oh, Rioux's all right, I guess. What I was wondering is whether you guys think the Liberals will be as influenced by lobbyists as the Ross Hamilton government was."

Stan waved a piece of cutlery in the air, while Avie abruptly sank back into his padded chair, clearly uncomfortable with my question. Stan noticed Avie's sudden reticence right away. "Now *that* is an in-in-interesting question!" Stan declared. "Hamilton's gang were virtual h-h-hostages of the lobbyists. What do you th-th-think, Avie?"

Avie looked away distractedly. "Oh, um, I don't know," he said. "Um. I think this whole anti-lobbyist thing has been overwritten."

"Why do you say that?" I asked him.

"There are plenty of lobbyists who are honest," he replied. "Look at guys like Dick Thorsell, or Mark Petryk. They're good guys."

"Petryk is a great guy," Sherry said. "What's he doing, now that the Grits are in power?"

"He's always g-g-good for a quote, that's for certain," Stan said. "I h-h-heard he was setting up a new p-p-partnership somewhere."

"I would venture to say that a great number of Mr. Rioux's associates are found in the lobbying industry," John Moore said. "Perhaps too many."

"What do you mean, John?" I asked.

"There has been perhaps no Minister of Finance in decades with as many corporate directorships as Mr. Rioux had," Moore said. "And, because the Department of Finance is the final arbiter over every department's budgetary allotment, he is susceptible to the criticism that lobbyists — or his past corporate affiliations — will unduly influence the budgetary process. It is my understanding that Mr. Rioux's own finances have kept the conflict-of-interest bureaucrats at the Deputy Registrar General's office quite busy."

Avie was looking defensive. "But they have given him a clean bill of health," he said.

Stan eyed Avie closely. "How d-d-do you know that, Avie? Is Global pl-pl-planning on reporting that?"

"Um, no," Avie muttered.

Stan and I watched Avie; he looked exceedingly uncomfortable. After a few moments, the Global News producer announced that he needed to get back to the corporation's Press Building offices. He quickly left. "Our g-g-good friend Avie seems kind of d-d-defensive about certain subjects," Stan said, while the others talked about what lobbyists earn.

"I'll say," I said. "What's eating him?"

"The Liberals are desperately trying to fill press secretary posts in about a dozen min-min-ministerial offices," Stan replied. "They're h-having difficulty, from what I've h-h-heard. And one rumour is that Avie is about to leave Global to join s-s-someone's office."

That surprised me. "Wow. Why are the Liberals having so much trouble finding press secretaries?"

"Laurier is still stuck in the sixties when it c-comes to salaries," Stan said, rolling his eyes. "And he re-refuses to allow ministers to p-p-pay more. So all the g-g-good ones are staying in the pr-private sector, doing c-c-communications consulting."

That didn't make sense to me. "So how could they afford Avie, then? He's got to be earning a lot as the most senior Global guy in Ottawa."

"That's where the rumour doesn't m-m-make any sense to me, either," Stan concurred. "Who could afford a $90,000 p-pay cut?"

"Not me," I said, laughing. "My Hendrix bootlegs are too expensive."

Stan laughed, too. "Chris, y-y-you're stuck in the s-s-sixties as much as Laurier is."

*   *   *

The following day, a Saturday, I woke in my Metcalfe Street apartment to the sound of the phone and the first snowfall of 1993. I had fallen asleep the night before on my IKEA couch, plodding through my usual allotment of papers: the *Star*, the *Globe*, the *Citizen*, the *Gazette* and the *New York Times*.

It was Stanley Silversides. "Chris," he said, "I th-th-think I know why Avie was acting s-s-so strange yesterday."

"Why?"

"You're not going to b-b-believe this, but he's quitting Global to join some c-c-consulting firm."

"You're kidding. He's been with Global his whole life. What does he know about consulting?"

"That's not all," Stanley said, clearly pleased with himself. "George Cunningham is leaving the *Financial Times*, too."

"That's probably not a bad move," I replied. "The *Times* probably won't last another year, it's so much in debt. Where's he going?"

"He's going to become a s-s-senior policy adviser to our new Minister of Employment, Tom Aspinall."

"He's crazy." It was widely believed that Bobby Laurier had made a big mistake in asking Aspinall, a well-known social democrat, to rejig the country's social-security net.

"Y-y-you're telling me," Stanley said. "Talk about tr-trading chairs on the deck of the *Titanic*."

"So, does anyone know where Avie is going?"

"I f-f-forget the name of the place. It's new," Stanley said, pausing. "Something like Pr-pr-prince. The Prince something."

I felt my heart sink. There goes *that* story. After a brief discussion of the likely contenders for Avie's post, I said goodbye to Stanley. I quickly threw on my parka, and started walking through the snowflakes towards the office. It was time to find out who, or what, this Prince Group was.

CHAPTER FIVE

The cluttered offices of the national bureau of the Canadian Press are located at the corner of Wellington and O'Connor streets, facing the entrance to the West Block on Parliament Hill. Our bureau, as cramped and as crowded as a rats' nest, occupies most of the ground floor. From our desks, we have a pretty good view of the Hill — so that we can readily observe the comings and goings of our nation's parliamentary élite. During the latter part of the Ross Hamilton regime, demonstrations were fairly commonplace across the way, so we observed plenty of those; the bigger demos would occasionally involve thirty or forty thousand people filling up the lawns and roadways in front of the Centre Block. The best-attended event, of course, was the Canada Day celebrations, which regularly drew more than a hundred thousand patriots to take in the fireworks and mumble their way through the national anthem. When things were quieter, the employees of the Canadian Press would look up from their computer screens to see a dozen or so navy Buicks belonging to cabinet ministers idling near the Centre Block or West Block, and tourists craning for a better shot of the Peace Tower.

On the snowy Saturday in late November that I stepped into the bureau, the Bobby Laurier government was into its fourth week of governing, and a perceptible change was already well under way. Whereas Ross Hamilton's Tories had often seemed intent on creating the impression that they were in a perpetual state of manic activity — drafting trade agreements, tinkering with the Constitution, stirring up linguistic and cultural passions for no apparent purpose — the Laurier Liberals were positively *laissez faire*. After an initial flurry, in which they cancelled a couple of large defence procurement contracts, Laurier's gang seemed to slip into a kind of self-induced governmental-policy coma: they weren't doing *anything*, and they were *proud* of it. In one of my encounters with Bobby Laurier in his final year in Opposition, he had hinted at this approach, describing his political credo as "Undersell, Chris, and den overperform." So I suppose the Grits were underselling. But I frankly hadn't seen much evidence that they were all sequestered in some back room, somewhere, overperforming.

I hadn't seen a lot of my former Liberal sources lately, either, since a sizable number of them had become cabinet ministers. When members of Parliament are languishing in Opposition, I had learned, they spend as many of their waking hours as they can chasing reporters for coverage, shamelessly prostituting themselves for a quote or — better yet — a clip on the TV news. In government, those same MPs will devote equal amounts of energy to running away from reporters. Unless the press encounter was in a highly controlled environment — the Wellington Street press theatre, for example, with its many well-marked exits — government-side MPs could not be counted on for much in the way of candour. So, in just a matter of days, my sources seemed to have dried up.

Given the sorts of "media sluts," as Joey termed them, who had made up my stable of Liberal contacts, this was surprising. One of the chief sluts, metaphorically speaking, was Annette "Annie" Frosini, the third-place finisher in the Liberal leadership race, and a formidable pit bull in the House of Commons and just about everywhere else. Annie was the product of a long line of Sudbury nickel miners, and she could certainly curse like one when the situation warranted it. Annie, who never met a microphone she didn't like, harboured a dislike of Jean Rioux and his ilk that bordered on the pathological. In our occasional get-togethers in the cafeteria on the fifth floor of the Centre Block, Annie would refer to Rioux as "that one-eyed rich cocksucker," or "that silver-spoon cocksucker," or, simply, "that cocksucker." Whenever I thereafter heard the word "cocksucker," in fact — no matter who was uttering it — I thought of Annie and Jean Rioux. In the new government, Annie had assumed the entirely ceremonial post of Deputy Prime Minister, because Laurier privately regarded her as a younger version of himself. She also took on the role of Secretary of State, because Flash Feiffer — a notorious sexist — despised her, and had convinced Laurier that she couldn't be trusted with anything more substantive. I hadn't heard from Annie in months, since before the commencement of the election.

Another great source, back in the days of Tory government and Grit Opposition, had been good old Flash himself. Not that he would ever admit it to anyone — particularly Bobby Laurier, who was known to dislike leakers — but Flash could pander to the media with the best of them. He had a different style, however; he wasn't obvious about his pandering. Flash had most people convinced that he was little more than a well-hung policy wonk with no interest in the petty affairs of the news media. But behind his thick glasses, and beyond his thinning pate, Flash was, in fact, one of the biggest media sluts of all. For instance, whenever a story came out about the Liberals that Bobby Laurier did not like, Flash would immediately become convincingly disapproving of it himself — even though, more than once, he had been the guy who had leaked it. He was, in a sense, a double-spy kind of leaker: he could leak, and then complain mightily about leakers, all at the same time. It was quite remarkable.

Most often, his leaks would be aimed at MPs who had crossed him, or Liberals who had done an end-run around him to get to Bobby Laurier. Like a silent cruise missile, he would fire off some nasty tidbit to me — or one of the other reporters he favoured — and then await the fallout. Everyone was fair game in Flash Feiffer's get-even media strategy, except Laurier, of course, and, shortly after the leader-ship, Jean Rioux. "He used to slag Rioux all the time, the bugger," said Joey, remarking on this change in behaviour. "Not anymore. He won't say a bad thing about Rioux, and I know why. He's screwing Donna Curtis."

"How do you know that?" I asked Joey. I couldn't believe it.

"Well," he said, shrugging, "everybody else has screwed her, so why not Flash?"

One media slut who had always been available for a quote or two — or three or four — was John Derbyshire, a former TV reporter from near Goose Bay, now an MP. Derbyshire was possessed of a glowing mane of thick black hair, a mellifluous baritone and an unerr-ing sense of what reporters needed to make a story work. In my three years on the Hill, I had often seen second-tier portfolios being handed to other Liberal MPs in Opposition. These men or women would toil away in obscurity for years, earnest as monks, trying unsuccessfully to get the media to pay attention to their particular area of expertise — postal service, say, or airline regulation in the regions. But then, when-ever Bobby Laurier or the Liberal House Leader, a humourless and tough P.E.I. lawyer named Mary Kennedy, wanted to give the postal or airline regulation issue some prominence, he or she would turn to John Derbyshire. The Newfoundlander would get briefed on the issue for all of ten minutes, my sources told me, and then he would step out into a scrum. He would charm reporters, he would cajole them, he would use the kind of language real people use. And, in the process, he would get quoted and clipped everywhere — achieving in a few short minutes what his Liberal colleagues had been unable to do, once, in many months of sweaty effort.

I settled in at my desk and checked my voice mail. There was only one message, from John Derbyshire. I hadn't seen Derbyshire close up since the day of the swearing-in at Rideau Hall, when he was anointed the Minister of Public Works as well as Supply and Services.

"Chris, you old scalawag," Derbyshire said, in his best coastal brogue. "Why don't you ever call me anymore, m'boy? You have forsaken me, brother." He paused to laugh. It sounded as if he had been swilling a bit of screech. "Listen, Chris, in all seriousness, I'm just giving you a heads-up, and I'm hoping to sweet Jesus God that your voice mail is secure. Here's the tip, buddy: Rioux's gang are all atwitter about some story you are working on, about a company that is about to open, or has just opened, or something like that. I don't know the name of the company, but I'm certain you do, and I can tell you that little terrier Mike Mahoney and his minions are in a state. You've touched some raw nerves, m'boy, and I'm proud of you. Just don't ever touch my fuckin' raw nerves over at Public Works, y'hear me? Now go back to sleep." *Click.*

I laughed aloud and played the message again, getting more excited as I did so. Derbyshire, like all of the long-time Bobby Laurier loyalists, hated Jean Rioux's guts, and vice versa. In Opposition, Derbyshire had often taken me aside to pass along some critical tidbit about Rioux. Nothing dramatic, but enough to ensure that Rioux and his 829 Club kept their ambitions within the bounds of propriety.

I thought about calling Derbyshire at his Ottawa home, but decided against it. The Newfoundland Grit was enough of a media pro to tell me exactly what he wanted, and no more. Instead, I flipped through a couple of notepads, looking for the stuff I had dug up earlier on the lawyer in Montreal who had registered the Prince Group.

Roger Fournier. That was it. When one of our copy people — a Carleton Journalism student on an internship — had brought me the results of my requested corporate search a few days earlier, I had been surprised to find anything at all. Most of the lobbying outfits in Ottawa were simply loose associations of influence-pedlars, frequently unincorporated. Some of them would occasionally register themselves provincially, but not often. The fact that the Prince Group — whoever they were — had decided to go to the trouble of incorporating themselves suggested that they took themselves somewhat seriously. Companies incorporate themselves to take advantage of tax loopholes, or to shield their directors and officers from lawsuits, or both. But in lobbying circles, incorporation was rare. After all, most of the time, the lobbyists were simply charging people to arrange meetings with cabinet ministers or top-level bureaucrats, or to rewrite departmental documents someone had handed them. No need to incorporate for stuff like that.

But the Prince Group *had* incorporated. And, what's more, it had done so federally, in the province of Quebec. That, too, was a bit strange. If the shadowy types behind the company were planning to ply their sleazy trade in Ottawa, why not just incorporate under provincial laws, in Ontario alone? Why bother to go up the highway to Montreal for a federal incorporation that is done by the Consumer and Corporate Affairs bureaucrats back in Ottawa? It was all very strange.

I looked at the Prince Group's printout. Apart from Roger Fournier's name, his boulevard René Lévesque office address and when the incorporation had been approved — two months earlier — there was no other information of consequence. Nothing about what the Prince Group did, what its share structure was, who owned the biggest piece of it. Nothing. I again tried the phone number I had been given by directory assistance. Again, a recorded message stating that the number was not in service.

I walked across the bureau to the library. Only Luc Bergeron and two or three other people were in, all of them weekend copy-editors. I gave them a wave and went looking for the telephone directories.

Every investigative reporter worth his or her salt knows the value of the city directory, or "reverse directory," as some call it. It is a weighty tome, for some major Canadian cities about eight inches thick, containing tons of helpful information. One section lists phone numbers, followed by names and addresses, so one can track down someone by looking up just a phone number. Another section lists addresses first, followed by names and numbers. And a third section lists names, alphabetically.

I pulled out Montreal's most recent reverse directory and turned to the names section. As I had expected, there was no shortage of Roger Fourniers. In all, about a hundred of them, in very tiny type, all over the island of Montreal. I started examining the names, line by line.

The reverse directory is wonderful for a couple of reasons. First, unlike the regular telephone directory, the reverse directory sometimes prints unlisted numbers — how it gets them, I don't know, but it does. I've called enough people with unlisted numbers to know. After the initial barrage of profanity, I'm inevitably told that the number is unlisted, and asked how I obtained it. I always decline to say. Second, the reverse directory is wonderful because, after a name entry, it usually contains a few abbreviations indicating what a person does for a living. "Ret" means retired, "stdt" means student, and so on. And "barr" means lawyer.

I went through the list of Roger Fourniers once, then twice. There were all sorts of professions and occupations listed beside the names. But none appeared to be a lawyer. I looked a third time. Nothing.

Then it dawned on me. "What an *idiot* you are," I said to myself. In Quebec, the French equivalent of a lawyer is an "avocat," or a "notaire," but not a "barrister." They don't even have the same system of law as the other nine common-law provinces. I grinned, thinking about what my mother would say: *If you had gone to law school, Christopher, you wouldn't have wasted all that time.*

I went down the list again, looking for "not" or "avt" beside one of the names. I found three, retrieved the telephone numbers and returned to my desk.

The first number was wrong. The Roger Fournier I reached — who spoke English — told me that he taught law at the Université de Montréal, and that he hadn't actively practised law in a decade. I tried the second number. After a lot of rings, a woman came on the line. Her voice sounded muffled; the connection was bad, too.

"Allô?" she said.

"Uh, bonjour," I replied, cursing my inability to keep up with my French studies. "Parlez-vous anglais?"

"Non," she answered, curtly.

We went back and forth like that for a minute or two, me trying to connect with her in my mangled French, she sounding pissed off. It became apparent that she did speak English, but that she didn't seem to want to speak it to me. She, it turned out, was Roger Fournier's wife.

"Qu'est-ce que votre nom, monsieur?" she asked me, her tone icy.

"Je m'appelle Christopher O'Reilly, avec Canadian Press," I replied.

"Vous êtes un journaliste?" she said, her voice growing louder.

"Oui, oui," I answered, suspecting the call was rapidly nearing an end. It was.

"Merde," she spat, adding another few curses I didn't understand. Something about a tabernacle, and something being "fini" and "mort." "Vous êtes un dégradation!" She slammed down the phone.

I sat there for a minute, listening to the dial tone. What had I said that was so offensive? At the end of the conversation, she seemed to have hollered something about our discussion being finished, or dead. Something like that. And that I was a disgrace, I think.

I replayed the tape. *Il est mort* I thought she had said. *It's dead.* What's dead? The Prince Group?

I decided to check it out with a copy-editor. Luc Bergeron was listening to music on a Walkman in front of his computer. I waved to him and he removed his headphones.

"Hey, Luc," I said. "What does 'Il est mort' mean? 'It's dead'?"

"Boy, they sure don't provide you Western Canadian boys with much in the way of a liberal-arts education, do they?" He laughed. "Yeah, it can mean some*thing* is dead. Or it can mean some*one* is dead."

"A person?" I asked. "As in, 'He is dead'?"

"Oui," he said.

"Great. Thanks."

I went back to my desk and replayed the tape. Did Mrs. Fournier mean that her husband was dead? That Roger Fournier, the Prince Group's lawyer, was dead? How could someone incorporate a company when he was dead?

I decided to again check out Fournier's name on our automated library system, which I could gain access to by using my own computer terminal. A couple of years before my arrival, the Canadian Press had finally developed a system whereby reporters could search for every CP story — and, if they wanted, every Southam News or *Globe and Mail* story — containing certain key words. The system was of fairly recent vintage, so it didn't contain any stories earlier than about 1988. But it was a useful tool.

I plugged in Fournier's name, along with the words "Montreal" and "lawyer," and waited a minute. Nothing came up on the CP system, as had been the case when I had checked before. A search of the *Globe*'s database also revealed nothing. I tried Southam.

Two stories blinked onto my screen, taken from the Montreal *Gazette* around the start of the month, when Bobby Laurier's cabinet had been sworn in. The first story was only three paragraphs long, but I read it a dozen times, my heart racing.

> *Montreal Urban Community Police are treating the death of a city lawyer as a homicide, following the discovery of a body in an underground parking lot on René Lévesque Boulevard yesterday evening.*
>
> *The body of Roger Fournier, 43, was found slumped behind the wheel of a car at 954 boulevard René Lévesque by a security guard. Insp. Etienne Cadieux said Fournier had practised law in an office at the same building for about ten years.*
>
> *Cadieux added that the circumstances surrounding Fournier's death are suspicious enough to treat it as a homicide. He would not provide any further detail.*

The next story the *Gazette* had printed about Fournier was equally brief. It came two days after the first.

> *Montreal Urban Community Police are continuing to investigate the murder of a 43-year-old city lawyer, found Monday evening in a boulevard René Lévesque parking garage.*
>
> *The body of Roger Fournier was found behind the wheel of the lawyer's car by a security guard. "Initially, we had thought it was a suicide," said police Insp. Etienne Cadieux. "But evidence located at the scene indicates that Mr. Fournier was murdered."*
>
> *Cadieux said that the motive did not appear to be robbery. "His keys were still in the ignition, and it was a nice car, so it*

could have been stolen very easily," said Cadieux. "And noth-ing had been removed from his wallet, either."

Other evidence found at the scene pointed to foul play, but Cadieux refused to give any further detail. A private memorial service is to be held for the lawyer next week, he said.

I printed out hard copies of the stories. Neither of them contained a byline, which wasn't unusual for stories that were so brief. I figured that a cop reporter at the *Gazette* would still be following the story, which the newspaper obviously did not regard as a big deal. I wasn't wild about calling a rival news organization; their interest might get piqued if they learned of my own interest. So I decided to contact Etienne Cadieux myself. I knew he wouldn't talk over the phone with a reporter he didn't know, so a trip up to Montreal was in order. I checked my watch. Buses left the Voyageur station every hour for Montreal.

I dialed up the local of my editor, Kevin Ritchie, and let it ring until the voice mail kicked in. "Kevin, it's Chris O'Reilly," I said. "It's Saturday, about two o'clock. Listen, I've come across something good on that Prince Group lead I mentioned to you the other day. But I need to go up to Montreal to check it out with the cops. I promise I won't charge you too much overtime, okay? And I won't use room service at the Ritz-Carlton too often. I'll see you Monday morning."

I threw on my coat and dashed home to pack a bag for a quick trip to Montreal.

*   *   *

Roger Fournier's office building at 954 boulevard René Lévesque was an unremarkable modernist structure: lots of mirrored glass, shiny marble, that sort of thing. The building was perhaps a dozen storeys high and, as I loitered in the deserted lobby near the tenant index, I saw that the list was filled with a sizable number of accounting firms, dentists and lawyers.

I had worn a suit and a tie, and I had filled an attaché case with the tools of my trade — a few Hilroy reporter's notepads, a tiny German 35-millimetre camera, a fistful of batteries and two micro-cassette tape recorders. One of the recorders was fastened to the case's interior, near a tiny hole. I used it on those occasions when I needed to tape a conversation without the focus of my attentions learning of my interest in what was being said.

In my suit and tie, and with my shortish hair and the briefcase, I looked a lot like a lawyer — which was the general idea, when I dressed back at the Howard Johnson's. When I did the court beat, in B.C., I had discovered that court clerks and cops were a lot more willing to gossip among themselves when they believed no reporter was eavesdropping nearby.

A throat cleared behind me. A tiny, pimply-faced young man in a Pinkerton's uniform stood frowning at me, attempting to convey his concern that a stranger was loitering in his lobby on a Saturday evening. It was about 7:00 P.M.

"Monsieur?" he said. "Est-ce que je peux vous aider?"

"Oui," I replied. Then, switching to English: "Do you speak English, by any chance?"

"Yeah, sure," the guard said. "No problem."

I extended my hand. "My name is Christopher O'Reilly, and I've come from Ottawa to conduct an investigation of Mr. Fournier's death. This is where he worked, right?"

"Yeah, he worked here," the security guard said. His name turned out to be Gaston Petit. And he certainly was *petit*: he couldn't have been more than five feet tall. "Are you ——"

I didn't let him finish. I assumed that he was probably going to ask me if I was a cop, which was a question I did not want asked. As an investigative reporter, I had learned two immutable rules: one, never ask a question to which the answer might be "no." Two, never lie about who you are. It *was*, however, fair to use guile and trickery to prevent anyone from learning that I was, in fact, a meddling journalistic snoop. Which was why I cut Gaston Petit off. "I work on Parliament Hill," I said, quickly. This, of course, was literally true. But Gaston could certainly not be blamed for assuming, for instance, that I toiled for our nation's spy service, or the RCMP, or the Department of Justice — all of which maintained offices on Parliament Hill, too.

I plunged on, before Gaston could ask any other questions. "Gaston," I said, moving closer, "we have been following this case very closely in Ottawa, and we are disturbed by what happened here. It does not seem" — and here I paused and peered around the lobby, lowering my voice — "that the local police are devoting enough time to the case."

Gaston brightened noticeably. "No shit!" he exclaimed. Like most adolescent security guards I had met, Gaston harboured a secret longing to become a detective. "The fuckin' guy was killed almost a month ago, and they still haven't solved the fuckin' case! Our tenants are all freaked, you know. Some of them want to move out, and I don't fuckin' blame them."

"Exactly," I said. "We have the same view of the case, you and I."

I was in full investigative-reporter mode, wherein my usual insecurity dissipated and I became, in a sense, someone else. Typically, this chameleon routine would see me adopting whatever style of dress, manner of speech or behaviour that was necessary to make someone feel comfortable enough to talk. Security guards, I knew from past experience, saw a lot of things that went on in the buildings under their care. And on Saturday night, I had figured, I would perhaps find one who was bored enough to chat.

So we chatted. Roger Fournier, Gaston explained, was "one of the most unfriendly fuckin' guys I've ever met." Gaston had provided security alone at 954 boulevard René Lévesque from 6:00 P.M. to 2:00 A.M. for three years. He knew most of the building's tenants, he said, on a first-name basis. Fournier, however, had always remained aloof, as had the three elderly secretaries who worked for him. Fournier had been a sole practitioner, relying only on the three women to service his many well-heeled corporate clients.

"No partners or associates or students?" I asked Gaston, as he sat at his desk in the lobby. My briefcase, with the tape recorder whirring away inside, was sitting on the floor between us.

"Nope," Gaston said. "That Fournier guy was a fuckin' mystery man. Never worked with anybody except them three bitches."

"Where are the secretaries now?" I asked.

"Out of fuckin' work, I hope," Gaston retorted, snorting.

"Ever see any clients coming in?"

"Nope," Gaston answered. "Not many during my shift, anyway. Lots of couriers, though."

"Ever sign for any of the couriers?"

"A few times, yeah," he said. "When his office was shut down, which wasn't often. They were big packages, from Europe and Africa and places like that."

"Really? Where in Europe?"

"You know, the Gran' Canyon or Gran' Cayman or places like that," said Gaston, who clearly should have paid more attention in his geography class. "So I'd sign for the package, and I'd have to call one of them fuckin' secretaries."

"Have to?"

"Yeah," he replied, shaking his head. "She would come over here with her hair in curlers, didn't matter what time it was, and she'd get the package from me. Could be one in the mornin', it didn't matter. Nasty old bitch, that one."

"Which one?" I asked.

"Maryse Boivin, right here," he said, pointing to a piece of paper taped beside the phone on his desk. There was a telephone number beside Maryse Boivin's name, which I read upside down and quickly memorized.

"I see." I let a few moments pass in silence while Gaston awaited the next query. "Doesn't all of this seem very unusual to you, Gaston? Doesn't Mr. Fournier seem to be a very mysterious fellow to you?"

"Fuck, yes," Gaston said, stretching his diminutive frame so that his feet no longer touched the floor. "It seems mysterious to me, that's for fuckin' sure. That's what I told the cops, too."

"Has Cadieux finished with Mr. Fournier's office, yet?" I asked Gaston.

"Cadieux?" he said, giving me a pimpled frown.

"Inspector Etienne Cadieux. The investigating officer."

"Oh," he said. "That's not the name of the guy I talked to." He held up a business card that had been tucked under his desk blotter and offered it to me. The officer's home and business numbers were conveniently printed on the card.

"Robert Chiasson," I said, reading aloud the name and numbers on the card so that my tape recorder could pick it up. "He's the officer you spoke to?"

"Yeah," Gaston replied. "They finished up at Fournier's office about a week ago." Gaston eyed me for a minute. I waited.

Finally he spoke. "Want to see the office? It isn't rented yet."

"That would be a great help to our investigation, Gaston."

Gaston fished out a ring of keys and crossed to the entrance to the building. He locked the doors and led me to the bank of elevators. We stopped at the eighth floor, which was dark. "Wait a second," Gaston said, disappearing through a door beside the elevators. The lights blinked on and Gaston returned. We moved down the hallway to a single door, beside which a small brass plate had been posted: "ROGER FOURNIER, AVOCAT." Below the sign was a doorbell.

"The cops were here for a few days, going through the files, talking to Fournier's secretaries," Gaston said, unlocking the door. "Once the cops left, the secretaries came back to start packing the place up. They'll be out this week."

We stepped inside and Gaston flicked on another light. Dozens of cardboard boxes were stacked neatly against the far wall. The furniture had already been removed; indentations could be seen in the carpeting where chairs and desks had once stood. Off to one side, overlooking the street, was a small meeting room. Beside it was a large office, covered in dark wood panelling. It was Fournier's office.

Opposite the boxes, on the floor, were a few dusty computer terminals and dictation machines. "No shredding machine?" I asked Gaston.

"I never saw one," he answered, then gave a conspiratorial grin. "Oh, okay, I get it. You want to know if they threw anything out, right?"

"Right."

Gaston walked across to Roger Fournier's vacated office and looked around. "Here they are," he said, pointing.

Fournier's office had been stripped of everything — except for three green plastic garbage bags piled beside the door. I looked at the bags, then at Gaston Petit. The security guard peered at his watch. "I've got to do my tour of the building," he said. "I don't think I'll be back here for an hour, at least. You can stay here."

"I really appreciate this, Gaston," I replied.

"No problem," he said, walking out. "It's about time somebody figured out who killed that fuckin' guy, right?"

✳   ✳   ✳

About three hours later, I was back in my room at the Howard Johnson's, standing over the bed. Spread across the blanket were two dozen papers I had extracted from the garbage bags. I pored over them while listening to the tape of my discussion with Gaston Petit.

Gaston, it turned out, had been the nameless security guard referred to in the first Montreal *Gazette* story about Fournier's murder. He had found the lawyer's body just before midnight on November 1. Gaston was on one of his hourly tours of the building, strolling through the parking lot, when he heard a faint pinging sound. "*Beep beep beep*," Gaston said. "It was the sound a car makes when you leave the door open and the keys in the ignition. *Beep beep beep.*"

Gaston approached Fournier's black Lincoln Continental from behind, he recalled. The car's dome light was on, and a dark shadow could be seen across the dashboard.

The dark shadow, Gaston told me, was "a lot of fuckin' blood." Wearing a fur coat and an expensive suit, Roger Fournier was sprawled across the car's leather front seats, the left side of his face a mass of gore. His left hand was twisted back, almost as if it had been broken, holding a large-calibre handgun. "It looked like a fuckin' .45 to me," Gaston said. "Whatever it was, it wasn't a fuckin' pea-shooter, because half the guy's head was all over the glove compartment."

Gaston dashed upstairs to dial 911, he told me, and await the arrival of the police. At first, the detectives seemed to be convinced that Fournier's death had been a suicide. "What changed their minds?" I asked him.

"Well," Gaston said, probably repeating what he had overheard the police discussing that night, "one of Fournier's secretaries told the cops that he was right-handed, but the gun was found in his left hand."

"What else?"

"No suicide note. No reason to do it — he was fuckin' rich, no financial problems. On wife number three, this real hot chick with big cans."

"Maybe he was depressed," I said.

"Yeah, and maybe he was a fag," Gaston replied, shrugging. "But why did he start to turn the ignition on, and *then* shoot himself? Why was the door open? And, besides, there was the tape."

"Tape? What tape?"

"The closed-circuit-camera tape," Gaston said. "The cops have it now. But I played it for them before they took it away. It shows a couple of guys walking out of the garage just around the time Fournier was shot."

"Couldn't see their faces?"

"Nope," Gaston said. "No cars, no briefcases, just a couple of guys heading out the door, totally fuckin' oblivious to the fact that Fournier had supposedly just committed suicide a few feet away."

"Not bad, Gaston," I told him. "Not bad."

I clicked off the microcassette recorder and continued surveying the papers. Most were in French, and would require someone with a greater appreciation for the language than I possessed. I wondered why nobody had bothered to pick them up. Wouldn't Fournier, himself a lawyer, have had a lawyer? Or a relative? What about his wife? Yet, here were his personal possessions in a green garbage bag. I opened up a large manila envelope marked "CARTES." Inside were neat photocopies of a score of business cards, about a dozen to a page. The photocopied sheets had been three-hole-punched.

There were cards for process servers, automobile mechanics, a fur-coat storage company. There were cards for other lawyers, most of them in Montreal. And there was an engraved card marked only with an address — 39 Park Avenue, Outremont, P.Q. — and a phone number.

The address looked familiar. I placed a yellow Post-it note on the page, to remind me to check it out, and continued flipping through the sheets of photocopies.

And there, on the second-to-last page, it was:

J. DONNA CURTIS
Barrister and Solicitor
Suite 442 — 59 Sparks Street
Ottawa, CANADA
K1P 5A0

J. Donna Curtis, Jean Rioux confidante, hot babe and all-round political sleazebag. In the papers of the murdered lawyer who had incorporated the Prince Group.

"Gotcha, J. Donna," I said aloud. "Gotcha!"

CHAPTER SIX

The next morning, I was up early. I hadn't been able to sleep much.

I called our national bureau in Ottawa, but — it being Sunday — nobody was in yet. I looked at my watch: it was 9:00 A.M. The only Montrealers up at this hour on a Sunday morning were those few who still subscribed to the tenets of Roman Catholicism. Grabbing my notepad, my jacket and Fournier's photocopied sheaf of business cards, I headed out the door. It was clear and sunny, but cold; a good day for a walk in Outremont. Around Park Avenue.

A little later, my tour of Outremont's upscale streets complete, I was standing inside the entrance to a cluttered *dépanneur*. After a moment's reflection, I pulled out my address book, and I did something I almost never do — I called my boss, Kevin Ritchie, at his home. One of his children answered.

"Hello, it's Christopher O'Reilly. Is your dad there?"

After a bit of shouting and general confusion, Kevin came on the line. "Mr. O'Reilly," he said, in his much-imitated monotone. In our news bureau, Kevin Ritchie was widely regarded as the dictionary definition of unflappable: stoic, calm, cool in a crisis. He was also a hell of an editor.

"Kevin, I'm sorry to get you at home so early on a weekend," I said.

"I have twin four-year-olds, Christopher. Around here, 'early' is a relative term."

I laughed. "Okay, then, I don't feel so bad. Listen, it's a long story, but I'm in Montreal ..."

"I know you're in Montreal," he said. "I heard the message you left on my voice mail. And I want to hear the long story."

"Okay," I said. "Here goes." I went through what I had learned: Roger Fournier's death, my encounter with Gaston Petit, the Prince Group incorporation. "And, um, I found some interesting papers. They, uh, had belonged to Fournier."

Long pause. "I see," Kevin said. "And how did you obtain these papers, pray tell?"

"Well, they were in the garbage."

"As in, they had been thrown out?" he asked.

"Yes. In garbage bags in Fournier's office. The security guard let me look through them. He said they would be tossed out by the janitors first thing Monday morning." I paused, awaiting judgment.

"All right," Kevin said, after another pause. "As long as they were in the garbage, and as long as your new friend Gaston will testify to that effect in court. Removing papers from Mr. Fournier's desk is theft, as you know. And even touching them as they lay on his desk is trespass."

"Yeah, I know," I said. Kevin was a veritable encyclopedia of law as it applies to journalists. "So the papers include photocopies of a bunch of business cards. And one of the cards has Donna Curtis's name on it."

"And Donna Curtis is?"

"She was one of Jean Rioux's gophers during the Liberal leadership campaign," I said. "Pretty good-looking."

"I see. That is interesting, but hardly front-page news, I'm afraid."

"I know," I said. "But there was another card there, containing only an address and a phone number. In Outremont."

"Let me guess," Kevin said, giving a dry laugh. "You are in Outremont now, on your way to said address?"

"Nope. I've already been there. And I think it may be Jean Rioux's house, or the house he used to live in. It looks as if he's renting it to the Bahamian consul general now. But he still owns it, from what the neighbours tell me."

There was a silence at the other end of the line. One of Kevin's twins started to shriek. "I see," Kevin said, finally. "Isn't that interesting."

"Today I plan to meet with the cops, and Roger Fournier's widow and one or two of his secretaries. And then I'll head back to Ottawa. Probably tonight," I said.

"I doubt Mrs. Fournier will tell you very much, if anything, given your last conversation with her. And, based upon the six years I spent reporting for the Canadian Press in Montreal, I know the police will tell you even less. You speak the wrong language."

"Well, it's worth a shot," I said.

"It is, yes. But I don't want you dilly-dallying too long in Montreal, Christopher. I think it will be a busy week for you."

"Why?"

"You weren't the only person to leave a voice-mail message on my line at the bureau," he said. He sounded less amused. "You may not know it, but Avie Fleischmann is an old friend of mine."

"I didn't know that."

"Yes, he is," Kevin said. "And Avie left a message on my machine to tell me that he was leaving Global to work for this Prince Group."

"Yeah," I said. I was a bit disappointed, too, because I also regarded Avie as a friend. And lobbying was a sleazy profession. To a reporter, leaving the news business to work for a politician was bad enough. But to become a lobbyist was beyond the pale. "I had heard that."

"Avie's message indicated that the Prince Group is having an opening-day party at its new offices, this coming Thursday," he said. "An invitation is being sent to me."

"Oh."

"Well, as I said, don't dilly-dally in Montreal," Kevin finished up. "I think we may be onto something here."

❊   ❊   ❊

Kevin Ritchie and I made plans to convene for breakfast at 7:30 A.M. Monday at the Imperial Lunch, a wonderful greasy spoon tucked at the back of an old office building on Albert Street, a couple of blocks south of the Canadian Press's national bureau. He arrived fifteen minutes late, as I was making my way through copies of the *Star*, the *Citizen*, the *Sun* and the *Globe*.

Kevin stood beside the booth, removing his overcoat. "My apologies, Christopher, but I had to drop the twins off at the Kids on the Hill," he said. Kids on the Hill was a daycare facility that operated out of the Confederation Building. It was used by MPs, Hill employees, members of the Parliamentary Press Gallery and any senators with a trophy bride young enough to produce offspring. We went to get breakfast.

"So how were the Montreal constabulary?" he asked me, as we moved through the cafeteria's lineup.

"Like you said they would be," I said, ordering a big omelette, bacon and toast. "They don't *parlez* very much with nosy anglophone reporters, do they?"

"The distinct society," Kevin said, before ordering the breakfast special. "And Mrs. Fournier?"

"She wouldn't even buzz me into their apartment building. Told me to go fuck myself — in French, of course," I said. "But the security guard told me she was stupid, and wouldn't have known much anyway."

"You have an excellent rapport with security guards, don't you?" Kevin looked amused. He paid for our meals.

"They are an investigative reporter's best friends," I said. We sat down to eat.

Kevin Ritchie was the guy who had hired me away from CP's Victoria bureau more than three years earlier. I hadn't experienced many bosses in my journalistic career, but he was already the best one I could imagine. Kevin refused to let the national bureau revert to what it had been for many years — namely, a news service that merely rewrote everybody else's copy and distributed it across the country. He wanted his reporters to write stories with personality. He wanted news features and investigative work.

He was a thin, reedy sort of guy in his mid-forties, favouring John Lennon–style eyeglasses and button-down shirts from Brooks Brothers. He was prematurely grey and a pipe smoker. His own reporting career, in places like Montreal, Toronto and Calgary, had been unremarkable; it was as an editor that he had excelled. Unlike many of the species, he understood that an important part of his job description was management. He constantly prodded us — without being too critical, or too pushy — to produce better copy. For me, he was an ideal boss: he encouraged me to do investigative stories, but he seemed to comprehend that I possessed a bit of a self-confidence problem. So he didn't push too hard.

From my first tantalizing encounter with the outlines of the Prince Group story — the tip from my commissionaire friend, Ray Aquin; Joey Myers's hints over dinner at the Press Club; the message from John Derbyshire; Mike Mahoney's cautious reaction when I let slip the name of the firm — I had told Kevin what I was up to. I had even told him about Jean Rioux's job offer. That had resulted in a lot of uncharacteristic laughter from Kevin.

"That's the oldest trick in the book," he told me, snorting. "Politicians making job offers to reporters, or hinting at job offers, knowing that it will flatter some reporters into providing lots of good coverage. Or neutralize them."

"Well," I said, momentarily embarrassed, because I *had* been flattered. "It won't work with me."

"The other great old trick," Kevin said, ignoring me, "is for a politician to call a reporter up about something he or she has published, and tell them how brilliant it is, how the politician wishes he had thought of something like that, and so on. Or hiring a reporter's relative or friend on a contract. Unfortunately, that sort of nonsense works with too many reporters in this town. That, and cozy breakfast meetings — off the record, of course — and golf games and weekend getaways."

We had decided to keep the circle tight on my Prince Group investigation. Apart from Kevin — and Joey Myers, who admired Kevin tremendously, and John Derbyshire, apparently — my hope was that nobody else knew what I was up to. As I chewed on a piece of toast, Kevin suggested that I attend the Prince Group opening-day party, using the invitation Avie Fleischmann was sending over.

"The fact that Jean Rioux was in contact with Roger Fournier — and that that Curtis gal was — is interesting, but we need more," Kevin declared. "You obviously need to find out what the Prince Group is planning to do with all of these high-powered friends. Does Jean Rioux have a financial stake in the Prince Group? Which companies and individuals does it plan to lobby for? If it is simply a lobbying firm, why bother to hire a professional journalist like Avie?"

I scribbled down some of his questions in my notepad. I had already thought of most of those things, but it didn't hurt to be attentive to what the boss said.

"I'd wait until after the Prince Group's little launch," Kevin said, pulling on his coat. "You never know what you might find out at an Ottawa cocktail party."

✳   ✳   ✳

In the four working days leading up to the Prince Group's party — the invitation arrived Monday afternoon, by courier, and requested an RSVP — I busied myself with some investigative work, along with my regular beats, which had remained Finance, Treasury Board and the Privy Council. The fact that the House of Commons wasn't sitting made it easier.

The address printed on Donna Curtis's business card — the one I found in one of Roger Fournier's garbage bags — turned out to be a little bit of a fraud. The "Suite 442" noted on Curtis's card was no suite: it was a post-office box. And the Sparks Street address belonged to the main downtown postal station.

The papers I had brought back were, for the most part, useless. Luc

Bergeron had translated all of them. Nothing useful. Kevin, meanwhile, had arranged for one of his former colleagues from the Montreal CP bureau — a francophone who was assisting former *Globe* reporter Stephanie Caldwell in her book that would expose corruption during the Ross Hamilton years — to question the Montreal police about Roger Fournier's case. Word came back that countless reviews of the closed-circuit security cameras had revealed nothing; nobody had been able to identify the men leaving Roger Fournier's underground parking lot on the evening of November 4. "The case remains open," Kevin told me after being briefed by his friend. "But they don't expect to solve it anytime soon. To the police, it looks like a professional hit that was disguised, almost as an afterthought, to look like a suicide."

My Hill sources, when questioned, were singularly unhelpful. Nobody wanted to talk about the Prince Group. This was either because they were afraid to cross Rioux's people, or — as I later learned — they were among the hundreds invited to the party.

*   *   *

The Prince Group couldn't have chosen a location closer to the national bureau of the Canadian Press if they had tried. They were on a floor high above street level in the tower of the World Trade Centre, which is approximately a thirty-second walk from my desk. A search at the Land Titles Office revealed nothing; the Prince Group Inc. was listed as a tenant, effective November 1, a couple of days before the swearing-in of the new government.

I strolled over to the Trade Centre building the day before the party. The Prince Group's offices were located on the thirteenth floor of the centre's business tower. On two oversized aluminum-plated doors, I read:

GROUPE
PRINCE
GROUP

I tried to open the doors, but they were locked. I thought I could hear some hammering inside, but nobody answered when I knocked.

Late the next afternoon, after consulting with Kevin, I slipped one of my microcassette recorders into my inside jacket pocket. In the unlikely event that I persuaded anyone to talk to me about something that was newsworthy, we would at least have a taped record of it. Kevin had RSVP'ed and told the woman who answered — she turned out to be a consultant who specialized in throwing parties on the Hill on behalf of diplomatic and corporate clients — that he would be attending.

"So what happens when I show up with your invite?" I asked him.

"Nothing," he said. "This is Ottawa, and gate-crashing is a way of life here. Besides, if they try to throw you out, it will make for a better news story."

I showed up at the party at 7:30, half an hour after it began. Before the elevator doors opened, I clicked on my tape recorder. On the thirteenth floor, a flock of well-lubricated and loud Liberal assistants was crowding the hallway; there were a few former Tory assistants here and there, too. Along one side were a few coat racks. I hung mine up. At the doorway, two curvy young women sat at a table. They smiled, and one of them greeted me in both official languages. I handed the first one the invitation; she didn't ask me if I was Kevin Ritchie. The other woman, however, asked me my name. I decided to try a joke. "Jimi Hendrix," I told her.

"Okay," she said, printing JIMMY HENDRICKS on a name tag. She handed it to me. "Welcome to the Prince Group, Jimmy!"

I pinned the name tag to my lapel and squeezed through the metal-encased doorway, which looked like something out of an early *Star Trek* episode. The entire office — which was large, and crammed with a couple of hundred political hacks in various stages of inebriation — was very much in the style of Captain Kirk's personal quarters. Everywhere was shiny metal, except on the floor and ceiling. The receptionist's station closely resembled the mother ship from *Close Encounters of the Third Kind*. It was all perfectly ridiculous, and pretentious as hell.

I looked around. There was Randolph Jennings, the Liberal's septua-
genarian House of Commons rules expert, deep in conference with
Victor Green, a former minister in one of Maurice Johnson Bechard's
cabinets. Green was married with children, but was also known to
participate in the gay rough-trade game. Not far from Jennings and
Green was a group of people from the office of newly minted Industry
minister Albert Bierce, the former chairman of Winnipeg's Metro
Council; towering above them all was Bierce's leggy, mini-skirted
personal secretary.

I asked for a soda water at one of the many bars and scanned the
room. Holding court on the far side of the waiting room was Lewis
Schull, a figure in Liberal backrooms for most of the past two
decades. Schull, though not much to look at — he reminded me of a
high-school physics teacher — was a bright fellow who had helped to
pilot the Grits to their election victory. The fact that he had been
asked to toil on the party's central campaign was something of an
achievement; a few years earlier, Schull had been at Queen's Park,
working for yet another Liberal government, when he had been
caught in an apparent scandal involving some bedroom furniture —
as in, someone alleged he had been given a waterbed in exchange for
some perceived political advantage. The whole affair — which had
been called "Waterbedgate," of course, by the Queen's Park Press
Gallery — was pretty silly. No one ever proved that Schull had, in
fact, been given anything by anyone. But that didn't prevent his resignation in disgrace. Politics is a cruel game sometimes.

Surrounding Schull were other hacks and flacks of note. These
included McKinley Morley, the Liberal Party's official pollster. Morley,
who had done a good job of forecasting the party's election fortunes,
looked every bit the picture of a man who is about to plunge his snout
into a vast trough of political slop. Also present was Jim McGinnis, the
national bureau chief for the *Sun* tabloids. McGinnis, along with being
notable for his daily trips to the taxpayer-subsidized gymnasium in
Wellington block — so that he could showcase his biceps in tight T-
shirts — was basically a mouthpiece for most of the dirt dished out by
John Derbyshire, the Minister of Public Works. McGinnis's biggest

achievement, to date, had been a snooze-inducing quickie biography of April McTavish, the woman the Tories had selected — for a few short weeks — to lead them to an historic election rout.

I moved around. All of the assistants were better dressed — and cockier — than I had remembered their being before the election. They spoke more loudly, for one thing, as attested to by the volume level in the Prince Group offices. And they seemed to be delighting in flashing around, peacocklike, the emblems of their new office: cell phones and beepers and thick books of taxi chits.

I spotted Avie Fleischmann over in a dark corner with Donna Curtis, the *Globe*'s Stanley Silversides and Morris Dittmore-Wills, *Maclean's* national bureau columnist. Stan and Morris, I knew, were mulling over an offer to write an insider book about the new Bobby Laurier government. The two of them were old school chums. The way they were laughing at whatever Avie and Donna Curtis were saying, however, I wouldn't have been particularly surprised to hear that *they* were working at the Prince Group, too. I decided to visit them later.

Sipping on my soda water, I made my way through the gaggle of political aides to the receptionist's desk, which was now unattended. Behind the desk, but out of sight to those now crammed into the waiting area, was a large electronic bulletin board. On it were a dozen names. I made note of them on a napkin.

"A. FLEISCHMANN" — our friend Avie, now gone over to the Dark Side. "D. CURTIS" — J. Donna, of course, now employed full-time for the first time in her young life. "M. PETRYK" — media-savvy lobbyist. There were other names: "G. AILES" — Gore Ailes, one of Ross Hamilton's former press secretaries, and a one-time columnist for the Toronto *Sun*. Although a veteran reporter, Ailes was now a take-no-prisoners Tory, and was rumoured to be one of the authors of the infamous campaign ads that had mocked Bobby Laurier's face.

There were other names on the board — among them pollster boy-wonder Skip Flynn, a tousled-haired number-cruncher who had been one of Ross Hamilton's favourites for a few years — but I did not recognize all of them. I had just completed scribbling all of the names onto the napkin when I caught a hint of perfume nearby. Not very strong, but nice.

The room was getting more crowded. I was pocketing the napkin and turning away from the receptionist's desk when she spoke.

"You know," she said with a laugh, "I thought about doing that, but I was worried they would throw me out."

And I turned to see France Lajoie, who possessed The Most Beautiful Face I Have Ever Seen. And I flipped for her, right on the spot. *Ka-boom.* Just like that.

"It's a pleasure to finally meet you, Mr. Hendrix," she said, pointing at my name tag. "I've enjoyed all of your albums."

"Call me Jimi," I said.

*　　*　　*

France Lajoie, as I was soon to learn, was twenty-five years old, partly of Chinese descent, and employed as a junior Quebec assistant in Bobby Laurier's PMO. Her father was a former Canadian diplomat who had met her mother in Hong Kong. France's ultimate boss, she told me, was Charles Lafontaine, Laurier's chief of staff. "But I don't see him very much," she said. "Then again, nobody sees him very much."

She laughed. She had a great laugh — it was quiet, and effortless. Not forced or phony.

France Lajoie was about six feet tall, with long, long black hair, which, on the night we met, was pulled up. She was wearing a double-breasted pinstripe suit over a white blouse. She didn't seem to favour jewellery much. Apart from a tiny pair of sapphire earrings, she didn't wear any. And she had the greatest smile. I couldn't take my eyes off her.

We stood talking in the middle of the Prince Group's crowded waiting area for a long time. She didn't seem the slightest bit interested — or put off — by the fact that I was a reporter. In Ottawa, that alone made her remarkable: very few politicos are neutral on the subject of journalists. We continued to chat.

"So, tell me," she said, facing the doors, "are you on business or pleasure tonight?"

Her question surprised me. "Why do you ask?"

"Well," she said, "there are a couple of guys over by the door, behind you, who have been staring at you for a few minutes now. And they don't look very happy."

I shrugged. "Maybe they don't like reporters," I responded. Not wanting to get into a discussion of my story with an employee of the man who had put Jean Rioux in cabinet, I added: "I'm just here to see the sights."

"I doubt it," she replied, still smiling. "You were taking notes of the names behind the desk over there. You don't look as if you're having a very good time. You are using a ridiculous pseudonym on your name tag. And you seem to have come alone."

I was impressed and slightly put off at the same time. France Lajoie was pretty bright. "I always come to parties alone," I said, then regretted saying it.

"Maybe," she said, after regarding me for a moment or two. "But my hunch is that you are here for some story."

"Okay, I'll tell you what," I said, surprised that I was acting so boldly with a woman. "Why don't you walk around with me for a few minutes, and you can see for yourself whether I'm working or not." I paused, and blushed. "I mean, that's if you're here on your own, or whatever."

France slipped her arm through mine. "I came alone, too," she said, and steered me through the crowd towards the rear of the offices. "Let's check this place out, Jimi."

The din of the party grew. The Prince Group had spared no expense: an actor dressed like a medieval prince was handing out bags of candy bearing "The Prince Group" in gold print. A half-dozen young women decked out in clingy outfits that emphasized their considerable bosoms — presumably royal ladies-in-waiting — handed out little bottles of screech. Each was surrounded by a hormonally charged herd of young male ministerial assistants, grinning like idiots. Every second or third office door was open. In each, a well-stocked open bar was doing a brisk business. I spotted the florid Eric Pottingsgill, long-time columnist for whatever rag would take him, instructing a bartender on the creation of the perfect martini. For Pottingsgill, parties like this often passed for research; we could expect a shit-eating column on the Prince Group in his next effort.

"No expense has been spared for this little do," I said to France, still thrilled to be walking around with a beautiful woman on my arm. She was literally turning heads.

"I'll say," she said, nodding in the direction of one of the open office doors. Beyond the bar, a metallic modular-style desk had been set up; expensive-looking computer equipment covered its work surface. "That is a top-of-the-line computer. It must have cost a fortune."

Before we could escape — before I had even spotted him — the pink hand of Mac Lee had grabbed my free arm. "Chris O'Reilly!" Lee exclaimed, his rotund, Michelin-man figure pressed against me, and his eyes glued to France. "What is such a disreputable reporter doing with such a beautiful young woman?"

"Uh, Mac, this is France Lajoie," I said.

"And where do you work, sweetheart?" Mac asked, shaking France's hand for much longer than was necessary. "I haven't seen you around before, have I?"

"Oh, I work for a member of Parliament, Mr. Lee," she said, extracting her hand and smiling as she gave me a look. "Christopher and I are old friends."

"That so?" He sounded disappointed. "Hey, France, let me introduce you to some of *my* friends, okay?"

"Well, okay," she said, allowing herself to be led a few feet away, to where CBC anchor Patrick Stone was swilling Scotch. Standing around him were the *Globe*'s John Moore, who regularly appeared on Stone's various televised political navel-gazers, and CBC radio's Ralph Nearing, a Mother Corporation veteran with the political acuity of your average farm animal. (Nearing had been moved to CBC radio from the television service when his hair started to thin).

Hovering beside Nearing was Gus Stimpole, a former magazine editor. Stimpole, who derived near-sexual pleasure from any piece of gossipy nastiness, was also a regular contributor — anonymously, of course — to the capital's misogynistic and homophobic satirical rag, *Hank*. (Everybody was, if the truth be told.) Also present was Toronto's chrome-domed Stephen — never Steve — Allenby, whose father had been British, and whose mother had been anglo-Indian. Allenby, the author of assorted books few people ever read, claimed to be a member of a visible minority, a status that he believed entitled him to repeat racist stereotypes on his Toronto radio talk show. He styled himself as a gadfly, but I thought of him as more of a tick.

Rounding out the group was Lilly Nicolescu, a sixtyish Romanian who was powerful in Can Lit circles. Lilly was the owner of Nicol Press, which had published Bobby Laurier's monosyllabic — and ghostwritten — autobiography some years earlier. Her presence at the party confirmed her desire to snag Jean Rioux as her next book subject. For some unknown reason, she had a bookseller from the UBC bookstore in tow — Greg Willett — the poor man was no doubt wondering what he had wandered into. Into this odd group France was propelled by Mac Lee.

I hovered on the fringes, not wanting to interrupt the conversation. Stimpole and Allenby, who secretly despised each other, were busy carving up Robert Fulford, a *Globe* columnist. Nicolescu, a long-time pal of Fulford's, swept her unfashionably long hair over her shoulder, inscrutable.

I was about to rescue France from endless, coma-inducing stories about Toronto's chattering classes, when there was a tap on my shoulder. I turned around to see Donna Curtis, Dick Thorsell, Mark Petryk and Avie Fleischmann watching me. Apart from Curtis, all of them had big smiles on their faces. The smiles looked forced.

"Chris!" Avie said, almost shouting over the noise of the party. "It's great to see you here! What a surprise!"

I'll *bet* they were surprised, I thought, shaking Avie's hand, then Thorsell's and Petryk's. Curtis ignored me. Thorsell, who had clearly been drinking, looked as if he had just been squeezing a dead fish. The four of them appeared to have decided to see what I was up to.

"Congratulations on your new job, Avie," I said. "What are you going to be doing here?"

"Oh, thanks," he replied. He shot a look at Petryk. "I'll be doing communications consulting, that sort of thing. You know."

"That's great," I said, turning to Petryk, and hoping that my little tape recorder was still functioning. "But I had heard the Prince Group only did lobbying."

"Nope, we're going to be a full-service little firm," Petryk responded, all *bonhomie* and good spirits. "We'll be doing it all — consulting, communications, even some P.O.R."

"P.O.R." meant public opinion research. "Wow. Even polling? Who will be doing that?"

"Skip Flynn," Petryk said. "Howie Atwater and I did a lot of work with him in our old firm."

Skip Flynn, a pollster who looked like a high-school pep squad captain, had become very wealthy during the Ross Hamilton years. It surprised me that Petryk would align himself with Tories as well known as Atwater and Flynn. "Are you going to be doing a lot of government polling, Mark?" I asked.

Before he could answer, Thorsell leaned towards me. "I hear you've been a busy boy, Chris," he said. He was trying to sound menacing, I guess, but it wasn't particularly effective.

"Well, funny you should mention that, Dick," I said. "I *do* have one question. Have any of you heard of a guy named Roger Fournier?"

Curtis, Thorsell and Petryk stared at me. Nobody said anything. Thorsell looked as if he was about to slug me. Petryk, meanwhile, was watching Thorsell, worried that a bad situation was about to get worse. It was.

"Hey, O'Reilly, why don't you just go fuck yourself?" Thorsell yelled at me. A lot of heads turned our way.

"Can I quote you on that, Mr. Thorsell?" It was a dumb line, but it was the best that I could manage under the circumstances. Thorsell leaned even closer, his features bright crimson. As I stood there, a little disbelieving that all of this was taking place, Thorsell placed one of his hands on my chest.

A lot of people were watching us now. "Get your hand off me, Mr. Thorsell," I said, as Avie advised Thorsell to do the same — and as Mark Petryk tried, vainly, to pull the drunken hack away.

"Or else what, asshole?" he said.

I started to answer, but I didn't get a chance to get another word out, because Dick Thorsell had punched me.

CHAPTER SEVEN

Even as I was making my inglorious descent to the Prince Group's plush carpet, bowling over one of the chesty young women dressed as a lady-in-waiting as I did so, I was annoyed with myself. By letting my exchange with Dick Thorsell escalate into an actual physical confrontation, I had made my life a good deal more complicated. I wasn't the first reporter to have gotten too up-close and personal with a political type in Ottawa, of course. Just last year at the Parliamentary Press Gallery dinner, in fact, an unamused Bobby Laurier had told Jean Laurendeau, the rabid columnist for *Le Journal de Montréal*, to fuck off in a crowded hallway after Laurendeau had made some bigoted remark. But I knew that the collision between Thorsell's fist and Christopher O'Reilly's nose would complicate my pursuit of the Prince Group story. It would, I calculated, enable Jean Rioux's good spinners — and he had a couple of the best, in the form of Mike Mahoney and Mark Petryk — to claim that my investigation had been motivated by malice, or spite, or something like that.

My nose hurt.

As I slammed to the ground, Petryk and a couple of other guys were already frantically pushing Dick Thorsell away. Within moments, a number of hands reached down to help me up. From my ankle-level vantage point, I could see that about a dozen males were also pulling the whimpering lady-in-waiting to her feet.

I let myself be helped up. Nothing was broken, but my nose was bleeding like a stuck pig, as an Albertan would say. France Lajoie appeared before me, a veritable Florence Nightingale, a wad of napkins in her hand. She held them against my nose. Mac Lee tried to hand me a glass of water — or gin, I'm not sure which — but I declined.

"Chris, are you okay?" France asked, looking horrified. "Are you okay?"

"Yeah, I'm fine," I said, even though I wasn't. "It's okay. Is the, uh, girl okay?"

"She's fine," France replied. "Is your nose broken?"

"Hey, slugger!" Mac Lee bellowed, beaming at me. "What does the other guy look like?"

France was furious. She glanced over her shoulder at the figure of Dick Thorsell, who was being hustled into an office by Mark Petryk. The door slammed shut behind them. "Who was that asshole?"

Mac Lee was heartily enjoying himself. "Christ, Chris, that was the most dramatic 'no comment' I've seen since Maurice Johnson Bechard shoved John Moore down a stairwell during the October Crisis! Yee haw!" He laughed maniacally, and I started to laugh, too, despite myself. It hurt my nose.

Avie Fleischmann, looking pale and frantic, pushed through the circle of political assistants who had surrounded me, seemingly intent upon warding off another physical attack by any other drunken lobbyists in the vicinity. "Jesus Christ, Chris! Are you okay? Is it broken?"

"No, I don't think so, Avie," I said. "Do you think I could sit down?"

"Christ, yes! Come to my office," he said, leading a procession that included France, Mac Lee, Gus Stimpole and a few others I didn't recognize. Stimpole, I felt sure, was already composing his anonymous *Hank* magazine contribution on the O'Reilly vs.

Thorsell bout in his head. Avie led us in to his large corner office, its walls unadorned by a single photo or picture, and directed me to a ghastly black leather chair.

I dabbed at my nose while Avie sent for ice. After questioning me about my state of health, Avie said: "What the hell are you working on?"

"I think you know already, Avie," I said, glancing up at France and Mac Lee. I sensed that Avie seemed to be legitimately in the dark. I almost felt sorrier for him than I did for myself. "Avie, why did you choose this place, of all places, to work?"

He looked away, obviously uncomfortable with the question. "It's a long story," he said.

I watched him for a minute, as Mac Lee gave Stimpole and whoever else was within earshot an exaggerated account of what had just transpired between Thorsell and me. There would be no more investigative reporting on this particular evening. I said: "Look, Avie, let's talk tomorrow, okay? I think I'm going to call it a night."

Avie reached for the phone. "Well, let me call you a cab, at least. We owe you that much."

"No, thanks," I said. "I think I'm going to walk."

And out we walked, me and France Lajoie.

*   *   *

Forty-eight hours later, on Saturday night, I stood outside my Centretown apartment building, waiting for a Blue Line cab to arrive. Apart from the incident involving my proboscis — not broken, but larger and redder than is usually the case — a lot had happened since the party at the Prince Group.

After the party, and after my nose had stopped bleeding — but over France's objections — I coaxed her into going for a drink. Given all of the embarrassment I had already been through at the Prince Group's offices, I could live with a few more puzzled stares from strangers. So we took a cab to Vineyards, a quiet and dark wine bar in the Byward Market. I figured my bright red Rudolph-like nose was less likely to be spotted there. And it was a good place to talk. I wanted to know everything about her.

France Lajoie told me that she had been born in Montreal and, following a stint by her father as a trade counsellor at Canada's embassy in London, she and her family returned to Montreal. There, her father worked as External Affairs chief representative at the International Civil Aviation Organization — the body that serves as the United Nations' airline regulator. Her mother, an artist, painted and exhibited in Toronto and Montreal. France and her younger sister, Sophie, attended the private Catholic girls' school Villa Maria. France decided to study political science at Queen's in Kingston when her father accepted a new posting to the World Bank in Washington.

At Queen's, which she loved, France became active in Young Liberal politics. Like most young Quebecers I knew — the anglo or more worldly ones, anyway — she regarded the Liberal Party of Canada as the only political grouping capable of dealing with the endless issue of Quebec nationalism and separatism. Under Ross Hamilton the Tories would accept into their midst a sizable number of long-time separatists (all of whom later abandoned the Conservatives to form the Bloc Québécois). The New Democrats, too, were far too accommodating towards Quebec's nationalists. *Ipso facto*, she and her peers voted Liberal.

At the end of her second year at Queen's, France became involved with a poli-sci grad student, some guy named Ryan. In their fourth year, they lived together in a flat in the student ghetto, much to her parents' horror. They broke up shortly before she graduated, which was also around the same time that France's father was transferred back to the aviation post in Montreal. She returned home to take a master's in political theory at McGill and live with her folks.

While she was working on her thesis, on political communication, her father introduced her to Bobby Laurier — they were old friends, she told me breezily — and she was charmed. "I loved his ability to reduce all of these complex political issues I had been studying to little bite-sized pieces," she said. "And he still seemed to possess an enthusiasm for public life, which surprised me." When Jack Gibson threw in the towel, and the leadership race started to heat up, France called Flash Feiffer and offered her assistance.

I couldn't resist. "What did you think of Flash when you met him?" I asked.

She laughed. "He had the worst handshake I had ever experienced," she said. "And he couldn't stop staring at my breasts. He thinks himself quite the lady's man, you know."

"You're kidding."

"No, it's true," she said. "And I think he would have asked me out, had I given him the slightest opportunity."

"Flash Feiffer, Stud-about-Town. Amazing."

Following the leadership campaign — she attended it as a delegate — France worked in Montreal at a polling agency as an analyst. She dated a few guys, but nothing serious developed.

After the election, Charles Lafontaine called her to offer her a position on the Quebec desk at PMO. It was her first political job.

Listening to her, I could feel my journalistic antennae twitching slightly. Her biography was that of a young woman from a privileged background, or too pat, or both. Why would she be interested in the likes of me? I decided to test her.

"Listen," I said, after we had canvassed our respective family and academic histories — and after I was confident she wasn't seeing anyone in Ottawa. "I love my job."

"I can see that already," she said. "You almost got your nose broken for it, earlier this evening."

"And I love doing the investigative-reporter stuff," I said, toying with a glass of Beaujolais nouveau. "So when I tell you what I'm about to tell you, I want you to be totally honest, okay?"

"Sure," she said.

"I'm working on a story about something. A potentially big story," I said.

"Is it about the Prince Group, by any chance?"

"Maybe. That's a pretty good guess, if you're right."

She regarded me a bit suspiciously. "It's just a guess," she said.

"*Are* you working on a story about the Prince Group?"

"Maybe, maybe not. My editor gets mad at me when I talk to people in politics about stories I haven't published yet."

"Well," she said. "It's rather obvious you *are* working on a story about the Prince Group. When you were leaning over the receptionist's desk earlier this evening, for example, I could see the little red light on the tape recorder in your jacket pocket." She laughed, and I did, too. "Next time, I'd recommend doing something about the little red light, so that no one can see what you're up to. Or wear double-breasted suits."

I was impressed. "Are you sure you don't work for CSIS, and not the PMO?"

"I'm just a peon at the Prime Minister's Office, don't worry," she said. "Now, what were you going to say?"

I continued with my test. So far, all that I was sure about was that France was completely gorgeous, and that I wanted to sleep with her at the first available opportunity. But I don't meet gorgeous women this easily. Not usually, anyway. "Well, the story I'm working on could be very embarrassing for your government. Or at least one part of it."

"I see," she said. "I can't say I'm surprised. You are a political reporter, after all."

We looked at each other for a moment, saying nothing. She seemed to know more than she was saying. And she seemed to know that I certainly suspected as much. But my hormones, and the wine, were wreaking havoc with my journalistic compass. Screw self-restraint, I decided.

"Well, usually I'm Mr. Lacking-in-Self-Confidence," I said, playing with my now-empty wine glass. "But ... I would like to see you again. If that's okay." I felt like a fool.

"It's okay by me," she said, smiling. "Just don't get into any more fist fights, okay?"

We both laughed. "But if we see each other again, and if my story goes the way I think it might go, I don't want to get you into trouble," I said. "There were a lot of people there this evening, and they saw me with you. If they get mad about my story, they might get mad at you, too."

"That's a lot of 'ifs,'" she said, looking thoughtful. "I'm fairly certain that we won't be the first two people in politics and journalism to see each other socially, Christopher."

She had a point there. Ottawa was littered with examples of cross-fertilization between political hacks and journalistic hacks. But a relationship with an investigative reporter — or someone who aspired to be an investigative reporter, anyway — is dangerous for a politico. Investigative reporters, by definition, are always exposing some unpleasantness about someone in authority. That makes life a little bit riskier for someone like France.

"I just don't want to get you into trouble with Flash Feiffer or Charles Lafontaine," I said.

"If it makes you feel any better, we can keep our friendship Top Secret, okay?" She laughed. "You're a worrier, aren't you?"

"I am the World's Biggest Worrier. I'm also paranoid," I said. "But the people I am after are not without influence."

"Christopher," she said, placing a hand on mine. "I haven't been here long, but I already know that secrets don't stay secrets for very long in Ottawa." She paused. She looked as if she was deciding whether she should tell me something. "From what I've heard, some of the Rioux people are very nervous. They don't like what you're doing. And everybody else ... they're just waiting to see what you find."

*   *   *

Waiting. I got fed up with waiting for my Blue Line cab, and I started to walk over to Bank Street to wave one down. In Ottawa, taxi-cab stories are part of the local folklore. When a young person is hired to work for a minister on Parliament Hill, he or she is supplied with a cell phone, a Hill security pass and a book of taxi chits. And, on the Hill, stories circulate all the time about political assistants who use departmental taxi chits to take a cab two blocks to the laundromat or to a restaurant — or use them to take cabs all the way from Ottawa to Montreal, just for kicks.

After a few minutes of vigorous arm-waving on Bank, I was on my way to France's apartment in Sandy Hill. She lived in a nice old limestone six-unit building on Wilbrod, not far from the University of Ottawa. I paid the cabby and went up to ring the bell above France's name. She buzzed me up.

She looked beautiful, just as she had every time I had seen her since Thursday night. When she opened the door, she was wearing a pair of jeans, a turtleneck and Birkenstocks. Despite the fact that I come from B.C., I hate it when people wear sandals anywhere other than the beach. I decided to keep that to myself. "I'm almost ready," she said, giving me a kiss on my cheek. "Come on in." She disappeared into her bedroom.

Her apartment was a mélange of mementos from all over the world — tapestries and shadow puppets from the Orient, watercolours of market scenes in London. Mixed in with it all were a few cardboard boxes containing things she hadn't had time to unpack yet. On the mantel, there was a collection of photos of what I assumed to be her family. There was a graduation photo of France. Another of the photos, poorly shot, featured a smiling France and a tall, thin, bearded man — her father, I guessed — flanking Bobby Laurier. All three were wearing cowboy hats.

She walked back into the living room while I was examining the photos. She looked fabulous.

"This is your father, I assume," I said. His face was almost completely shadowed by the brim of the cowboy hat.

She peered at the photo. "That's my dad, and me, in Calgary at the leadership convention. I'm not sure who the guy in the middle is," she said, smiling.

"He looks somewhat familiar," I said. "Was your dad a delegate, too?"

"No," she said. "That would have been difficult, given the fact that diplomats are supposed to be scrupulously neutral. But he was in Calgary the weekend of the convention, so he dropped by." I sensed, and not for the first time, that she was being deliberately vague.

"Great shot," I said, returning the photograph to its place on the *faux* fireplace mantelpiece. "So, are we ready?"

"All ready," she said. "Let's go!"

*   *   *

The movie wasn't very good — it was one of those ridiculous Hollywood romantic comedies, a chick flick — but that didn't prevent a huge crowd from coming out to see it on a frosty December evening. In Ottawa, there isn't a lot to do after work. Once the political day had faded away, the choices were basic: go out for dinner, go out to a movie. There wasn't much theatre, or anything else, to speak of.

After the movie, we walked along Bank Street to a nice Italian place on Gloucester I had been to with Joey and his wife. It was snowy and, as usual, few people were out on the streets. In Ottawa, on any given night, only the Byward Market seems to possess any life after working hours.

We were walking shoulder to shoulder, my gloved hand brushing up against hers, when I decided to take what — for me — was a big step: I held her hand. She squeezed mine, and we kept walking.

We stepped into the restaurant, and were waiting to be seated, when I saw someone frantically waving at us. It was no less than Annie Frosini, the Deputy Prime Minister of Canada, PC, MP. Annie was sitting with her husband, Pietro, and her chief of staff and close friend, Debbie Cresson. Debbie, who had always been helpful to me, had worked for Annie as long as she had been an MP. Annie waved us over.

"Uh-oh," France said to me in a whisper, "our little secret is out."

We walked over. "Well, hello there, Christopher and France. Isn't this a nice surprise," Annie said, looking delighted she had found us together. "Isn't this a nice surprise, Debbie?"

"It sure is," Debbie said. Everyone laughed, except me. I blushed, I think.

We all chatted for a minute or two about how much fun Annie was having as a minister, and how hard Debbie was working as a chief of staff. As we turned to go, Annie said, "Chris, can I talk to you for a minute?"

France, taking the hint, had already retreated with the waiter to our table. Annie took me over to a shadowy spot beside the kitchen doors, out of sight of any of the restaurant's patrons. "So," she said. "Word is you're after that silver-spoon cocksucker."

"Mr. Rioux, you mean," I said, grinning. "It's less him, really, and more the people around him."

"Well, go get 'em," Annie said. "That one-eyed fucker's people have stabbed me in the back plenty of times."

"I had heard that."

"If there's anything I can do, let me know, okay?" she said. She smiled. "And next time you get in a punch-up with that little prick Dick Thorsell, make sure you belt him a couple times for me, okay?"

"Uh, okay," I said, mortified. Even cabinet ministers had heard about my encounter with Thorsell. Ottawa, as Joey had told me more than once, is like a gigantic party line, with everybody listening in on everybody else. No secrets. As I made my way back to the table, I remembered the first call I received at the bureau the morning after the Prince Group opening. It had been Dick Thorsell, wanting to apologize. I didn't say much as Thorsell grunted his way through his expression of contrition. It sounded as if he was being forced to apologize, and — according to Kevin Ritchie, who had been furious when I called to tell him about the Thorsell incident — Avie Fleischmann had apparently informed Mark Petryk that he would be quitting if Thorsell didn't apologize to me, and soon. Or so Kevin said.

Thorsell had called, Joey later opined, because "he is scared shitless you're going to sue his ass for assault." But neither Kevin nor I had given a moment's deliberation to suing Thorsell or the Prince Group. To do so would turn *me* into a story — and effectively disqualify me from pursuing the story I wanted to pursue.

I joined France at our table, apologizing profusely. She waved it off. "When the Deputy PM wants to talk, you talk," she said.

Before we ordered, I told her I wanted to show her something. "It's in the wine list," I said, offering it to her. "Take your time."

It was my story. After I got it lawyered for any potential libel concerns — and after I was interrogated about it, and the Thorsell incident, by Kevin — the decision had been made to place it on the wire late on Sunday night, so that it would run in all of the Monday papers under a Christopher O'Reilly and Canadian Press byline. That way, none of the Central Canadian papers — such as the *Toronto Star*, which was notorious for the practice — would have enough time to do a rewrite of my work, interview one more person and publish the story as its own.

I wasn't entirely satisfied with the story, but it was a start. Usually, the publication of one of these things leads to other tips, which leads to other stories, and so on.

Finance minister denies connection to lobbying group
By Christopher O'Reilly, the Canadian Press

OTTAWA — *The office of Finance minister Jean Rioux is denying it has any connection to a high-powered lobbying company that opened its doors in Ottawa last week. And Rioux's office would not explain the Minister's relationship with a murdered Montreal lawyer who incorporated the lobbying firm, called the Prince Group.*

"Jean Rioux divested himself of all his holdings, or placed them in a blind trust, before he became a cabinet minister," said Mike Mahoney, Rioux's chief of staff. "He has no connection whatsoever to the Prince Group, or any other lobbying firm. We have no further comment."

The Prince Group, which was launched at a party in Ottawa last week, will offer communications advice and polling services, said Mark Petryk, one of the company's partners. Petryk was Rioux's campaign manager during the 1990 Liberal leadership race. The firm also employs Donna Curtis, one of Rioux's senior advisers during the leadership race, as well as other individuals who have worked for companies in which Rioux possesses an interest.

An apparent reference to Rioux's unlisted former Montreal address in Montreal's posh Outremont neighbourhood — along with Curtis's business card — was found by a Canadian Press reporter last week among the personal papers of Roger Fournier. The 43-year-old lawyer was found shot to death at his office building in downtown Montreal on November 1. A few weeks prior to his murder, which remains unsolved, Fournier had incorporated the Prince Group.

Petryk would not comment on Fournier, other than to say: "Lots of people know Jean Rioux and Donna Curtis. They are well-known people, and the fact that they may have met Mr. Fournier means nothing. There are probably thousands of Canadians who have met Mr. Rioux," he said ...

The story went on for a few more paragraphs. As France read it, I recalled my telephone conversation with Mike Mahoney, when I had called him for a comment by Rioux. He hadn't been as cool as I expected him to be — in fact, he had been even more chummy than before. It was all fake, of course, but I was impressed with his ability to maintain *sang-froid* when his boss was at the centre of a negative story. After politely informing me that Mr. Rioux would not be speaking on the matter directly, he read out the quotation contained in my story. Every time I asked him something, in fact, he read out the same thing. This was a news-management technique pioneered at External Affairs, and it ensured that a reporter was obliged to report only the message the government wanted out. The only way to circumvent this sort of stonewalling was to corner a minister on his or her way to or from Question Period. But the House wasn't going to be sitting until the New Year, and I didn't know where Rioux hung out.

"I guess this means you *won't* be accepting our job offer, Chris," Mahoney said, as I was preparing to sign off. He sounded genuinely disappointed.

"I guess so, Mike," I replied. "Thanks for the offer, but I think I'll stick to reporting."

"Well, all the *best*, Chris! Talk to you soon," he said.

Ten minutes after we rang off, I was called by the PMO's director of communications, Walt Hume. This was the Hume–Mahoney tag team I had been hearing about in the Press Gallery: whenever someone was about to write or broadcast something slightly critical of Rioux, the PMO–Finance axis would swing into action and scurry to protect the thin-skinned cabinet minister. It wouldn't have been unusual, were it not for the fact that Walt Hume seemed — to some reporters, anyway — to be much more focused on protecting Jean Rioux than he was on protecting Bobby Laurier. And Mike Mahoney, of course, had never been known to call anyone to defend Laurier.

"Chris-baby," Hume said, once he got me on the line. "Howzit goin'?"

"It's going fine, Walt, thanks," I said. "How can I help you?"

"Well, I heard through the grapevine that you're working on something about Jean, and I thought maybe I could help," he said, in full spin cycle. "What can I do for you, Chris-baby?"

For the next thirty minutes, Hume wouldn't let me get off the phone. He did all that he could, short of threatening me — which was an approach that had already been embraced, then discarded, by Dick Thorsell — to dissuade me from pursuing the Prince Group story. It was only after I started to ask *him* why the PMO was so nervous about the story that he abruptly developed a case of political laryngitis. He said we should get together for lunch some time, blah blah blah, and signed off. Presumably to report on our conversation to Mike Mahoney.

✻ ✻ ✻

I watched France read the story, from behind the wine list. It was a bit of a breach of the rules to show someone a story before it was published, of course — even if publication was just a few hours away.

The reason I was showing it to France, I suppose, was because I knew it was weak, and I wanted to see if she would be willing to help make it better. I was using her but I couldn't help myself: I saw the possibility of a scoop. I continued watching her. She finally handed the story back to me, and I returned the printout to my jacket pocket.

"Honest opinion?" she said.

I nodded, knowing that she had concluded it was not strong enough.

"It's a good start," she said. "But I can't see the smoking gun. So Rioux and Curtis know this dead lawyer. Is that a crime?"

I sighed. "That's what Kevin said, too. He has agreed to let it run on Monday, but he doesn't seem overwhelmed with enthusiasm, to be honest. He said it could use a bit more. Something." I waited.

"I have to agree with him, and I'm not just saying that because I'm a Liberal," she said. She squeezed my hand. "Are you mad at me?"

"No! No way," I said. "I just wish I had more." An image of my father flitted through my mind's eye. He wouldn't be pleased with what I was doing here: using a relationship to get information for a story. I forced myself to focus on the story.

She waited until I ordered for both of us. Then she leaned closer.

"Here's the deal: I may have something that will help you with your story," she said, taking the bait. She paused and then suddenly looked very serious. I had not seen her this way before. "I was mad after that incident with Thorsell on Thursday night. So I asked someone a couple of questions. Don't ask me who. And that person gave me something."

Just as suddenly, she looked mischievous. "But it's at my place. If you want it, you have to come back there with me, I'm afraid."

I ate fast. Really fast.

* * *

The next morning, while France took a bath in her big cast-iron tub — she refused to let me watch, saying she had been too revealing already — I reached under her futon to locate the piece of paper she had given me the night before. I had already read it a half-dozen times, but I couldn't help myself.

Even though we had spent the night together, and shared some intimate moments, I was still suspicious of one detail. I hadn't known France very long. Why would she just drop such a document in my lap? Where would she get it? It didn't make a lot of sense, but it was certainly what I had wanted — more dirt on Rioux from the Laurier loyalists. Political people were so predictable: they couldn't resist sticking it to a rival. That part hadn't been a surprise. But where had a junior PMO staffer obtained such a document? It didn't make sense, but I wasn't about to give it back. If it checked out, I would be making enthusiastic use of it.

The piece of paper was not on any departmental letterhead. But France had assured me it was all true. It certainly had the feel of authenticity. "SOLE-SOURCE, SPLIT, RETROACTIVE OR AMENDED CONTRACTS AWARDED TO THE PRINCE GROUP BY THE OFFICE OF THE MINISTER OF FINANCE WITHOUT COMPETITION" was the document's lengthy, but self-explanatory, title.

Essentially, the piece of paper detailed contracts passed along to Petryk, Curtis et al., in ways that were certainly intriguing. For example, the government's own rules did not permit a department to sole-source a piece of work to a company if the value of the contract exceeded $30,000. But four of the contracts on France's list had been well above the $30,000 threshold, and they had been sole-sourced. About eight of them had been "split"— that is, a single contract for, say, polling, had been divided up into two or three separate contracts with dollar amounts that each fell under the $30,000 limit. Three of the contracts on the list had been "amended" — work had been contracted in the mid-$20,000 range and, after the paperwork had been signed, the work in question had suddenly become much more pricey than anyone had thought, and the contract had been "amended" to three or four times its original value.

What made the figures on France's list all the more remarkable was the time frame they covered. The Prince Group, after all, had only been in legal existence since the beginning of November. But, according to her list, a few of the contracts had even been passed along to the firm during its first week of business. All told, the piece of paper documented a remarkable amount of work going to a single firm in a remarkably short period of time. And the values on the piece of paper added up to more than a half-million dollars' worth of patronage.

It was early. After breakfast, I had told her, I was going to have to meet with Kevin at the bureau to completely rework my Prince Group yarn.

"I know," she said, wearing only my button-down, and towelling her hair. "Go get that Pulitzer Prize, Chris."

"We don't have Pulitzer Prizes in Canada, France," I replied, reaching for the phone to call Kevin.

She shrugged. "Whatever."

✻   ✻   ✻

My first story on the Prince Group — the rewrite was headlined "Contracting rules bent to benefit Grit insiders," so you get the general idea — elicited a curious response around Ottawa. Joey Myers, to whom I had read the story late Monday night, declared it "page-one stuff." I, of course, hoped he would be right. Kevin Ritchie, even after France's material was confirmed by a highly reluctant bureaucrat and added to the story, wasn't so sure. "Not a whimper, but not a bang," he said.

"Don't starting quoting poetry to me now," I retorted.

I started to worry that France would get blamed for the leak. She, after all, had been seen arm in arm with me at the Prince Group function. After I showed her the final draft, she remained unsure that the story would cause a big sensation. "You journalists love to declare a government's honeymoon over," she said. "But I think the Liberal honeymoon is still in full bloom. I can't see your story being big enough to affect the government's approval ratings. Besides, this story is Rioux's problem, not Laurier's."

"But you are all in the same big, happy Liberal government, aren't you? And, besides, aren't you a little worried that the Rioux people will accuse the Laurier people of leaking that contracting information to me?" I asked her. We were in my apartment, eating spaghetti, the only dish I could reliably prepare without sending someone to the hospital. It was Tuesday evening, and Canadian Press had placed my story on our news wire. "I don't want you to get hurt by this."

She sucked up a couple of strands of pasta. Great mouth. "I wouldn't have given it to you if it could be traced back to me, number one," she said. "Number two, nobody knows who I am. I only moved here three months ago, when they hired me to help out on transition, remember. And, number three, the Rioux people will be convinced that it came from a Laurier person, even it didn't. Laurier and Rioux have been leaking stuff on each other ever since the leadership. That's politics."

"That is true," I replied, recalling the dozens of times Annie Frosini or John Derbyshire had passed along some nasty morsel about Jean Rioux or a member of the 829 Club. It wasn't a uniquely Liberal affliction, either. During Ross Hamilton's reign, his people regularly defamed Pat Stanton, his immediate predecessor as Tory leader. And vice versa. As Joey once observed, "People in the same political party usually hate each other more than they hate people in other political parties."

I watched France for a bit. "You know, if I had put in an Access to Information Act request for that information, I seriously doubt I would have ever gotten it," I said. "I guess I shouldn't ask you how someone on the Quebec desk was able to get her hands on that document."

"No, you shouldn't," she said, her mouth full.

"Okay."

We took in the news together. The story had been shipped to Canadian Press subscribers late on Tuesday afternoon. Kevin had decided to get it out as quickly as possible, once the lawyers gave it their stamp of approval — and once an assistant deputy minister at Finance had unwillingly verified the information I had been given.

The first national news organizations that would be making use of the story, after CBC radio, were the television networks. I didn't like TV news at the best of times, but Kevin had made his decision, and I wasn't about to argue with him.

CBC radio completely ignored the story, which I attributed to the fact that we had sent it out only about an hour before their six o'clock broadcast. At the appointed hour on CBC television, however, Patrick Stone covered tragedy in the former Yugoslavia, an RCMP investigation into a Tory kickback scandal in Saskatchewan, a blizzard in the Maritimes and a dozen other stories. But nothing — not a word — was uttered about Jean Rioux's apparent willingness to break the rules to line the pockets of his lobbyist pals. Not a word. Her Majesty's Loyal Opposition had not helped matters much: the Bloc Québécois, because they didn't see a sovereignty angle, did nothing. The rump Conservatives, of course, also kept quiet — knowing as they did that the Prince Group was also home to the likes of Gore Ailes and Howie Atwater, big Tory hitters both.

The Reform Party's response, unfortunately, went to the opposite extreme: they did too much. No fewer than three Reform MPs faxed out press releases on the issue. One of them, a boneheaded mouth-breather from B.C., referred to the company as "Prince Incorporated" in a release that was rife with spelling and grammatical errors. Another Reformer, a leggy brunette from Vancouver named Reba MacLeod — who would later be linked romantically, and incredibly, to one of Bobby Laurier's high-profile ministers — held a press conference in Room 130-S of the Centre Block early on Tuesday evening. Room 130-S, in the basement, is a small press theatre favoured for its proximity to politicians' offices. Given the hour, I wasn't entirely surprised when only two media people showed up for Reba MacLeod's presser — me and the pool cameraman. Though Reba laboured mightily to be news-worthy, it was clear that she did not know anything beyond what I had already written in my story.

"This is, um, an outrage," squeaked Reba. "The Reform Party demands an inquiry." Like the Reform Party itself, it was a case of too much too soon. Reba was helping to bury my story with her over-the-top rhetoric. I put on my overcoat and trudged back to CP's national bureau.

All of this was unfortunate — because, as I had learned during my stint in Ottawa, stories are rarely pushed onto the front pages on their own merit. Other factors need to be present. The Press Gallery needs to hate a governing party's guts, for example. This had certainly been the case towards the end of Ross Hamilton's Tory regime. But Bobby Laurier was still enjoying a honeymoon of surprising resilience, even in traditionally anti-Grit territory like B.C. and Alberta. Another necessary ingredient, if one wants a story to acquire legs, is for the television-news power brokers to find it compelling; the sad fact is that a lot more people get their information from TV than they do from Canadian Press news-wire stories. But the presence of the much-liked Avie Fleischmann at the Prince Group effectively ensured that was not about to happen anytime soon. In the Press Gallery, Avie was still seen as one of us, and not one of them.

The best way to ensure that a story takes off, in fact, is to get the Opposition to take on the issue — in a concerted, organized and loud fashion — in Question Period. But the House wasn't sitting.

Joey gave me a call a minute after Patrick Stone signed off with his trademark pretentious closer — "And that was today" — and while I was in the bathroom. France answered. I returned to the living room, where she handed me the phone with a shrug.

"I'll grill you later, young man, about the identity of the person who just answered your telephone, and what she is doing in your apartment on a school night," Joey said. "I just wanted you to know that you should not have been surprised to see CBC take a pass on your story."

"Well, I was, a bit," I replied. "Surprised, I mean."

"Don't be," he said. "These people all travel in the same circles."

"I know, I know," I responded. "But I figured this one stood up on its own merits, you know."

"Christopher, Christopher, my boy," Joey said. He was making me feel better, in spite of myself. When he started making jokes about Flash Feiffer's penis I felt distinctly better.

We chatted some more, and he assured me that CTV — which he called "Canadian Tory Vision" — would cover the story. Joey, like most of the senior Liberals I knew, saw CTV, along with the *Globe*, the *Sun* chain and the knuckle-draggers at the *Financial Post*, as a resolutely anti-Grit organization. CTV, he reasoned, will always leap at the chance to broadcast something unhelpful about the Liberals.

I hung up the phone and returned to the couch with France.

"What's this about Flash Feiffer's penis?" she asked, looking horrified and puzzled at the same time.

"It's a long story," I replied. "No pun intended."

*   *   *

There was a Newfoundlander politico — I forget his name, but he was a great bullshitter and orator, like most of them from the Rock — who remarked that not much happens around Ottawa once the Christmas season approaches. "Once they're up to their arseholes in jingle bells, you can fucking forget it," he said. And he was right.

CTV covered my story, all right, but with a lame voice-over by their Grecian Formula announcer. That was it. My wire copy got a fair amount of play across the country, but nobody seemed too interested in pursuing it. The Liberals were still popular and — besides — Christmas was coming. Nobody cares about politics at two times of the year — during barbecue season, and during Christmas. So my Prince Group story just sort of died.

Under any other circumstances, I would have been pretty ticked off about that. But France Lajoie and I were spending more and more time together, and I could not remember being happier. She was as intelligent as she was beautiful. When I finally agreed to let Joey meet her over drinks at the Château, he was so smitten he even abstained from sexual innuendo and references to Flash Feiffer's appendage. I watched as they talked about the best museums in London, where both of them had lived, at different times, and for different reasons. Afterwards, he pulled me aside. "She is lovely," he said, all solemn and proper. "If you do not propose marriage soon, I shall assume you are a homosexual."

The Prince Group slid to the back burner for another reason. Another Finance Department–related story was occupying a lot of my time, and a lot of government time, too: the Value Added Tax, or VAT, for short. Despite their election promises to dismantle Ross Hamilton's despised consumption tax, the Grits had learned that governing is a lot tougher than screaming from the Opposition benches. Bobby Laurier, a former Minister of Finance, had gone through the Liberal leadership campaign without once stating that he would scrap the VAT. But Jean Rioux and Annie Frosini — plus the Grits' addled chorus of fossils in the Senate — had all vowed to eliminate the tax once the Liberals were returned to their rightful place in government.

Expressing more than a little annoyance, Laurier had confided to me, in our first off-the-record discussion in 1990, that Rioux and the rest of them were "goddamn stupid." Waving his big hands through the air, Laurier huffed: "Jesus Christ, Chris! Do dese guys tink de Tories put de tax in because dey want to lose popularity? Dey put it in because de country is bankrupt an' needs de revenues! That friggin' tax is worth at least $10 billion!"

"Well, your Liberal colleagues have made it a big issue, Mr. Laurier," I said, surprised. "What are you going to do now?"

"There's not much I can do but go along wit' dem," he replied, scowling. "If dey had all jus' shut up, we could have kept de revenues when we got back to government, and the Tories would have taken all of de shit. But Rioux has already said he'll quit if I don't back de caucus position. So I will have to go halong."

So he went along, and, according to my sources, they were now regretting it, big time. As Laurier had told them, the billions in taxation revenue brought in by the VAT were all that separated the government from a visit by the International Monetary Fund bean-counters — which would mean the end of Medicare, and a few other social programs, too. So the story was simple: how were the Liberals going to justify keeping the VAT, after so many of them — Laurier had been a notable exception — had promised to kill it?

I wasn't the only reporter working on the story. A few of my colleagues, such as Stan Silversides and John Moore, were also calling around town about the *volte-face*. Over eggnogs at various Christmas parties, Liberal MPs were confirming that the PMO was planning a communications offensive to justify keeping the VAT. A lot of the Grit backbenchers were nervous about the flip-flop, and so were more than a few cabinet ministers. John Derbyshire, for one, told me he saw it as one of those bedrock credibility issues: "Jesus, Chris, those fuckin' pencilheads over at PMO actually seem to think the Canadian people are going to just roll over on this one! I was at one of my Tim Hortons on the weekend, and some of the boys were ready to stick me arse in the fuckin' doughnut-making machine over this VAT business," he said. Derbyshire regarded chats with constituents at Tim Horton franchises in his riding as a more accurate way of gauging public opinion than the most expensive polling or focus-group exercise. He was probably right.

*   *   *

In the last few days before Christmas week, and after a few of us had filed speculative stories about the VAT-related machinations, I got a call from Flash Feiffer's secretary. "Mr. Feiffer was wondering if you would join him for lunch at the Parliamentary Restaurant tomorrow," she said.

"Sure I would," I said.

The next day, after being briefed about the perils of watching Flash Feiffer consume food by Joey, Kevin and France, I took the elevator up to the sixth floor of the Centre Block. I was surrounded by a couple of lecherous old senators from Nova Scotia and their buxom secretaries, also on their way to the restaurant. For many occupants of the Red Chamber, the Parliamentary Restaurant provided them with their only opportunity to get seen by — or, if they were lucky, exchange a word with — someone from the PMO, or one of the bigwigs from the Press Gallery, or a cabinet minister. It was very much a Be Seen kind of place, which was precisely the kind of place I disliked. I was a few minutes early. I stepped out onto the carpeted hallway and took a seat beneath a large black and white photograph of Pat Stanton. Photos of all of Canada's Prime Ministers lined the walls outside the Parliamentary Restaurant.

I wasn't there long before I heard a commotion. Flash Feiffer's figure could be seen scampering down the hallway and the Nova Scotia senators were trying to block his path. From what I could overhear, they were trying to get him to talk about some sort of Department of National Defence contract. Flash obviously wasn't very interested in discussing military procurement with a couple of boozy old Grit bagmen.

After disengaging himself from the grasping senators, Flash scurried over to me. He shook my hand and, if I didn't know better, I would have assumed he was paralysed below the wrist. "Hi, Chris," he said, his breath a tad ripe. He was not one of the most attractive fellows in Ottawa, *sans doute*. Flash hung up his rumpled overcoat, and we moved into the restaurant.

To his credit, Flash didn't seem to notice the commotion his appearance caused, but I sure did. Past the long table on which the buffet had been laid out, at almost every table — and at many of the tables in the alcoves found on the east and west walls of the restaurant — heads turned, and conversations stopped, as Flash Feiffer's presence was noted. It was remarkable. Months before, during the Ross Hamilton government, Flash would have been lucky to get a second look from a *sous-chef*. Now he was being accorded the status of Princess Diana.

The foppish maître d' nearly swooned when he spotted Bobby Laurier's disembodied brain. "Oooh, Monsieur Feiffer," he gushed. "Your table is ready. Please follow me."

Flash and I were seated at a table in the alcove in the restaurant's northwestern corner. This was normally where the Prime Minister of the day sat, when he or she ate at the restaurant. But not many of them did that anymore. I had seen Ross Hamilton there once, but never Bobby Laurier. One rumour had it that he sent his personal assistant out to pick him up something at the local Harvey's, his fast-food favourite. He would then eat his double cheeseburger and fries at his prime-ministerial desk, alone. With coffee.

The preliminaries over, and our food obtained at the buffet table, Flash turned to the matter at hand: spinning the Grit flip-flop on the VAT. Between mouthfuls of roast beef — which he slurped up with fewer manners than the kid who was raised by the animals in *The Jungle Book* — Flash eyed me from behind his thick glasses. "So, what's your view on the VAT, Chris?" he asked me. Kevin Ritchie had warned me about this tactic: the politico will attempt to solicit advice from the reporter, thereby suggesting to the reporter that he or she has helped to find whatever "solution" the government, in reality, has been planning all along.

"Well, I'm awaiting the announcement on when we can all expect to see the VAT eliminated, Bernie," I said. I never called him Flash, at least not to his face. "That was your party's election promise, after all."

Flash grinned or winced; I couldn't be sure which. "Well, as you know, Chris, Mr. Laurier always made it clear that the VAT would be replaced with something that brought in equivalent tax revenues," he said. "You remember that from the campaign ..."

"Sure I do. He was always careful. But Jean Rioux and Annie Frosini sure weren't," I said. "If they said the VAT was going to be scrapped once, they said it a thousand times."

"Neither one of them is the Prime Minister," Flash said. He could do better than that.

"That's true, but one of them is the Finance minister, and has responsibility for setting taxation policy," I said. "And I'm hearing all over the place that you guys at the PMO are getting ready to change your stand on the VAT. Is that true?"

Flash kept eating. The spin session was not going well, I guess.

"So, how is France?" he abruptly asked, looking up from his roast beef at me.

This, of course, was A Low Blow. Nasty guy, Flash was. As France's boss — indirectly, anyway — he was letting me know: one, that he knew about our relationship; two, that he was higher up the pole than she was; and three, that he might make life difficult for her if I got too adversarial. I was pissed off, but tried not to show it. Before I could say anything, however, the maître d' swished up to our table. I assumed it was a telephone call for Flash — cell phones were *verboten* in the tony confines of the Parliamentary Restaurant — but it wasn't. It was for me.

Excusing myself, I made my way to the telephone behind the cash desk at the entrance to the restaurant. I picked up the receiver, half-expecting to hear Joey tell me some pornographic joke. But it wasn't Joey.

It was a male voice. It sounded distant and muffled. The sounds of some sort of machinery could be heard in the background.

"Christopher O'Reilly?"

"This is he," I said. "Who is speaking, please?"

There was a pause. "How is Mr. Feiffer today? Is he behaving himself?"

"I'm sorry, but I don't know who this is," I said. Only Joey and Kevin and France had known about my lunch with Flash Feiffer. Maybe it was one of the guys from the bureau trying out a practical joke. "Who is this?"

There was another pause. "If we wished to be dramatic, you could call me Deep Throat," the man said, then gave a dry laugh. "But you can call me whatever you like. If you wish to discuss the Prince Group and its unique relationship with Mr. Rioux's office, you will look for a Blue Line cab parked at the rear of the Brewer's Retail outlet on Somerset Street at precisely six o'clock this evening. I will be in the cab. The back doors will be locked, but you will find the front passenger-side door unlocked."

"Wait a second, is this some kind of ..." I stammered, scribbling out what he'd said onto a message slip.

"This is not a prank, Mr. O'Reilly," the voice said. "It is all quite real. Don't be late. And, if I were you, I would not tell anyone about our conversation."

Click. The man had hung up.

I returned to the table, but Flash Feiffer was absent. I looked around the restaurant, and spotted him getting seconds at the buffet table. He was chatting up one of the Nova Scotian senators' secretaries as he did so.

I looked down at the message slip. "Deep Throat" I had written, plus his instructions about where to meet.

I got up and went back to the phone, to call Kevin.

CHAPTER EIGHT

It was more than a little ironic — and, as I later learned, quite intentional — that my putative Deep Throat had chosen a spot near the intersection of Somerset and Kent streets to meet. I would not have known about the significance of the location had Kevin Ritchie not explained it to me, a few hours before I was scheduled to meet my new source. We were in his office, overlooking a snowbound Wellington Street. I had told him about my phone call in the Parliamentary Restaurant, and he agreed that it all sounded like something out of the Watergate era.

"He wants you to meet him at the Brewer's Retail on Somerset Street? The one near Kent?" Kevin asked me, after we had gone over what I should and should not say during my rendezvous with the mysterious Mr. X. Kevin seemed more interested in the location of the meeting than in the meeting itself. "Are you sure?"

"Yeah, I'm sure, Kevin," I said. "So what's the big deal about that?"

Kevin gave one of his rare laughs. He shook his head. "Well, it might be a coincidence, but that beer store is right next door to an old apartment building," he said. "And that apartment building was the home, many years ago, to none other than Igor Gouzenko."

"You mean the Russian spy?"

"Yes," he said, grinning through the pipe smoke that filled his office. "The Russian spy."

Gouzenko had been a Red Army officer and cipher clerk at the Soviet Union's Ottawa embassy, where he had toiled in the mid-1940s. In 1945, when he learned that he and his family were to be shipped back to the frosty climes of Mother Russia, he decided to defect. Unfortunately for Igor, nobody in the then-Liberal government of Mackenzie King initially took his attempted defection very seriously. (This didn't surprise me: after a certain length of time in power, Grits always seem to take the position that nothing is worthwhile unless they thought of it first.) It was only after the Soviets botched an attempt to kidnap him that Gouzenko was finally believed. His later testimony — and the documents he smuggled out of the Soviet embassy — resulted in the arrests of a number of Soviet spies. And, Kevin explained, at the time of his defection, Gouzenko lived in a three-storey brick apartment building on Somerset Street, near Kent.

I approached the intersection through a park directly across the street from Igor's former home and the Brewer's Retail outlet. In warmer times, the park was littered with empty beer bottles and men passed out on the grass. In late December, however, all that covered the ground was a lot of snow. Some of the trees had been decorated with Christmas lights.

It was already dark, and — being a Friday night — a steady stream of cars were moving in and out of the beer store's parking lot, carrying revellers to Christmas parties. I was early, but I could see that the Blue Line cab containing my source had apparently arrived earlier. It was parked on the west side of the parking lot, away from most of the other cars. I studied the cab for a while. It was a standard-issue Ottawa taxi: four-door Chev sedan, painted black, ubiquitous salt stains on the sides. The windows were tinted, so I could see nothing inside it. I could, however, see exhaust billowing into the frigid air, so

I knew that the car was running. I reached inside my coat and clicked on my microcassette recorder.

Jaywalking across Somerset, I approached the automatic doors of the Brewer's Retail outlet. I made a mental note of the taxi's licence plate, then started picking my way through the mounds of slush towards it. Although I had been told they would be locked, I tried one of the rear door handles anyway. It was locked, all right.

I went to the front passenger door, opened it and slowly moved my head inside. No dome light had come on. In the gloom, I saw that there was no driver. In the back seat, I could make out a human form — he was large, I saw that much, but not much more. My host was wearing a dark overcoat, and he had a wide-brimmed hat pulled down low over his face. "Get in, Mr. O'Reilly, and face forward," he said. It was the same voice from earlier in the day. There was the faintest trace of an accent, but I couldn't place it. For the first time, I noticed that a Golden Oldies station was playing — loudly — on the car's radio.

I did as he said, slightly bemused by the Cold War–era theatrics. "Isn't this all a bit much?" I said, turning my head slightly towards Maxwell Smart.

"Face the front, please, Mr. O'Reilly."

"Okay, okay," I said. A moment passed. "So, what should I call you? Mr. Gouzenko?"

There was a muffled sound; it almost resembled a laugh. "I'm impressed," he said. "So you know where we are, I take it."

"Yes."

"I was told you were bright," he said. "Perhaps you are, after all."

"Who told you I was bright?" I asked.

He ignored my question. "You may call me Igor," he said. "It will be our private little joke."

"So, Igor, why did you want to see me? Given the fact that you obviously don't want to be identified, it doesn't make a lot of sense to me that you didn't just tell me what you want to tell me on the phone."

"I think you know why I want to meet with you, Mr. O'Reilly," Igor said. "But your question is a good one. Let's just say that I wanted to meet in person because I have a flair for the dramatic. And that I never trust telephones. Neither should you, for that matter."

"Okay," I said, still facing forward. "So what is it you want to say? And why to me?"

"You could say that, fundamentally, I am a democrat," Igor said. "I am unenthusiastic when I see the opposite at work."

"Fine, whatever. Why me?"

He didn't say anything for a bit. "I was told you could be trusted," he said, sounding unconvinced of that.

"Thanks, I guess," I said. I reached for the radio. "Mind if I turn this down? I'm having difficulty hearing you."

"You may turn it down if you turn off the tape recorder you are carrying," Igor said.

I sat there for minute, then decided against debating with Igor. Maybe he had seen me reaching inside my jacket before I crossed Somerset Street. I reached inside it again and flicked off the micro-cassette.

"Thank you," he said. There was a pause.

"Do you feel someone is being undemocratic, Igor?"

He sounded entertained by that one. "Mr. O'Reilly, politicians are, by their very nature, ambitious," he said. "If they achieve one post, they immediately set about achieving the next, more senior, post. It is something they do. They cannot help themselves."

"Thanks for the political-science lesson, but I'm not getting your point," I replied. Igor had read one too many John le Carré books. And this whole scene was getting too silly. Maybe Igor Gouzenko had come back from the grave. Or maybe Joey Myers was playing a seasonal practical joke.

"Political ambition is natural, and it is the nature of the beast," he said. "And as long as it is maintained within certain parameters, it is fine. But when it starts to exceed those parameters, the system can be placed at risk."

"I get the feeling we are talking about Jean Rioux."

"We are," he said. There was another lengthy pause. "Mr. Rioux, even at this early stage in the life of this government, is possessed by an ambition that threatens the entire system. He would do virtually anything, it seems, to achieve higher office."

"Yeah, and the same goes for any politician I have ever met," I responded. This Igor guy was starting to get on my nerves, notwithstanding my own growing aversion to Rioux's gang. "What is he doing that makes him such a bad guy?"

Igor shifted in his seat. From the periphery of my vision, it seemed as if he was looking at his watch. "The holidays are coming," he said. "Early in the New Year, Mr. Rioux will attempt to eliminate one of his chief leadership rivals, Ms. Frosini, using illegitimate means. He is a very ambitious man."

Tap tap! I almost jumped out of my skin; someone was knocking at my window. I whirled around and saw a man standing out in the snow, looking in.

"That is the driver of this vehicle," Igor said. "He wants you to leave now. Please do so and, when you get outside, I will slip you something through my window."

I wanted to stay and talk some more with Igor, but I also wanted to see what he had for me. I stepped out into the cold and slammed the door; simultaneously, the driver was opening his door and slipping inside. A second later, Igor's tinted window rolled down an inch and a legal-sized envelope appeared. I took it.

"Merry Christmas, Mr. O'Reilly," Igor said. "I will speak to you in the New Year."

The taxi backed up and drove off, slowly, through the slush in the beer store's crowded parking lot. I watched it go, then looked at the unmarked envelope in my hands. I shook my head.

"Weird town, is Ottawa," I said aloud, to no one in particular. "Weird town."

*   *   *

I puzzled over Igor's gift for most of the holidays, some of which were spent in Victoria with my mother, sister and brother-in-law.

Normally, leaks were communicated to me in a variety of ways. Often, a disgruntled bureaucrat would pass on some embarrassing document to an Opposition MP — like the NDP's Nils Andersen, for example, who received a lot of such papers — and then the MP would pass it along to me in exchange for some sort of quote in the resulting story. Or I would get an anonymous phone tip, usually from one ministerial aide with an axe to grind about another ministerial office. These were becoming less and less common, however; many leakers were afraid of having their call traced, now that technology was cheaply available to identify callers. Or, most often, I would simply get told something over lunch, at a restaurant far removed from the inquisitive eyes found on Parliament Hill.

It was relatively easy to determine in advance if a lunch-time leak was likely. If the politico insisted on paying for lunch out of his or her expense account, he or she probably wasn't going to be telling me anything important — it was obvious that, when the proverbial shit hit the fan, expense records might be scrutinized to see who had last had contact with that snoopy O'Reilly fellow. But if I was expected to pay, I could also expect there was a reasonable chance of some tantalizing tidbit landing in my notepad. Never, however, had I received information in circumstances as Byzantine as those surrounding my parking-lot encounter with Igor.

The unmarked envelope contained a single sheet of paper. It looked like a sixth- or seventh-generation photocopy, so I could not tell if it was authentic just by looking at it. It also looked as if it had been faxed somewhere at least once. But I couldn't make out any of the numbers. At the top of the photocopy were the letters "J.D.C." I took this to be the private stationery of J. Donna Curtis, the Rioux crowd's chosen concubine. Here is what the memorandum said:

> M: I recommend the wk before House re-opens. F.M. looks contrite, truthful, gd pre-Budget pre-conditioning, etc. Potato Head will stick to PCO line. And she will be left twisting in the wind. Vaporize A. Tax claims its first victim. Ha ha! D.

By the time I returned to Ottawa — and leaving Victoria's temperatures for the capital's ridiculous winter weather is never easy, believe me, but seeing France for a New Year's dinner made it manageable — I had pretty much figured out the meaning of the memorandum. While the jury was still out on whether it was genuine or not, the memo appeared to be from Donna Curtis to her pal Mike Mahoney. It seemed to suggest that Jean Rioux — the "F.M.," as in Finance minister — was going to make some sort of announcement in the last week of January. The announcement concerned the fate of the Value Added Tax. And, based upon what Igor had related to me, my bet was it would have some sort of implications for the political future of Annie Frosini. Perhaps she was the "A" referred to in the memo.

"Potato Head," of course, was easy: that was Bobby Laurier. Potato Head was the name the Rioux forces had given Laurier during the leadership convention. "PCO" was the Privy Council Office, the Prime Minister's bureaucrats. A few of my colleagues and I had been told that the PCO had developed a comprehensive communications plan for the flip-flop on keeping the VAT. Using the Access to Information Act, I had obtained one or two of these communications plans in the past — always heavily censored, of course. The "comm plans," as bureaucrats called them, laid out the various public-relations consequences of different policy choices. Each choice was looked at for its positive and negative consequences. Polling data, surveys of editorial opinion, even analyses of the tone of news stories, were all factored in. And there was always a separate section examining the communications impact a particular decision would have in the province of Quebec. As a Westerner, that part always galled me; despite our years of complaints, Quebec still called the shots.

New Year's Eve was spent over a very expensive meal at Café Henri Burger. The upscale restaurant was famous for its French cuisine; it was located on the Hull side, across the Ottawa River from the Château Laurier. Usually, the place was packed with ministers and lobbyists. On this date, however, all MPs were back in their ridings, pressing the flesh — or on a beach somewhere. Once we had ordered and received our first course, I showed France the photocopy. The last time I had shown her something on the Prince Group, she had given me something better. I was hoping history would repeat itself, although I was starting to feel a lot guiltier about using her in this way. I was falling for France, I think.

Between bites of salad, she frowned over the memo. "I don't get it," she finally said, handing it back to me.

"For most of my time in B.C., I didn't either," I said. "When my mother wasn't nagging me about law school, or about having forgotten to bring along a photo of you, I read it plenty of times. But I think I've figured it out, sort of."

I gave her my interpretation of the document, explaining that many reporters were expecting the VAT announcement to come at a time when it would be difficult for the Bloc or the Reformers to capitalize on it. It was a smart strategy — a Running-Shoes Theory of politics, if you will. That is, the first one to lace on his or her Nikes, race to an available microphone and blurt out that the Liberal decision to kill the VAT had been a mistake would look — as Donna Curtis had apparently noted in her cryptic memo — as if he or she was being the most truthful. Candour with the public: it was all very "new politics." The rest of the Liberal team, meanwhile, as they tried to decide whether to break ranks or not, would appear as if they were still trying to hide something from the public. The Running-Shoes Theory wasn't a very team player approach, of course, but nobody had ever accused Jean Rioux of being one of those.

"Sounds plausible," France said. "I don't suppose I should ask you where you got the memo."

"You can ask all you want, but I won't tell you," I said. "Not unless you want to tell me who gave you that document on the illegal contracting Rioux's office had done with the Prince Group."

"Not a chance, sweetie," she said.

Our Christmases had been quite similar. Our respective sisters had grilled us about our new romantic interest. Our mothers had asked a lot of questions about how serious the relationship was. And our friends from high school and university had asked each of us why we had chosen to make a home in a place as awful as Ottawa. We had joked about this when we exchanged Christmas gifts, belatedly, on the hardwood floor of France's apartment on the morning of New Year's Day. I gave her a scarf from Holt's, plus a Haida print I had picked up on Granville Island in Vancouver. She gave me an 18-carat-gold key fob — in the shape of a pair of boxing gloves. She squealed with laughter when I opened the tiny box containing the key fob. "That's to remind you of the night we met, when you duked it out with that jerk at the Prince Group!" she said.

"Very funny," I said.

In the intervening weeks, my brief meeting with the end of Dick Thorsell's fist had turned into the stuff of local legend. As I had expected, Mike Mahoney and Mark Petryk had successfully spun the incident in *Hank* and various gossip columns as mainly my fault — that I had been drinking too much, that I was obsessed with Rioux, that I had an axe to grind. I had heard a variety of accounts of what had taken place in the lobby of the Prince Group offices, and in all of them I was the bad guy. Mission accomplished, Mike. You have now made my job a lot harder.

✻   ✻   ✻

Apart from my time spent with France — and I was spending more and more of it with her — January was very frustrating. Like half the reporters in town, I was chasing stories about the Budget, trying to figure what would, and would not, be in it. (The other half were chasing stories about what would be in the Throne Speech.) People like John Moore, Stan Silversides and Sherry Bickle were getting lots of bylines about the Budget's contents. According to Joey, those three — and a few others who worked for right-wing papers — were receiving briefings from Mike Mahoney that came perilously close to a violation of Budget secrecy. But I was getting nowhere, and I knew why. On one particularly bad morning in mid-January, when I had been scooped yet again in the *Globe*, I trudged into Kevin Ritchie's tiny office.

"Kevin, you might as well take me off the Finance beat," I said, slumping in a chair facing his desk. "The Prince Group story has turned me into *persona non grata* with Rioux's department. Nobody is giving me anything. I've been cut off."

"I know that," Kevin said, looking up from the papers piled high on his desktop. "What did you expect was going to happen?"

"Certainly not this."

He waved a dismissive hand at me and went back to his papers. "Every Budget needs to be approved by the Prime Minister's Office," he said. "Work your sources there. Ask them what will be in the Speech from the Throne, and that way you'll know what we can expect in the Budget."

I took Kevin's advice. Later that same day, I was perched on a chair in the *sanctum sanctorum*: Flash Feiffer's office. When I had called, Flash came on the phone himself. He wasn't stupid, of course. He knew I was calling him about the Budget because I had been cut off by Mike Mahoney and the 829 Club for having the temerity to print something critical about Rioux. But Flash, unbeknownst to many, had an ego, too. He liked it when I told him that the PMO would be vetting everything that was in the Budget as well as the Throne Speech. And he didn't try to suggest otherwise.

As I waited for Flash to return to his office after a brief conference with his secretary about a daunting mound of pink telephone-message slips, I looked around. For the most part, the room looked as if it had been furnished and decorated by someone with absolutely no sense of colour, design or proportion: it was vintage Flash Feiffer. Piles of paper were littered across the desk. On the walls were a couple of photographs, crookedly hung, of a smiling Flash with Maurice Johnson Bechard, whom Flash idolized — according to France — for his sterling anti-separatist credentials. One of the photos pictured Bechard and Feiffer beside a lake somewhere, each man clutching a canoe paddle. A few Native art pieces were placed here and there; these, apparently, had been gifts from various aboriginal bands Flash had dealt with while he was Bobby Laurier's chief political aide at Indian and Northern Affairs.

Flash hurried back into the office, smiling, shaking my hand again. If you call what Flash does a handshake, that is.

Up close, and away from the cauldron of egos found in a spot like the Parliamentary Restaurant, where I had last seen him, before Christmas, Flash was much more relaxed. In his own clumsy way, he was even charming. His little eyes gleamed with cordiality. He smiled a lot, too, especially as he told me about how he came to be photographed with Bechard at the lakeside. One summer, he told me, he and Bechard and a number of very senior Liberal bagmen and hacks had travelled up north, to the Yukon, to portage above Kluane Lake, near the Alaska border. It was evident that Flash was very proud of the photograph.

Conversation turned, eventually, to the VAT, and Flash became more serious. I recalled from the Liberal leadership that Flash had been one of the few big-name Liberals — along with his boss, Laurier — who had quietly argued for the retention of the despised tax. Listening to him now, I surmised that he was still annoyed that Laurier had been talked into a pledge that he couldn't keep: namely, ditching the VAT. I also sensed that scrapping the tax was simply a non-starter. Throwing off my usual lack of self-confidence, I cut to the chase. Who, I asked him, was going to break the bad news to the Canadian public?

"Taxation policy, as you have told me yourself, is the responsibility of the Minister of Finance," Flash said, the faintest trace of a grin playing on his lips. "Jean will do that. *If* that is what happens, and I'm not saying that it will happen."

"It will happen, and we both know it," I said, unsure whether he was pleased that Rioux was about to take the fall for the VAT. Flash grinned some more and said nothing. I pressed on: "When? When will he make his announcement?"

"Soon enough, *if* it happens at all," Flash said, twitching in his swivel chair. "But I'm not saying that it will happen."

For a little while, we talked about other things. In my three years in Ottawa, I had noted that Flash had a tendency to like those people Bobby Laurier liked, and dislike those his boss didn't. The only exception, of late, was Jean Rioux. As Joey had told me, Flash was bending over backwards to say all manner of nice things about the fickle Finance minister. There were two theories about why this was so: one, that Flash expected Rioux to become leader one day, and he wanted to curry favour with the new regime. Or, two, that he wanted to avoid the sort of back-stabbing nastiness that he himself had subjected poor Jack Gibson to.

The Laurier people had not been entirely content to wait for Gibson to gracefully step aside, you see; instead, they frankly did all that they could to hasten the day that Gibson returned to the exile of many a defrocked politician — corporate law. No one had been more involved in the Delegitimize Gibson effort than Flash Feiffer, who probably dined with every Liberal staffer in town during the dark days of Gibson's leadership, trying to win converts. At these little get-togethers, usually at a Chinese restaurant many blocks from the standard Hill hangouts, Flash would sing the praises of Bobby Laurier, and subtly point out Jack Gibson's many faults.

Many of the Gibson people never forgot or forgave this. When Jack Gibson finally threw in the towel — a fitting metaphor for the failed Grit leader, who never quite seemed to have grown out of high-school athletics — a good number of them turned to Jean Rioux. Gibson and Rioux had long been friends; both favoured a pro-business, pro–Quebec nationalism stance. It was a natural fit. I decided to ask Flash about it.

"Bernie, how is the relationship between the Prime Minister and the Finance minister?"

He looked slightly uncomfortable. "It couldn't be better," he said. "They have a lot of respect for each other. And Mr. Laurier believes Jean is doing a good job."

"Has all of the leadership rivalry ended?" I asked.

"That's a long time ago," he said, not meeting my gaze. "That's all forgotten."

"But some of Rioux's people say they plan to do to the Prime Minister what your team did to Jack Gibson. You know, undermine him," I said.

Flash looked genuinely wounded. "Who said that?" he demanded, not waiting for me to answer, because he knew I wouldn't. "That's just not true. Jean supports the Prime Minister. No doubt about it."

I couldn't tell if he was promoting what he believed was the truth — or what he hoped was the truth. I decided to drop it. If Flash Feiffer and his boss were dumb enough to believe that Jean Rioux was onside, then they probably deserved to lose their hold on power. Jean Rioux, in my view, was about as loyal as your average cobra at a sock hop.

We talked about the Budget for a while. Flash was writing it, I figured, and he didn't disagree when I said so. We also talked about the Throne Speech. Sounded as if he was writing that one, too.

*　　　*　　　*

The New Journalists convened at the Château Laurier late on a Thursday afternoon, after we had filed our stories for the day. In attendance were Kurt Tasse from Southam News; Sherry Bickle from the *Post*; Stan Silversides and John Moore from the *Globe*; Gord McAleer from CBC television news; the *Star*'s Roxanne Perry; and me. Absent were Avie Fleischmann, of course, who had moved on to the rarefied air of the Prince Group, and George Cunningham, who had left the *Financial Times* to help Tom Aspinall ready the Grits' planned revamp of unemployment insurance.

The crew from the *Globe* were in great spirits; earlier in the day, they had been told by Mike Mahoney that Jean Rioux was preparing to make a major announcement on the fate of the VAT, probably tomorrow. As we would all see on Friday morning, Silversides and Moore had each filed a longish piece that was more analysis than news, filled with self-serving quotes from an anonymous Liberal identified only as "a senior Finance official" — a cover that Mahoney used so often with compliant reporters that "he should have it printed on his business card," Joey had said to me. Silversides's yarn, in particular, was overflowing with all manner of glowing adjectives about Jean Rioux, how he was a disciple of "the New Politics," that he personally favoured complete candour with the Canadian people, blah blah blah.

Stan told me a little bit about his story while we waited for our beers to arrive. "The Rioux announcement is q-q-quite unusual," he said. "Even y-y-you have to admit th-that, Chris."

I shrugged. "I guess so," I said, slightly resentful at his implication that I was some sort of an anti-Rioux reporter. "We'll see." Unlike my colleagues at the *Globe*, I had dealt with the flip-flop differently: the way my story read, Jean Rioux was being sent out by the PMO to take a bullet on the VAT. Three years ago, he had threatened Bobby Laurier with his resignation if Laurier had not gone along with the then-caucus position on the issue; now, I wrote, it was payback time. Rioux was being forced to reverse *his* position. That, in any event, was certainly how a lot of Laurier loyalists were seeing it. According to a few — John Derbyshire and Annie Frosini among them — Rioux's script for the press conference had been written for him, word for word, by Flash. And no deviation from the script would be permitted. I didn't mention any of this to Stan, however. I mainly just listened.

Sherry Bickle regarded me suspiciously. Since the publication of my Prince Group piece before Christmas, Sherry had been decidedly cool towards me. In fact, at one pre-Christmas party at Gord McAleer's place — we called him "God" behind his back, because that was generally how he expected to be treated by everyone else — Sherry had even made a couple of snarky remarks to me, calling my Prince Group investigation "pretty thin."

"What a bitch!" France had said, after Sherry wandered off. "What's her problem?"

"Beats me," I replied. "I guess I'm breaking with the conventional wisdom. Joey tells me that's a taboo in Ottawa."

Now, as the Château's waiter started dispensing our drinks, Sherry sat squinting at me. "So what do you think about Rioux agreeing to make the VAT announcement, Chris?"

"I dunno," I said, not wanting to get drawn into an argument. "Depends on whether he actually agreed to do it, I suppose."

I suddenly had the full attention of Sherry and of the *Globe* crew.

The possibility that Bobby Laurier's team was actually managing a file, and not Rioux's 829 Club fanatics, obviously hadn't occurred to any of them.

"What do you m-m-mean, Chris?" Stan said. "I'm t-t-told that Rioux insisted th-that he make the announcement."

Before I could reply, God McAleer jumped in. God, a former investigative guy with the *Gazette*, was about seven feet tall, with thinning hair and massive, bushy eyebrows. He was widely reputed to have the best-nourished ego in the entire Parliamentary Press Gallery. That, in a town as full of pomposity as Ottawa, took some doing. I liked him, however, because he rejected the orthodoxies of both the Olde and the New Journalism. He moved in and out of each journalistic circle, never fully belonging to one or the other. And he was as smart as he was self-absorbed.

God snorted at Stan and Sherry. Nobody said anything because he was picking up the tab. "Jesus fucking Christ, Stan," God said. "You guys have been spun so hard by that little sneak Mike Mahoney, your heads are on backwards ..."

"Oh yeah?" Sherry said, jowls suddenly aquiver. "Well, screw you, Gord! At least Rioux will talk to *us* ..."

God laughed heartily at that one. Sherry was referring, undoubtedly, to an incident about ten years earlier, when God had quoted Ross Hamilton saying something stupid on the Tory campaign plane. According to the Conservative spin-meisters, this was unacceptable conduct, because God McAleer should have known that everything said on a campaign plane or bus is always off the record. The incident had thrown Hamilton into a towering rage, and the Olde Journalists in the gallery had been pretty unimpressed, too. So God McAleer was cut off, on Hamilton's personal instructions. Having partly built her journalistic career on cozy relationships with those in power, Sherry was never cut off.

Kurt Tasse, who was on the management track at Southam, and was taking lots of courses at the University of Ottawa to improve his negotiation skills, tried to mediate. "Hey, guys," he said. "We'll find out tomorrow, right?"

"Don't be such a fucking Pollyanna, Kurt," God said. "That Rioux guy is the biggest bullshitter I've seen around here since Ross Hamilton."

Roxanne Perry, who mostly said little, suggested that Rioux's plan to embrace the VAT "wasn't exactly risk-free." Said Roxanne, who was one of the Hill's brighter reporters: "It could go either way for him," adding, in her trademark monotone, "I think the downside is pretty large."

John Moore stirred. "And I, for one, must confess that it is refreshing to see a senior minister being prepared to express himself with such candour," he said, sipping at a small glass of port. "And that is how I have expressed myself in tomorrow's column. I believe Mr. Rioux deserves some credit here."

God sneered. "Jesus, John, you sound like Stan," he said. "Is it possible for you guys at the *Globe* to write anything about One-Eyed Johnny without suspending your collective critical faculties?"

Stan was the author of a little political gossip column that ran in the *Globe* on Saturdays, called "Rumoured on the Hill." Since well before the election, the column had been resolutely — and egregiously — pro-Rioux. It was typically overflowing with accounts of some clever idea that Mike Mahoney or Mark Petryk had contributed to governmental policy, or some heartwarming little story Mahoney had made up to make Rioux look more human. At the end of it, Stan would declare which politico was "hot." Rioux was usually hot; Annie Frosini, John Derbyshire and other pro-Laurier ministers most often were not. So Joey, not unexpectedly, called Stan's column "Rioux on the Hill."

Remembering this, and listening to God McAleer, I laughed out loud; I couldn't help myself. Since almost the first day of the new Liberal government, the *Globe*'s Parliamentary Bureau had been sparing no effort, or glowing phrase, to depict Jean Rioux as the real brains behind the Laurier government. It was almost embarrassing. Why Laurier was putting up with this sort of thing was beyond me, but I suspected his press flack, Walt Hume, had something to do with it.

Sherry turned on me. "What's so funny, Chris?" she demanded.

I shrugged. "Nothing," I told her, still entertained by what God

McAleer had said. "So who do you think is giving Rioux communications advice on tomorrow's event?"

"The Prince Group, of c-c-course," Stan said, and then he remembered my story. "They ..." He trailed off.

Everyone looked at me and there was an uncomfortable silence. Finally Sherry said: "Do you think they still have that frigging no-smoking rule here?"

*   *   *

At the appointed hour, the announcement came across "the blower" — an internal broadcast system, set up to advise Parliamentary Press Gallery reporters about imminent press conferences or press releases. Jean Rioux, Minister of Finance, was holding a press conference in the press theatre, just down Wellington Street. At about the same moment, a fax came into our office, on Finance Department letterhead, saying the same thing.

Joey was in a chair beside my desk when the announcement was made. Every reporter on the Hill had known the press conference was to take place this morning; Joey and I had been waiting for it.

"The master calls," Joey said, standing to pull on his threadbare old overcoat. "Let us not keep him waiting, young Christopher."

Through gales of snow, we walked the fifty feet to the entrance of the press theatre. Once inside, stomping the snow off our feet, we were warmly greeted by Ray Aquin, my pal from the Corps of Commissionaires. We chatted briefly about Ray's Christmas holidays, spent with a daunting number of grandchildren. As Joey moved on to enter the press theatre, Ray touched my arm and waved me closer. "I have something for you, Chris," he said. "See me afterwards, okay?"

"Sure, Ray," I replied. I went inside and sat with Joey.

The press theatre contains about a hundred padded seats. Beside each is a small console that offers a choice of what is being said up on the small stage, or a translation in one's preferred official language. Ashtrays had also been fitted into the consoles at one time, but these had long since disappeared. The theatre was now proudly smoke-free. Above our heads, microphones had been strung from the ceiling, so that questioners could be heard by the questioned. At the rear of the room, on risers, camera people were setting up their equipment for the big event.

The stage contained a long and narrow desk, on which a few microphones had been placed. At one end would sit a representative of the Press Gallery, who would keep a list of those wishing to ask a question. On this day, the representative would be Roxanne Perry.

One of Jean Rioux's junior press assistants — a pretty young woman who was a daughter of one of the members of the 829 Club — politely offered Joey and me a brightly coloured binder. Inside it was a copy of Rioux's remarks, in both English and French; a legislative history of the Value Added Tax; a short summary of the unsuccessful discussions between Ottawa and the provinces on the fate of the tax; a spreadsheet showing VAT revenues, by province; and a biography of Rioux. "Isn't that interesting," Joey said, fingering the bio. "Does this guy ever quit?"

There was a flurry at the front. Jean Rioux entered and started chatting up Stan Silversides and Sherry Bickle, who were seated together near the entrance to the theatre. Joey and I watched them, saying nothing. Not far from Stan was Joan Starr, one of Bobby Laurier's senior policy advisers. Starr, a former Manitoba Liberal MLA, was bright but largely unappreciated in Ottawa's male-dominated corridors. She was there, I assumed, to ensure that Jean Rioux said exactly what Flash Feiffer and Bobby Laurier wanted him to say.

Rioux removed his deliberately downscale overcoat and made his way to the stage. Only one official was with him — Michel St. Laurent, the deputy minister at the Department of Finance. The two sat down, smiled broadly at everyone, and awaited Roxanne's signal. Once all the reporters had found their seats, she gave the go-ahead.

"Good morning," Rioux said. He looked controlled, and in control. "Since the government was sworn in, just a few short weeks ago, my officials and I have been engaged in a comprehensive series of discussions with business people, business associations and average Canadians. In these discussions, we have made good on this government's pledge to be a government that listens to the people. In those many meetings, which have taken place in every region, we have canvassed many alternatives to the Value Added Tax ..."

And so on. Like most of the reporters present, I was reading Rioux's text as he did. I noted that Rioux had said "the government's pledge," instead of what was printed in the official text, which was "the Prime Minister's pledge." Joey also noticed it. "Flash won't be very happy," he whispered to me, giggling.

Rioux's announcement had been so widely leaked around town by Mike Mahoney that it contained little, or no, news. The government had always been clear: the VAT could be scrapped only if an alternative tax could be found, one that brought in equivalent revenues. An infinitesimal number of alternatives had been examined. None could do it as well as the VAT. Ross Hamilton, wherever he was, must have been laughing uproariously to see the Grits finally parroting what his Tory government had said all along: namely, that the VAT — while hated, while despised, while a pain in the ass for small businesses — was the best anyone could come up with.

Once Rioux had repeated his statement in French, the first two questions came from Sherry Bickle. She stood up, and Rioux beamed at her.

"Mr. Rioux, with your announcement today, what are you saying here? Are you saying the Liberal Party made a mistake?" she asked. It was the obvious question.

Rioux didn't flinch. He had been expecting this one, and he was delighted that one of his favourite reporters was asking it. "Well, Sherry," he said, all chummy and convivial, "the bottom line is this: we made a mistake. We made a mistake in saying that we could get rid of the tax as easily as we had hoped."

From the corner of my eye, I could see that Joan Starr had literally jumped in her chair. I glanced at her. She was frowning, staring at Rioux, and she didn't seem to care who noticed it. Rioux ignored her.

Bickle knew that she had just been given the clip of the day. That night, on every radio and television broadcast, Rioux's remark — "we made a mistake" — would be replayed a hundred times. She plunged forward. "Mr. Rioux, let me read to you what Annie Frosini, the Deputy Prime Minister, said should be done with the VAT during the election. She said, and I quote, that it would be 'killed, hanged, drawn and quartered' when the Liberals got into power. She said she would resign if you didn't get rid of it," Sherry said. I wondered to myself who had supplied her with that particular quote. "Does that mean that Ms. Frosini should resign?"

Jean Rioux didn't even blink with his one visible eye. He looked as if he had been expecting this question, too. There was a long, dramatic pause. Finally, looking very grave, he said: "You would have to ask Annie about that. But I can tell you that all of us, as a cabinet, have agreed that our pledge to get rid of the VAT, in the way we communicated it, was a mistake. Next question."

Joey and I looked at each other. "Holy-y-y shit," Joey said, not bothering to whisper. "Did he just say what I think he said?"

✻   ✻   ✻

From what I heard afterwards, from France and others, Bobby Laurier was so angry at Walt Hume and Flash Feiffer he flung a heavy Native soapstone carving at his office door, cracking the wood. Walt had tried to argue that Rioux had only made a slight digression from the agreed-upon answers. Flash, for his part, had lamely stated that he had told Rioux not to deviate from the prepared text.

"Jesus Christ," the Prime Minister bellowed at them, "Annie is fucked now, do you guys realize dat? I never gave approval for dis!"

I, meanwhile, met with Ray Aquin an hour or so after the press conference, as he had asked me to do. "Chris," he said, "some big, tall guy left this for you." He handed me another envelope. "Said he knew you would be here today, and that we were friends," Ray added.

"What did he look like, Ray?" I asked, turning the envelope over in my hands.

"Hard to say," Ray said. "He was wearing a hat and a scarf over half his face. And glasses, too." He paused. "Oh yeah, he said his name was Igor."

"Igor, eh?"

I thanked Ray and opened the envelope once I was safely back at my desk. It contained another photocopy of a Donna Curtis memo. This is what it said:

> M: I rec using the line in Q & A. Make sure questioner is supplied with Annie's famous quote. The Vaporize Annie Tax is our best friend! She won't last a week. D.

Donna Curtis was right. Once the House reconvened, and Question Period began anew, the Reform Party and the Bloc Québécois came after Annie Frosini as if she were Judas Iscariot. On one news broadcast after another, Rioux's "mistake" line was juxtaposed against Frosini's "I'll resign" line. She didn't have a chance. Within a month, Annie had offered her resignation to Bobby Laurier. He refused it, at first, but Walt Hume and Flash Feiffer advised him that he had no choice.

Annie Frosini resigned one afternoon in mid-March, the first ministerial resignation under Prime Minister Bobby Laurier. That night, Joey told me, Mike Mahoney held a big party in his office to celebrate.

CHAPTER NINE

Bobby Laurier was in a deep, deep funk. For all of his adult life — and part of his non-adult life — he had slaved to achieve the post of Prime Minister. He had endured abuse about his looks, and his intelligence, and his ability to lead. He had consumed a metric ton of rubber chicken at fundraising dinners, and shaken countless hands mainstreeting in numbing cold. Through hard work, and not a little luck, he had risen to the highest post in the land. But he was miserable.

One did not need to be an insider to figure this out. Just watching Laurier in the House of Commons — where his attendance at Question Period was spotty, and his answers to questions lacked coherence or spark — it was obvious that something was wrong. During QP, those of us who still attended in the flesh (most reporters would watch the show over closed-circuit television, then amble over around ten minutes to three to scrum) could see it on the faces of Laurier's ministers: they knew that the Liberal leader was not performing well. John Derbyshire and the other Laurier loyalists — Transport minister Tom Byrnes, from Toronto, and Al Stewart, the

Minister of National Defence, from B.C., and others — tried to put the best spin on it. But, as I leaned over the railing above the Speaker's chair, I could see that they, too, were miserable.

Jean Rioux, on the other hand, was as happy as a pig in manure. He took every question that came his way, and even a few that were clearly intended for other ministers. He waved his arms expansively, as if giving a Sermon on the Mount. He told bad jokes, which the trained seals in the Grit backbenches found uproariously funny. And he preened outrageously to the hacks in the Gallery.

In the backrooms of government, his burgeoning reputation was in no small measure aided by the spinning efforts of Mike Mahoney, Mark Petryk, Donna Curtis and Dick Thorsell, pugilist extraordinaire. Reporters need information to survive; Mahoney, Petryk, Thorsell and Curtis provided the Gallery with as much self-serving information as they could, whether it was stamped "Top Secret" or not. Following Annie Frosini's resignation from cabinet — Bobby Laurier was determined to bring her back, I was told, after an appropriate period of penance had expired — an unprecedented number of leaks flooded the town. There were leaks about planned military-base closures. There were leaks about cuts to the number of public servants employed in about ten federal government departments. There were leaks about the fate of Tom Aspinall's social-services review.

In every case, the leaks served one of two purposes: they either made Rioux look good, or they made Laurier and his gang look bad. In the case of the military-base closures, for example — after Mahoney had used the Prince Group to conduct enough polling on the issue to show that it was a highly popular move with most cash-strapped Canadians — Mahoney got word out that Rioux had fought for the closures over the objections of Al Stewart. In the case of the layoffs of some 30,000 bureaucrats across the country — another highly popular move, given that the bulk of them were located in Ottawa — Petryk let it be known that Rioux had insisted that the "rationalizations," as he called them, be a centrepiece of the first Budget, whether big government types like John Derbyshire liked it or not. And in the case of poor Tom Aspinall — with whom the *Financial Times*'s George Cunningham had sought employment as senior policy adviser, in one of the more dramatic career-limiting moves I've ever witnessed — the much-touted social-services review had been an unmitigated disaster. Every difficulty in negotiations with the provinces, every blemish with the proposed legislation, every mistake, was happily recorded by Finance bureaucrats, then passed on to Rioux's office. If Mahoney didn't think it wise to leak it himself, he would make sure that Thorsell or Curtis knew about it, so that they could tell one of their own journalistic pets.

The leaks, of course, were fodder for most of the questions asked by the Reform Party or the Bloc Québécois. The Reformers, half of whom appeared to be mildly fascistic bible-thumping lunatics, ate these stories up. To them, the Liberals weren't doing nearly enough to eliminate the deficit and the debt. They directed most of their questions at Bobby Laurier, who seemed to be astonished by the mean-spiritedness of the party of self-described populists. To the Reformers, the poor were a coddled, drug-addicted, sex-crazed constituency of minorities who didn't have enough gumption to make something of themselves. Or to vote Reform.

The Bloc Québécois, on the other hand, went at the same issues from the polar opposite — *en français*, of course. To the Bloc-heads, as Joey called them, Canada was being run by a family compact of tight-assed, humourless WASPs who had no interest in helping the less fortunate — particularly the less fortunate drinking O'Keefe in front of video lottery terminals in nationalist ridings in Quebec. Whenever possible, they hurled vicious insults at Laurier, reminding him that he was a *vendu* — a sellout. The only wrinkle in the Bloc's theory of the Bobby Laurier government, of course, was the presence of Bobby Laurier himself, who could hardly be called a WASP. The Bloquistes, who were as intolerant in their own way as the Reformers were in theirs, remedied this inconsistency by insinuating that Laurier was not a *pure laine* francophone, having grown up in Alberta. *Quebec über alles.*

It was late March, and spring seemed far, far away. On one particularly cold and windy Thursday, as Joey and I strode through the wind towards Wellington Street with God McAleer, Joey said: "Christly

Jesus, how can a government fall so far so fast?" He looked as unhappy as Bobby Laurier.

"What are you talking about, Joey?" God asked, lighting a cigarette. "These bastards are still way up in the polls. And they aren't going to go down anytime soon, not as long as the Reformers and the Bloc continue to rob the Tories of two of their natural bases of support — the Quebec nationalists and the Western rednecks."

"Yes, yes, I know, Gord," Joey said impatiently, as we walked on. "But the country was looking to Laurier to repair some of the damage done by Ross Hamilton's wrecking crew, don't you think? And that certainly isn't happening. This is a government adrift."

God shrugged. "I'm not sure anyone voted for Laurier because they wanted to feel better," he said. "I think they just voted *against* Hamilton's party, that's all. Same old story."

"I have to disagree, Gord," I replied. "There was something different about the election last year. I didn't see any polling on it, but I got the sense that people felt that they could trust Laurier, you know? As if he was different."

"Give me an example," God said.

"Well, you were there that day in Saskatchewan, near the end of the campaign, weren't you?" I asked. "Remember that? When Laurier got up on that tractor, and gave that speech about the farmer whose kid had killed himself? Didn't you get the sense that the people there were still capable of believing in a political leader — and that they wanted to believe in Laurier?"

We stopped at a crosswalk at Wellington and O'Connor. God continued puffing away, frowning. "Yeah, I remember," he said. "I wanted to believe in him myself. Gave me fucking shivers down my spine that day, the old bugger. And I'm one of the most cynical bastards around."

I bid Joey and God adieu, and headed back to CP's national bureau. Shrugging off my overcoat, I dialled up my voice-mail messages. There was one from my mother, reminding me not to forget Sheila's birthday; one from France, reminding me that we were meeting some of her PMO pals for drinks at the Duke of Somerset pub after work; and one from him — Igor. From the sounds in the background, I figured he was calling from a payphone. It wasn't traceable, that way.

"Mr. O'Reilly," he said. "It is urgent we meet again. Six P.M. tomorrow evening, sharp. Do not worry about getting in. A gate on the Bank Street side will be open. I have left the location in a call I made earlier to one of your copy people." *Click.* That was it.

I was surprised he didn't mention that his voice-mail message would self-destruct after five seconds.

❊   ❊   ❊

After briefing Kevin Ritchie about the phone call from Igor, I returned to my desk. I had shown Kevin the two Donna Curtis notices that Igor had passed along to me; in both cases, neither of us felt that they were at all newsworthy. The fact the Rioux gang — his office, the Prince Group, the 829 Club, et al. — despised Annie Frosini was not particularly surprising. Nor was the fact that the Prince Group was giving communications advice to Rioux. I had written that in my first story on the firm, before Christmas. The suggestion that the Finance minister's office was supplying reporters with damaging material — the infamous Frosini quote about hanging, drawing and quartering the VAT, for example — that, however, was a bit of a surprise. But it wasn't the stuff of which front pages are made.

My investigation into the Prince Group had been slowed down by a variety of factors: the new Liberal government's honeymoon; the Christmas holidays; the pre-Budget frenzy; the reopening of the House of Commons, and the delivery of the first Grit Throne Speech in almost a decade. And so on. But with the Throne Speech as well as the Budget behind me, I could return my attention to the enigmatic Prince Group. That, certainly, was what Kevin wanted me to do. As he put it: "When a reporter gets punched in the nose for a story he's working on, you can generally assume that it's a story worth pursuing."

The message light was flashing on my phone when I returned to my desk where I found a pink message slip containing two words: "LANSDOWNE PARK." Igor wanted to meet in a football field. I punched in my code on the phone and heard Joey's voice. He sounded even more morose than he had been when we were walking down the Hill with God McAleer. "Christopher, my boy," he said in that overblown English accent of his. "Things are a little grim over here at Southam Corp. this afternoon. Would you be so good as to give me a call?"

As I dialled Joey's number at the Southam bureau, I had a pretty good idea what he was referring to, but I hoped I was wrong. For a number of weeks, reliable rumours had been flying that Carswell Spence III, the zillionaire industrialist and enthusiastic collector of newspapers, had his sights set on a hostile takeover of Southam. A product of the same private boys' schools that had given the Canadian public the likes of Gus Stimpole, Jack Gibson and Jean Rioux, Carswell Spence had made his fortune in the stock market. Later, he busied himself with community newspapers in and around Toronto. His approach was well known. He would take over a paper's owner-ship, then send in one of his minions from the Harvard Business School to tell the newsroom and production staff that they had nothing to worry about. A few weeks after that, a layoff list would be posted in the newsroom — letting go most of the expensive talent, along with those who were a tad too soft on social and economic issues.

That, in large part, was the biggest fear of many Canadian journal-ists whenever they heard that Carswell Spence III was sniffing around their employer's annual shareholder meetings: that he wasn't just interested in ownership, he was interested in ideological purity, too.

Carswell Spence was, to be polite about it, somewhat right-wing. Powerful, prosperous and perspicacious, he was the pin-up boy of Bay Street. The belief was that, whenever Spence assumed control of a paper, many of the writers who held views that were at variance with the new management — those, for example, who felt that governments occasionally had their uses — would be shuffled off editorial boards to be replaced by kooks from the Farber Institute or the like. Columnists who were also inclined towards social justice and against capital punishment for twelve-year-olds apprehended vandalizing school buses would be returned to a general assignment beat in the newsroom, or some other journalistic limbo. And so on. The Carswell Spence III era was not kind to journalists like Joey Myers.

Joey came on the line. "Hello, Myers here," he said. There was a lot of racket in the background.

"Hey, Joey," I said. "What's going on over there? It's awfully noisy."

"Oh, that," he said. "That's the sound of the gallows being erected in the middle of our little office, here. Some of the executions will be taking place forthwith."

"What are you talking about?"

"Christopher, haven't you heard? The acquisitive Mr. Spence finally possesses what he has always most desired — the Southam chain of newspapers," Joey said, trying his best to sound blasé. "And three of us have already received our pink slips."

"What? They fired you?"

"I believe that the proper term in the nineties is 'restructured,' Christopher," he replied. I could hear shouting in the background. "Or 'rationalized' ..."

"Joey, cut it out," I said. "They can't just fire you. You've got years and years of experience there! This is crazy!"

"To be fair to Mr. Spence's charming group, they told me I had a choice," Joey responded. "They told me that I could take an offer to write on general assignment for the Red Deer *Advocate*. Or I could leave. I chose to leave."

"I can't believe this, Joey," I said. "I'm so sorry. What are you going to do?"

"Believe it or not, I have already thought of that, which is quite unlike me," he replied. "And I called you for two reasons. One, to let you know about this somewhat unexpected new career change. And, two, to ask if you would arrange a meeting for me with Kevin Ritchie."

"Well, sure," I said. "Of course. When?"

"Right now, actually. I could come over right away."

I rang off and dashed into Kevin's office. Luc Bergeron and a couple of other guys were already there, with very worried expressions on their faces. Southam News was the biggest Canadian Press client; it was also our biggest contributor of news copy. If Carswell Spence pulled the plug on our contract with the Southam papers, we'd all be out of work, too. My co-workers were clustered around Kevin's desk, watching him as he read a copy of the Southam news release that had been faxed to us from Toronto. Kevin didn't look happy.

"Kevin, could I talk to you for a minute?"

He looked up at me. "Sure," he said, handing the Southam fax back to Luc. "Let's step outside." We moved a few feet from his office door.

"I assume you've heard the news," he said.

"Yeah."

"How is Joey?" he asked. "Have you talked to him?"

"I just got off the phone with him," I said. "They gave him a choice of Red Deer or a pink slip. He took the pink slip."

Kevin scowled. "Bastards," he said, which I think is the strongest word I have ever heard him use. "What is he going to do?"

"Well, actually, he wants to talk to you," I said.

"Me?" He thought about that for a moment. "He knows we aren't hiring, I assume?"

"I'm sure he knows that," I said. "He just said he wants to talk to you. Now, if possible."

"Give me his number, then."

And that, in short, is how my good friend Joey Myers came to work with me — first, for free, and then, shortly thereafter, on contract — on the Prince Group stories. For me, it wasn't much of an adjustment. For most of my time on Parliament Hill, I had been relying on Joey for his perspective on the stories I planned to write. I trusted him completely. As a team — and that is what we certainly became — we complemented each other well. His nature was to be much more forgiving about the people who ran for public life (with the possible exception of Jean Rioux, of course). In that respect, he encouraged me to be slightly less conspiratorial. I, meanwhile, gave him back an enthusiasm for toppling some political icons. Or at least that's what he told me.

Around the CP bureau, we came to be known as "the Odd

Couple." We dressed differently, talked differently, worked differently, looked different. But we made it work. It was a lot of fun, and there was very little competition between us. Joey, it seemed, was simply grateful to have a source of income.

They put a desk for Joey a few feet away from mine. One morning when I came in, he had posted a photograph of Carswell Spence III beside his computer screen. A bull's eye had been drawn over Spence's well-coiffed head. I laughed and asked Joey about it.

"Oh, well, that is just to remind me," he said. "When we have destroyed the career of Mr. Rioux, I will be turning my attention to my friend Carswell here."

❉   ❉   ❉

The Bank Street entrance closest to Lansdowne Park was, as Igor promised, open when I arrived at ten minutes to six on Friday evening. A couple of uniformed security guards were talking over by the Rough Riders ticket office, but neither of them gave me a second glance when I opened the gate and stepped inside.

I had been to only a couple of Rough Riders games during my time in Ottawa, and they had been plenty. Never before had I been witness to such spectacularly pitiful football.

I headed towards one of the entrances beside the north-side stands. It was locked. The next entrance over, however, was open. I went through it, and immediately found myself near one of the end zones. Football season was many weeks off in the distance, but the astroturf was free of snow. At the far end zone, on the east side, the night game lights were blazing like a hundred suns. At my end, on the west side, the lights were off.

I spotted Igor right where he had promised he would be, at centre field, casting a long, long shadow. As before, I could see that he was wearing a wide-brimmed hat and a scarf across his face. I started walking towards him. He was facing west, away from the lights. It was, I thought for not the first time, a very strange place to meet.

As I came closer, I noted that his face was completely wrapped in shadow. With the massive field spotlights at his back, his face was as dark as the dark side of the moon. I couldn't make anything out, other than that he was wearing an expensive-looking overcoat, rubbers on his expensive-looking brogues, and black leather gloves. Once again, he was wearing tinted glasses.

"Hello, Igor," I said, as I got closer. "How are you?"

"Very well, thank you," he said from behind his scarf. "And yourself?"

"Fine, thanks. Although, normally, I just come here to see football games," I said. "Is it you I have to thank for that last Donna Curtis memo?"

"It is. I trust it was useful," he said.

"It was, in a sense. It confirmed what I had been suspecting, anyway," I said. "How did you get it?"

"Never mind," he said. "What is the status of your investigation at the moment?"

"I'm still pursuing it, when I have the time," I said. "It's a difficult story to chase."

"That is true," he said. He glanced down at his wrist, at his watch. "Time is of the essence. I wanted to meet with you to inform you that you and your colleagues in the Press Gallery missed a very significant story, following the tabling of the Budget."

"What do you mean?"

"Here is a list," he said, pulling an envelope out of the pocket of his overcoat. He handed it to me. "On this list are the names of nine companies. Cross-reference these names with the names of corporate contributors to Mr. Rioux's campaign in St. Henri–Westmount. You should also cross-reference them with the list of companies in which Mr. Rioux held equity, or a director's post, prior to his involvement in politics. As well, you should cross-reference them with the list of companies that retained the Prince Group to lobby various departments — Industry, Defence and Transport in particular — in the period immediately preceding the Budget."

"I see. Will I find that all of these companies are on those lists?"

"You will also find them listed on various stock exchanges, if they are publicly traded. Most are. And you will find that each of them has enjoyed very substantial growth in its profitability since the Budget."

I didn't know what to say for a moment. "Is there any possibility that Mr. Rioux's office will be able to argue that all of this is a coincidence?"

He gave a humourless snort, which I took to be his attempt at a laugh. "They will certainly argue it, but not very convincingly," he said. "I do not think most reasonable people will believe them."

Igor, or whatever his name was, was handing me a major, major story here. If it could be shown that someone had manipulated the Budget process to benefit firms that Rioux had once owned, or helped to run, there would be a massive political scandal. I turned the envelope over in my hands, thinking. He spoke again. "You will also find, Mr. O'Reilly, that all of these companies are on lists you removed from the offices of Roger Fournier. Many were represented by him, before his murder."

That shocked me. How did he know what I had removed from Fournier's office? I had not shown anyone other than Kevin those papers. How could Igor have known what was in Fournier's garbage bags, for chrissakes?

"Who killed Fournier?" I asked him.

Before he could say anything, I heard voices on the other side of the football field, behind Igor. I looked over, and saw the two security guards who had been loitering near the gate when I arrived. At the same moment, Igor looked over, too. I can only assume he did this in error — because, as he turned, I saw most of his face in the light.

And, at that moment, I had a pretty good idea of who Igor might be.

✻   ✻   ✻

Joey and I worked on the list Igor had handed me straight through the two-week parliamentary Easter break. We did nothing else. Cross-referencing the companies contained in it against the various lists that Igor had mentioned was no easy task. But as we did so, slowly — bit by bit — a picture started to emerge.

The companies Rioux had once controlled, or had once helped to run, covered a wide range of business interests. Some were engineering consortia, involved in large-scale infrastructure upgrading — stuff like repairing large sections of the Trans-Canada Highway. Some were primarily involved in the production of computer components for light armoured vehicles, and other material our military used in peacekeeping missions abroad. Some were high-tech firms, aiming to get a big chunk of the federal government's upgrade for its antiquated, and incompatible, departmental computer networks. All of the businesses they were involved in were completely legitimate and legal — but how they increased their market share was highly suspect.

In the case of the light armoured vehicles, the companies involved had hired Mark Petryk, Rioux's former leadership campaign supremo — and a partner in the Prince Group — to lobby the Department of National Defence for a contract. What made the whole process unusual, one of Joey's military sources at DND told him, was that Petryk seemed to know that Finance was eager to purchase the light armoured vehicles' computerized control systems before anyone at the Defence Department did. And he had an encyclopedic knowledge of the technical requirements of the tender — even though the formal request for proposals was months away. The contract was worth close to a billion dollars.

It was the same thing with the Trans-Canada Highway upgrade. Donna Curtis had registered as the chief lobbyist for that one. During the federal election, the Liberals had promised to devote a big chunk of money to infrastructure across the country. But the specific programs — especially the big ones — were still being worked out by the three levels of government, federally, provincially and municipally. No one we could find at the Department of Transport had known that Finance was planning to set aside a couple of billion for the upgrade of the highway. And when Jean Rioux's curvaceous follower Donna Curtis arrived one day — well in advance of the

Budget — to tell them to prepare for it, they were surprised. Pleasantly surprised, but surprised just the same.

The whole process was repeated with the computer systems network integration. That one was also worth a whopping two billion. The lobbyist registered to represent the engineering firms involved — most of them headquartered in Quebec — was Howie Atwater. Howie was a big Tory, but he was also a partner at the Prince Group. A good place to work, these days.

The whole thing, if true, was analogous to a massive insider-trading scheme. Prince Group lobbyists would be briefed in advance by Rioux's department about which initiatives would be in the Budget. The lobbyists would in turn solicit the business of firms that had an interest in those initiatives, at presumably significant hourly rates, and with fat retainers. Changes would then be made to the Budget to suit the individual needs of the companies represented by the Prince Group. And all of them, on the day after Rioux's first Budget, would have a virtual lock on the few big-ticket spending items contained in the Budget. Other firms would try to compete, of course, but it would be a waste of their time. The ones represented by the Prince Group cabal — the ones who had known what the contract terms would be many, many months in advance, because they had helped to draft the terms — would score. Big time.

Only one or two of the companies on Igor's list had actually inked a deal with the federal government. Most were still waiting to be awarded a contract. But, according to some of the sources Joey was able to talk to — he had been around Ottawa a long time, thankfully, and was able to persuade a few terrified and/or bewildered public servants to open up about the whole scam — there was no doubt, in the bureaucratic world, that the Prince Group's clients would win at the end of the day. They simply knew too much.

"This is one of the sleaziest things I've seen in a long time," Joey said to me late one night, as we tracked the stock values of the companies we had taken to calling "the Gang of Nine." "It's extraordinary. The entire Budget process seems to have been manipulated to enrich the Gang of

Nine. It's like Rioux's office is running an alternative government within the one that Bobby Laurier supposedly is running."

"That's what I don't get," I said, pulling on another Diet Coke. "Where the hell are Laurier and Flash Feiffer in all of this shit? Aren't they supposed to be ensuring that the process is relatively clean? Is the Prime Minister of Canada asleep at the switch, or what?"

My phone rang; Joey answered. He listened for a minute, then hung up.

"That was Kevin," he said, looking pale. "He's coming in. He has received … a tip from someone."

"You look as if you've seen a ghost," I responded. "What's wrong?"

"The Prime Minister of Canada may have been asleep at the switch, as you say," Joey muttered. "But, if what Kevin's source says is true, he is also, at this moment, in a hospital in Florida, fighting for his life. Bobby Laurier has had a massive heart attack, Christopher."

CHAPTER TEN

In the United States, when the President skins his knee on a dock at Kennebunkport, or outside a cheap hotel room in Little Rock, it is national news. White House staff convene immediate press briefings, complete with detailed charts taken from *Gray's Anatomy*, and teams of white-coated physicians are made available to give their expert diagnoses. The geopolitical implications of the scraped presidential knee are canvassed at great length. The impact of the crisis is followed on the stock market. Every reporter's question, no matter how personal — no matter how irrelevant — is solemnly answered. Everything You Ever Wanted to Know about the President's Knee, and Then Some.

In Canada, as in most things, we do it differently. In Canada, when the Prime Minister — theoretically, the most powerful person in the country — experiences some sort of health problem, his officials are a good deal less than candid. They obfuscate. They prevaricate. They cover up, whenever and wherever possible. Above all, they do not let us know what is going on.

Unlike the President of the United States of America, the Prime

Minister of Canada is not the most powerful leader in the free world. That is not in dispute. But, that said, it would have been nice to know, at the time we learned of his heart attack, whether Bobby Laurier was alive or dead. And we didn't.

Kevin Ritchie rocketed back to the national bureau of the Canadian Press in record time. Luc Bergeron also appeared in rapid fashion, as did a couple of senior editor types. The night-desk copy-editors were still there, of course, but all of them were still unaware of what was going on. Joey, Luc and I were summoned into Kevin's office while the assembled editors started calling reporters at home, to tell them to report back to work.

The House of Commons was not in session the week we learned of Laurier's condition. Like many Canadians who could afford it, Laurier and his wife, Michelle, had repaired to a friend's timeshare somewhere in Florida, to soak up some sun and play some golf. That much we knew. According to Kevin's source — whom he would not identify, of course, but whom he insisted was very, very reliable — Laurier had mentioned chest pains earlier in the day, then later collapsed on a golf course. He was now in hospital, and his condition was unknown. Somewhere in Florida.

Kevin was calm and deliberate. "According to my source," he said, "the only other people who would know about this are the RCMP, who would have had a small security detail with Laurier, and a few senior people at the PMO. It is possible, my source said, that no other news agencies are aware of this."

He let that sink in. This was the Mother of All Scoops.

"Joey and Chris, I want you to get a confirmation out of PMO. Luc, I want you to work the RCMP," Kevin said. "The reporters who are being called back in will be assigned to finding out where Laurier is in Florida, what his condition is, and so on. I want to have a good story, with as much detail as we can find, on the wire within an hour." He glanced at his watch. "Any questions?"

There were none. We knew what we had to do. My first call was to France; she was at home, but the line was busy. Next, I tried Walt Hume through the PMO's switchboard, which operates twenty-four hours a day. The operator told me he was unavailable. Undeterred, I hauled out a copy of Ottawa's reverse telephone directory and found Hume's unlisted phone number. He lived in upscale Rockcliffe, naturally.

Hume answered. "Hey, Chris-baby," he said, his usual patter sounding forced, "how did you find my number?"

"Walt, I wouldn't be calling you unless it was something important," I said. "But we are seeking confirmation as to whether the Prime Minister had a heart attack in Florida earlier today."

There was a long, long pause. "I see," Hume replied. I couldn't tell whether he already knew or not. He sounded distant.

"Walt, can you confirm that? We need to know," I said. "It is obviously very important."

The line remained silent. After another long pause, Hume said: "I can't confirm or deny that," he said.

"What?" I responded, disbelieving. "Do you mean you *won't* confirm it, or you *can't*?"

"Sorry, Chris-baby, we have no comment," he said. "Anything else?"

"Jesus *Christ*, Walt!" I exploded, losing my cool for about the first time in my journalistic career. Joey was staring at me from his desk, where he, too, was on the phone. Smiling broadly, he gave me a thumbs-up sign. "What is this shit? The Prime Minister of Canada has a heart attack, and you won't comment ..." Before I could finish, Luc Bergeron came racing over to my desk, waving at me. He scribbled something on a message pad, then flung it on my desk. "SENIOR RCMP CONFIRM PM HEART ATTACK," the message read.

I counted to five, then returned to Walt Hume. "Walt, let's try this again," I said. "The RCMP, which presumably has at least one officer with the Prime Minister at all times, have told us that the Prime Minister *did* have a heart attack. *Now* will you comment, Walt?"

Silence. Finally, he replied: "What's your number? I'll have to get back to you." I gave him the number, and told him I would be calling back in ten minutes if I didn't hear from him. Joey, in the meantime, had somehow tracked down Flash Feiffer at Mamma Teresa's, a

Somerset Street restaurant favoured by Grits. As soon as Flash heard the question, Joey said, he swore and hung up. When Joey called back, two seconds later, a waiter told him that Mr. Feiffer had raced out of the restaurant, leaving behind his coat. "I'm pretty sure Flash didn't know, the poor bugger," Joey said. "And that is a story in itself."

"How did you know to call him there?" I asked, still amazed that Joey had figured out where Flash was.

Joey shrugged, smiling. "Flash is a notorious bachelor, my dear Christopher, and Mamma's is a notorious Grit hangout, chock-a-block with youngsters — female ones — seeking communion with Canada's political élite," he said. "I just made a guess."

Kevin walked over, looking grim. "Any developments?" he asked. We told him that the RCMP were confirming the heart attack, without attribution, while Walt Hume was playing games. Flash Feiffer, meanwhile, seemed to have been in the dark. Kevin told us to give Hume two minutes to call back, then start to write that RCMP sources were confirming it. After two minutes, I called Hume. His line was busy. I tried again in another couple of minutes and got through.

"Confirm or deny, Walt," I said. "Be part of the story, or be part of the cover-up."

"Ha ha ha — Chris-baby, the comedian," he said. He didn't sound as if he thought it was funny. "I can tell you that the Prime Minister experienced a health problem earlier today, and he is resting in hospital. That's all."

"Where?"

"Can't say."

"What's his condition?"

"Can't say."

"What, exactly, was the health problem?"

"Can't say that either."

"Is he competent to continue as Prime Minister, Walt? Yes or no?" I was getting pretty fed up with Walt's patented spin routine. There was silence. Apparently the geniuses in the PMO Press Office hadn't anticipated that question. "Yes or no, Walt?"

"Uh, yes."

He wouldn't say anything more. I told Walt I would be back to him later in the evening, and hung up. With Joey, Luc, Kevin and a growing number of arriving reporters standing behind me, I started to write.

URGENT URGENT URGENT URGENT
Prime Minister felled by heart attack
By the Canadian Press

OTTAWA — Prime Minister Robert Laurier collapsed on a Florida golf course earlier today, sources at the RCMP have confirmed.

An official at the Prime Minister's Office in Ottawa said late tonight that Laurier had experienced "a health problem," but would provide no other details about the Prime Minister's condition ...

That was the start of the main story we shipped out across the country. Over the course of the night — and twenty of us were there, reporters and editors, all night — we issued more than thirty updates to the first story I wrote. In that time, we learned that Bobby Laurier had collapsed on a private golf course outside West Palm Beach. And, according to one of our Washington correspondents, U.S. President Bill Clinton was aware of the situation, and had ordered that Laurier be flown by air ambulance to a nearby military hospital.

When I got home, at dawn, there was a message on my machine from Igor. A few days earlier, which seemed like a year ago, I would have wondered how he had got my number. But I didn't any longer. I showered, threw on some clean clothes and caught a cab back to the office, Igor's very brief message repeating in my head:

"Who is in charge, now, Mr. O'Reilly? Who is really in charge, now?"

*   *   *

By morning, by the time everybody had read the front page of their newspaper, everything had already gone crazy. The dollar dropped two cents in three hours, and trading in it was halted by the Bank of Canada at noon. Stocks plummeted. Reports were coming in about people flooding into churches, praying for Bobby Laurier. School kids were faxing thousands of get-well messages to the PMO. The CBC, CTV and some of the wealthier papers were flying reporters to Florida to search for Laurier's hospital — Flash Feiffer, we were told, was already there at his bedside. Midmorning, Gord (God) McAleer punched — and I mean actually *punched* — Walt Hume in a Centre Block hallway, when the PMO flack wouldn't say anything beyond the same horseshit he had peddled to me. And, at a meeting of some cabinet ministers — I wouldn't necessarily call it a cabinet meeting, because only a Prime Minister possesses the authority to call a full cabinet meeting — John Derbyshire, Tom Byrnes, Al Stewart and others apparently just sat around and wept.

Jean Rioux, not being stupid, was careful. He was crafty. Wherever he went, wherever he was likely to be spotted by someone who wasn't a certified member of the 829 Club, or partner at the Prince Group, Rioux was the very picture of melancholy. He moped through the marbled halls of the Centre Block, his shoulders slumped. He declined public appearances. And when a breathless Sherry Bickle actually asked him whether he would seek the leadership again if Laurier were to die, he looked suitably mortified and stomped away. Bickle was lambasted in editorial columns for two straight days, and Rioux was — of course — applauded for his sense of decency in such a difficult time, blah blah blah.

Behind closed doors, however, Rioux and his acolytes could hardly believe their good fortune. They were in a state of anticipation that most closely resembled that of a lust-crazed sixteen-year-old male intent upon losing his virginity. Four years of leaking, backstabbing and internal agitation had pushed the Finance minister no closer to the post he most desired. But in a single night — and without any unbecoming conduct by any of his retinue — his goal was finally within reach. The evening after we broke the story, another party was thrown in Mahoney's office. It was an even boozier one than that which had followed Annie Frosini's resignation. The Rioux people knew it would all be theirs, very soon.

And Annie Frosini's resignation, for the first time, was on other people's minds, too. Annie, along with being the former Secretary of State, had also been the Deputy Prime Minister. When she resigned, Laurier did not fill the post with someone else. It remained vacant. At the time, those of us in the Press Gallery took this to be another sign that Laurier planned to hand the title back to Frosini, once a few months had passed, and once she had said a few hundred Hail Marys. So the post of Deputy Prime Minister — the Number Two spot — was vacant.

Who, as Igor had said, was in charge now? Who? Because the position of Prime Minister is one that doesn't exist in our Constitution — by convention, the Prime Minister is simply the leader of the group of MPs possessing the largest number of seats in the House of Commons — the answer wasn't entirely clear. There was a void. And into that void, into that ambiguity, stepped Jean Rioux.

He was aided in this by the confusion that was reigning supreme all over the Hill. While Laurier's status remained shrouded in mystery, for example, the Opposition parties agreed to briefly suspend Parliament's rules and delay the recall of the House. The Reformers, however, loudly declared — and they were right to say so, in my opinion — that they would not agree to an indefinite delay. They stated, correctly, that the people of Canada deserved to know the health status, and whereabouts, of their Prime Minister. But Walt Hume continued to say little, if anything.

Rioux's spinners took advantage of this information gap and went into overdrive. They told journalists that Rioux was quietly, and modestly, ensuring that the affairs of the nation were being attended to. They told them that Rioux was providing stability and policy consistency, just as he had in the past few months. When news stories started to appear to that effect, Laurier's usually invisible chief of staff, Charles Lafontaine, reportedly went apeshit on Mahoney. Bellowing on the phone, he warned Mike that he — and his boss, too, if he was involved — was pushing the country towards a full-blown constitutional crisis. But Mahoney didn't care, and neither did Rioux. They continued the leaks about how utterly indispensable Jean Rioux was to Canada's governance. (My source on the Lafontaine phone call was sound, by the way — France had been present when Charlie placed the call.)

After I had gone seventy-two hours without sleep, France showed up at the CP news room and told me that I was being removed from the bureau, and pronto. I didn't argue — Kevin and Joey had left many hours earlier. Thirty minutes later, in Sandy Hill, as France was undressing me on her bed, I told her about my last interview with Bobby Laurier back when he had been Leader of the Opposition. We had sat on his sunny back porch at Stornoway, chatting, drinking lemonade, and he had said to me: "Chris, I don't need dis goddamn job. If de party doesn't want me, den my wife does. If dey want me to go, I'll go. *Pas de problème.*" He had sounded, at the time, as if he meant it.

I thought about that as I fell asleep on France's bed.

*   *   *

When I finally woke up, twelve hours later, I still felt exhausted. I wandered around her apartment for a few minutes, trying to clear my head. On the mantelpiece, France had left me a note — she was at the PMO, for yet another crisis meeting with Charles Lafontaine. I looked again at the family photographs. Something appeared to be missing, but I didn't know what.

Stacks of papers, both Saturday's and Sunday's, were on her coffee table. Sprawling out on France's couch, I scanned a few of them. Only the *Toronto Star* seemed to have any real news in it about Bobby Laurier — they had spoken to some American sources about where the Canadian Prime Minister was, and what his health status was. The Americans had been a good deal more open about the matter because, I assume, Americans tend to believe much more in antiquated concepts like freedom of the press. According to the *Star*, Laurier's condition was "guarded," whatever that meant. And Clinton would be visiting him on Monday.

Time to get back at it. Throwing on my somewhat grimy clothes, I let myself out, locking the door with a key France had given to me a few weeks earlier. I guess you could say we weren't playing house, yet, but we were getting serious. The trouble was that I was feeling guilty, still, about having used her in my earlier Prince Group stories.

I walked up to Laurier Avenue and found the Royal Oak, a pub near the University of Ottawa. There, I ate a huge helping of fish and chips. I was famished. Washing it down with a half-pint of lager, I dashed out the door and caught a cab back to my place. It was snowing slightly and Ottawa looked as if it was deserted. As I approached the door to my apartment, I saw that someone had taped an envelope to it. My first thought was that the sender was Igor — but, when I opened the envelope, I saw the telltale cream-coloured ministerial letterhead. It was from John Derbyshire. "Chris: Been trying to reach you for hours. Give me a call as soon as you get in. John." How the hell did he learn where I lived?

I unlocked the door and called Derbyshire. Another male voice answered — I assumed that it was Derbyshire's driver — and passed the phone to Newfoundland's lead political minister. "Chris, young fella," Derbyshire said. He sounded more tired than I was. "Where are you, brother? We need to talk."

"I'm at home. I just got your note," I replied.

"Oh yeah, that's right. We put it there," he said. "Jesus God Almighty, I'm one tired fuckin' cabinet minister. So ... do you mind if I come over, Chris?"

"No, not at all," I answered. What was going on, now? "Come on over!"

I jumped in the shower, shaved, and was frantically pulling my jeans on when there was a knock at my door. I opened it to the Minister of Public Works and Supply and Services. After Annie Frosini resigned, he was also handed the post of Secretary of State. At the moment, however, Derbyshire didn't look very stately. He was wearing a parka, jeans and a flannel shirt. He looked as if he hadn't slept in a week. We shook hands and he came in.

We sat down at the table in my minuscule kitchen. "Ah, the kitchen," John said, looking around, bleary-eyed. "Where I come from, all the really good political meetings take place in the kitchen, y'know?"

"Want a beer, John?"

"Now there's a fine suggestion," he said, brightening. "But only if you'll join me."

We drank from our bottles for a moment or two.

"Hell of a week, eh, John?"

"The worst fuckin' week of my life. The worst," he said. "It feels as if everything has just fallen apart in a matter of three days. The government is in a state of complete paralysis, nothing's getting done, no one even knows if the big guy is alive or dead. And Rioux ..." He trailed off.

"I imagine Mr. Rioux is just torn up about this recent turn of events," I deadpanned.

"Oh, yes, Mr. Rioux is terribly, terribly upset," John said, his voice dripping with sarcasm. "He is beside himself. No one in the cabinet wishes the Prime Minister a speedy recovery more than the fucking Minister of Finance ..."

"It's that bad, eh?" I asked.

"Yeah," he said, playing with the label on his beer bottle. "The only good thing about it is that even some long-time Rioux supporters are getting turned off by the way he and his people are acting. It's fuckin' sick."

I decided to say nothing and let him talk. I knew he was here for some reason, and would get around to it eventually. He did, right away.

"Chris, I'm here on behalf of a few people," he said. "A few members of the cabinet, a few senior members of caucus. We are all concerned about what is happening, and the impact it could have on the Prime Minister, of course, but also on the party and the country."

He looked me in the eye. "I've come to see you because, as I told some of the guys, you can be trusted. And your old man was one of Laurier's favourite Liberals, did you know that?"

I was a bit startled. "Actually, no," I responded. "I didn't."

"Well, it's true," he said, continuing. "And we know how the Rioux gang have run you down, and cut you off since you printed that story about the Prince Group. They're not too fond of you, or your buddy Joey Myers, either. He's working with you now, isn't he?"

"Yeah," I answered. "We've got him on contract at the moment."

"Good," he said. "Listen, we're totally off the record, right?"

"You know we are."

"All right, then," he said. "There is a special caucus meeting tomorrow morning. Usually, as you know, caucus meetings take place on Wednesdays. But a lot of members want to ask some questions, and get some things off their chest, so the caucus chair has agreed to hold this special meeting. We believe that Rioux is going to make his move tomorrow."

"Then I want to be there."

Derbyshire frowned at me. "Not even staff people are allowed in caucus meetings, Chris."

"I know that," I said, surprised at myself. "But isn't there a way I can listen in, or observe what's going on? It'll help you guys to have a reporter there, and it will sure as hell help me."

Derbyshire thought for a long time. "There's one way. And most of the members won't even know you're there," he said, grinning. "You'll be a translator."

"I'll be what?"

"A translator," he said, slapping the table. He started to speak rapidly as his excitement grew. "At the back of the caucus room, there are these soundproof, enclosed booths, where the translators sit behind one-way glass. There are three separate booths in a room. The first one is for the English translators. The second one is for the French translators. The third one is usually empty. Except that, tomorrow morning, you'll be in number three."

I was excited too. "And nobody will see me?"

"Not unless you stick your pecker up against the window," he said, giggling. "Nope, just keep quiet, take your notes, run your tape recorder, do whatever it is that you do. And watch the show."

I thought about his offer for a moment. To my knowledge, no reporter had ever been allowed into a caucus meeting, ever. The whole reason for having caucus meetings, in fact, was to allow members of Parliament to speak their minds without reading about it in Thursday morning's newspapers. By agreeing to Derbyshire's proposal, I *was* taking a risk, I suppose. But he and his unnamed pals were taking a bigger risk.

"I'll have to tell my editor," I said. "Kevin Ritchie."

"Kevin? That's okay, I guess. He's a good shit," John replied, rubbing his eyes. He looked exhausted. "But no one else yet, okay?"

"Sure."

"Okay," he said, leaning closer. "This is what you are going to do. Pay attention."

＊　　　＊　　　＊

At 7:30 A.M. Monday morning, I walked through the entrance of the Centre Block and the Hall of Honour. I was nervous, but no one was around. Before I reached the Parliamentary Library, I turned left, then left again down a tiny corridor to an unmarked door at the end. As John Derbyshire had promised, the door was unlocked. I quickly stepped through into a cramped and darkened space behind the translation booths. I hurried past the first two doors, and slipped through the third.

The translation booth was just that — a booth. It contained two chairs, and a small counter on which a French–English dictionary and a few pencils had been placed. That was it. I locked the door behind me. Beyond the tinted glass of booth number three, the Reading Room where the Liberals hold their weekly caucuses was dark and silent. There were ten rows of padded chairs; each row was twenty chairs long. Down the middle of the chairs — one hundred on each side — was a wide pathway. A single microphone stood at the front of the pathway, facing a raised table. There was room for four chairs behind the table. One for Bobby Laurier, one for the Deputy Prime Minister, one for the caucus chair, one for the whip.

I sat down, well back in what I hoped was the shadows, and waited.

At 8:15 A.M., the lights in the Reading Room suddenly came on, half scaring me to death. A couple of uniformed House of Commons employees wandered in, pushing carts containing cups, saucers, glasses, pitchers of ice water, coffee urns, and trays of croissants and muffins. I stared at them, motionless, wondering if they could see me. But they couldn't, as John Derbyshire had promised. They laid out the food and drinks on a big table at the back of the caucus room and left. A few minutes later, I heard voices a few feet away, speaking in French. It was the translators. I waited, not breathing, for one of them to try the doorknob on booth number three. But they didn't. They split up into French and English sections, presumably, and entered booths one and two.

At ten to nine, members of caucus started to move into the Reading Room. Not one was smiling. They wandered to the back, drinking coffee and speaking in groups of two and threes. I spotted Billy Skelton, a big former broadcaster from Manitoba, patting Leo Ramos on the back. Ramos was a tiny Filipino Liberal MP from Vancouver, and Laurier's Parliamentary Secretary. Ramos looked as if he was about to cry.

In another group, there was Senator Gage Cooper, a millionaire cowboy from Lethbridge, and a long-time Laurier backer. Beside him were a couple of other senators I didn't recognize. One of them was pointing at something on the front page of the *Citizen*. I suspected he was pointing at a front-page editorial about the need for the government to come clean, now, about the status of Bobby Laurier's health.

A few minutes passed. The room was filling quickly; this was probably the best-attended Grit caucus meeting in decades. Even the octogenarian senators, the lifers, were showing up — and they never showed up for anything.

John Derbyshire, Tom Byrnes, Al Stewart, Mary Kennedy, Annie

Frosini and a half-dozen other hard-core Laurier people strode in, together. A few members of caucus clapped when they spotted the group. Jean Rioux, meanwhile, came in at precisely nine o'clock, and one hundred heads turned his way. No clapping, but lots of murmurs. A few caucus members went over to speak with him — most were MPs or senators who had voted for him at the leadership convention.

It was a very strange scene, and frankly I could not believe that I was observing it.

I watched Derbyshire closely. He walked to the back, poured himself a coffee, sipped it just once — while facing my way — then placed the cup and saucer back on the table. He walked to his seat, which was only a few feet away from where Rioux had seated himself.

The little routine with the coffee was my signal. They were actually going to do it. I swallowed hard and turned on my microcassette recorder.

The caucus meeting began with the singing of "O Canada," in both languages. This was followed by a request by Gilbert Larose, the national Liberal caucus chair, for a prayer for Bobby Laurier, Leader of the Liberal Party and Prime Minister of Canada. Larose was a New Brunswicker, an Acadian from the Miramichi. As caucus chair, he was the person who ran the meeting and set the agenda. This morning's agenda concerned only one subject — Bobby Laurier.

"I don't have very much to say," said Larose, who was flanked by Mary Kennedy, the House leader and caucus whip. "I know as much as the rest of you. The Prime Minister is recovering from a heart attack in Florida, and his condition is stable. No one apart from his family has been allowed to see him, however. We do not know when he is coming back to lead us, or ..." He trailed off. "I called this special caucus because a number of members requested it. There are quite a few of you who have questions or comments. The microphone is open."

Caucus members started to line up at the microphone. Most of them seemed genuinely sorrowful, and recommended that the House remain closed until the Prime Minister had recovered. A couple of senators struggled to their feet, and cursed "those little bastards in the PMO" who had withheld information about Laurier's condition from the caucus. "It's not right, goddamn it, it's not right," said one from Prince Edward Island, waving a bony fist in the air. "We are parliamentarians, and we deserve some goddamn respect." That got some applause. As John Derbyshire had predicted, no members of the cabinet stood up to speak right away. Caucus meetings were an opportunity for average MPs to let ministers — and the Prime Minister — know what they were thinking.

But slowly, surely, a few members — Rioux supporters all — stood up to suggest respectfully that the government could not go without a Prime Minister indefinitely. When one of these, a slimy character from Montreal named Giovanni Perna, advised that an interim leader should be appointed right away, he got an angry response. A few MPs shouted at him; one or two told him to sit down and shut up. "I won't shut up," the baldheaded MP shouted back. "We need to get this question resolved once and for all. Is Laurier coming back or not?"

There was an eruption of shouting and curses. Laurier loyalists were apoplectic. "Show some respect, you bastard!" one senator hollered at Perna.

As Gilbert Larose struggled to restore order, I spotted one of the two staff members present — a member of Mary Kennedy's office staff, the only ones permitted to attend these meetings — racing in with a sealed envelope. The staffer had apparently been given the envelope by John Derbyshire's driver. To my utter amazement, Derbyshire pulled what looked like a CP release from the envelope.

The Newfoundlander gave a masterful performance. He opened the envelope, read the phony story, then leaned forward in his seat. He was leaning far enough forward for Rioux to notice him. Derbyshire seemed to be trembling. He ran one hand through his famous mane of hair, over and over. He wiped his eyes. Rioux, just a few feet away, was watching him closely. Derbyshire looked back at Rioux, hesitated, then waved him over. Rioux literally jumped out of his seat and dashed over to Derbyshire's side. What was written on the piece of paper that had so affected the mighty Newfoundlander?

URGENT URGENT URGENT URGENT
Laurier permanently brain-damaged by stroke in Florida hospital
By the Canadian Press

MIAMI — Clinton White House officials have told the Canadian Press that Prime Minister Robert Laurier suffered a debilitating stroke, late Sunday night, leaving him brain-damaged.

A team of physicians at the U.S. military hospital where Laurier has been recovering from a heart attack has been working all night, frantically attempting to determine the extent of the damage, the White House officials said. "It looks pretty grim," said one senior administration official, speaking on the condition of anonymity ...

The story went on like that for a few paragraphs, but it was pure bullshit. Every word. Someone on Derbyshire's staff had been able to produce a very authentic-looking — but fake — news story. When Derbyshire explained his little ruse to me later on, after the caucus meeting, I was annoyed. The Rioux people, if they ever figured it out, would think I had been part of faking a news story. But, because it was against the rules for me to be in the caucus room, I could hardly say anything to anyone. I was trapped.

Derbyshire handed Rioux the fake news story, then stood up as if the weight of the world were on his shoulders. He moved towards the microphone at the front. Although there were still quite a few members of Parliament in line ahead of him, Mary Kennedy — who was in on the sting, of course — whispered into the ear of Gilbert Larose. Larose frowned, nodded, then turned on his microphone. "I understand that John Derbyshire has something important he would like to say. Could the members let him speak?"

When those in the lineup saw the shell-shocked expression on Derbyshire's face, they didn't argue. Derbyshire grasped the microphone as if he were a drowning man and it was all that was keeping him from being pulled under.

"Mr. Chairman, Madame House Leader, fellow members," he said, his voice hoarse. Long pause. "I have been at Bobby Laurier's side for many years. I have been with him in freezing-cold nights, campaigning on the Rock — and on blazing-hot days, in separatist territory in Quebec, fighting for the country he loves. I have been with him on the ice in the Arctic, when he stared down an American destroyer that the Tories had allowed to violate our sovereignty. I have been with him for all-night votes in the House, fighting with all of his might to pass legislation that was just and right. And I was with him when he read the letter of a father whose son took his life because his daddy was not treated with the respect that is the due of every Canadian, from coast to coast."

It was maudlin and overdone, and I had heard Derbyshire do better on other occasions. But it was having the desired effect. Some members were sniffling.

"Mr. Chairman, my friends," he said. "I do not know if my leader, my Prime Minister, is coming back. I must admit to you all that I am starting to believe he will not ..."

"No, John, no!" Al Stewart hollered. He was in on it, too.

"No, Al, it's true," Derbyshire said, weary. "It's true, although I wish to Jesus God it weren't. We have a responsibility to the people who put us here. We have to come together, and find someone to lead us until we know whether he is coming back ..."

There was an unreal silence. Dramatically, slowly, Derbyshire turned in the direction of a red-faced Jean Rioux, who had long since finished reading the bogus news story. Derbyshire looked at Rioux for what seemed like an eternity, and virtually no one — especially Rioux — knew what was coming next. Finally, Derbyshire, still holding onto the microphone, said: "Jean? What say you?"

Time stood still. No one moved. No one breathed. With his one good eye, Rioux stared at Derbyshire, then moved forward. Taking the microphone from Derbyshire, Rioux said: "Yes. Yes, I will do it, if that is what you want."

The room went crazy. MPs were screaming, literally screaming. Some were clearly delighted. Many more looked shocked or angry.

Gilbert Larose banged his gavel over and over, calling for order. John Derbyshire, meanwhile, looked in the direction of translation booth number three and winked.

As Derbyshire had told me the night before: "Jean Rioux is the most egotistical guy I have ever met in my life, Chris. When he sees a chance to become leader, real quick, you can bet your bottom dollar he'll show his hand. And all of caucus will know that the guy is after the job, by hook or fuckin' crook. We'll flush out One-Eyed Johnny, right quick."

It seemed to me that I might have been flushed out, too.

*   *   *

By late afternoon, Jean Rioux was still under the impression that he had become acting Prime Minister of Canada. That, anyway, was what Mike Mahoney and the 829 Club were telling everyone, including reporters. Charles Lafontaine, however, was holding an unprecedented press briefing in his office — some of the journalists present had never actually seen Charlie before, and were surprised to learn that he existed — to state categorically that the Prime Minister was still the Prime Minister. The dollar plunged another couple of cents. Praying recommenced in the nation's churches.

My mother telephoned me at the office in a state. She was one of those people who had always believed that reporters actually withheld information from their readers. I told her that I did not know anything more about Bobby Laurier's condition than what she had already seen on BCTV, or read in the *Times-Colonist*. But I would call her as soon as I heard something, I promised.

At about the same time, as I would soon learn, Bobby Laurier was feeling much better, and, fully briefed on the chaos in Canada, preparing to fly home from Florida on a Challenger jet.

CHAPTER ELEVEN

In my journalistic career — which, admittedly, is not as long as that of somebody like, say, Joey Myers — I have covered two Royal visits, and one Papal tour. In each case, the esteemed personages were greeted by thousands of cheering, happy Canadians, virtually everywhere they went (except Quebec, of course, where the monarchy and the Roman Catholic Church are seen as the perpetrators of countless imagined humiliations). But never, ever, have I seen anything that remotely approached the sort of collective euphoria that accompanied the return to Canada by Bobby Laurier.

It was phenomenal. It was extraordinary. It was joyous. Take whatever happy adjective you can think of, and throw it, and it will stick.

The truly remarkable thing about Laurier's triumphant return, to a cynic like me, was how spontaneous it was. In the modern political era, this is indeed an achievement. While we are nowhere near the American model — in Washington, even the location of where a President spends his summer holidays is polled and focus-tested for its impact upon public opinion — Canadian politicos are pretty fond of scripting events, too. Seldom, if ever, is a detail left to chance.

In political parlance, the people who do this sort of work are known as "advance." Laurier's chief advance guy, John Fox, has been with him almost as long as Flash Feiffer. Fox is a tough, no-nonsense kind of guy, who wouldn't hesitate to holler at a group of singing nuns if they were slowing down a scheduled event. Typically, Fox's advance people travel to wherever the Prime Minister is scheduled to speak, or sleep, or whatever, and rigorously examine every possible thing that could go wrong. They examine the asphalt where the prime-ministerial feet are expected to alight. They test, and retest, microphones that are to be used by the prime-ministerial mouth. They spend countless hours viewing sites for the best optics — that is, which angle would tell the best story, and show the Prime Minister's best profile, and so on. Every little detail — the cars that are driven, the weather, the number of people who get to stand with the PM on-stage, you name it — is advanced by John Fox and his gang.

But Bobby Laurier's return to Canada wasn't advanced. He and his wife, Michelle, had expressly instructed Charles Lafontaine and John Fox, France later told me, that they wanted to slip into Ottawa's Uplands Air Force Base late on Tuesday night, and that they didn't want anyone to know about it, or make a big fuss. (Flash Feiffer was ordered to come on a later commercial flight, apparently.) But what Bobby Laurier had apparently forgotten, or at least underestimated, was the press. When the gentlepersons of the press wish to find something out, and are sufficiently motivated, they will find it out. This, ultimately, is what every failed politician, no matter how powerful, always forgets — you can cover up for some of the time, but you can't cover up for all of the time. Sooner or later, you get found out.

We found Bobby Laurier out. From what I could tell, the first to find out was an excellent young investigative reporter from the Toronto *Sun*, Scott Maguire, who had befriended a number of orderlies at the hospital where Laurier had been recovering. Scott had thus learned when "the Canadian dude being guarded by Secret Service guys," as one orderly put it, was being shipped home. He had also learned, the *Sun* announced in screaming eight-inch-tall headlines, that Laurier's heart attack had been a heart attack, but only sort of. It had been the most minor of heart troubles, what the doctors called "angina." A certain amount of heart pain, wherein insufficient blood is nourishing one's ticker. "Coronary insufficiency," the doctors called it. "BOBBY'S BACK!!" the loving *Sun* headline read, sounding to all the world as if it had always been pro-Grit (it hadn't, and it isn't).

As we stood in the setting sun on the roped-off tarmac at Uplands, Joey looked around at the people. There were thousands of them, carrying "WELCOME HOME BOBBY" and "WE LOVE YOU BOBBY" signs, mainly in English, and little Canadian flags. The crowd had gathered a few hundred feet away, behind a chain-link fence. Joey, who was an even bigger cynic than I was, was almost moved to emotion. "This is amazing," he said, as we stared at the crowd, which was growing by the minute. "I haven't seen anything like this since Beatlemania. They *love* him. If I hadn't seen it myself, I wouldn't have believed it."

"I'm not sure if they love him," I said. "But maybe his near-death experience reminded them how much they like him."

God McAleer, who was puffing on a butt beside us, was uncharacteristically quiet. "In-fucking-credible," he kept saying, as he watched the crowd. "In-fucking-credible."

There was a stir. In the eastern sky, lights were approaching fast; it looked as if it could be the Challenger that was ferrying Bobby Laurier back to Canada. A minute later, we saw that it was. Over behind the chain-link fence, people slowly started to cheer, picking up in volume as the plane came closer. As it landed, and taxied near where about two hundred Press Gallery types had been hastily penned, the cheering grew to a crescendo. "BOB-BY! BOB-BY! BOB-BY!" I laughed aloud. It was all very un-Canadian. Canadians are supposed to be sedate, and polite, and not given to this sort of thing. It was, indeed, incredible.

The door to the Challenger popped open, and an Air Force guy hurried out to secure the steps. And, a minute later, there was Prime Minister Bobby Laurier standing at the doorway, waving at the crowd. He looked paler, and thinner, and he was holding tightly onto the door frame with his other hand. But the crowd didn't mind. They were going crazy, chanting his name.

The Gallery types were going crazy, too. A few camera guys actually jumped over the restraining ropes and jogged towards the plane. Some RCMP guys started chasing after them, in a scene straight out of the Keystone Kops. Laurier laughed, pointing at the scene for Michelle.

We Gallery folks were hollering Bobby Laurier's name as loudly as we could, but the Prime Minister wasn't paying us much attention. As he walked slowly — very slowly — down the Challenger's steps and past us, leaning on his wife, he gave us a friendly wave, but didn't stop. Instead, he moved closer to the fence, where the crowd was in a more pronounced state of frenzy. After he conferred briefly with one of the Air Force guys who had been on the plane with him, someone somehow located a battered military-issue megaphone. The officer gave Laurier a brief lesson in how to use it. Laurier waved at the people, indicating that they should quiet down.

When the cheering finally stopped, Laurier held the megaphone up to his mouth.

"Hey, you Canadians! *Bonjour!*" he said, his voice booming across the tarmac. "Why don' you guys all come back home with us, 'cause Michelle says she's gonna make a big batch of cookies, hokay?"

The crowd went wild.

*   *   *

While the rest of the Press Gallery chased Bobbymania stories for a couple of days, Joey and I had other fish to fry. A big Finance minister fish, to be precise.

The list of companies Igor had passed on to me had proved to be a proverbial gold mine. As he had said, each of the firms — with the able assistance of the Prince Group, of course — had been involved in some fairly heavy-duty shenanigans. I had not heard of a case before where private firms had been complicit in crafting a federal Budget to suit their financial needs. But I was reasonably certain that it was totally unethical, if not worse. It was certainly a breach of trust on the part of a number of people.

Kevin Ritchie was nervous as hell about the story. He fretted endlessly about it, particularly the anonymous bureaucratic sources that held the yarn together. He quizzed us on every conceivable angle. When that was done, every word, sentence and paragraph was vetted exhaustively by the Canadian Press's lawyers, the same fellows who handle *Hank* magazine, the frequently libellous biweekly. This laborious process, which was conducted in a twentieth-floor board-room at the law firm on Elgin Street, took a lot of time. Joey, who hadn't worked on an investigative story in many years, was quite intimidated by the probing of the lawyers. Whenever we broke for lunch, or coffee, Joey would turn to me in the elevator and express his concern about getting sued. "The lawyers seem to think it's pretty thin, don't you think?" he'd ask. "Have we missed something?"

"Relax, Joey, for the hundredth time," I'd say, for the hundredth time.

Kevin was starting to get on my nerves about the story. On other stories, he gave me a lot of leeway. But, on this one, he was hounding me every hour. And his questions had an unpleasant undertone to them — as if he doubted what I was saying, even before I said it. On a couple of occasions, after late nights spent poring over documents, I had almost lost my temper with Kevin, but I kept my cool. I wasn't imagining any of this, either; even Joey noticed it. I wondered, briefly, if he had got wind of the fake CP story. I was too embar-rassed to tell him how naive I'd been.

I was also a little worried, of course, although I tried not to show it. The upshot of our story, once you distilled it down to its base elements, was that: (a) Jean Rioux was a crook; or (b) if he wasn't a crook, he was not paying enough attention to his pals, some of whom *were* crooks and getting rich because Rioux wasn't paying attention. Someone was going to sue us, I was pretty sure of that. In recent years, the tremendous number of libel lawsuits initiated by thin-skinned millionaires like Carswell Spence III, or prima donna politicos, had been one of the primary reasons investigative journalism had more or less dried up.

I was the one assigned to call Mike Mahoney for the official comment of the Office of the Minister of Finance. I was reasonably certain that he had already heard the Ottawa tom-toms going on Chris O'Reilly's latest Prince Group investigation. I was right.

Gone was any of the false cheeriness that he had used in our last telephone conversation. Mahoney, when he finally came on the line, was the Bitch Queen.

"Hello."

"Hello, Mike, it's Chris O'Reilly ..."

He cut me off. "I know who it is. What do you want?"

I checked my microcassette recorder to ensure that it was taping. I knew that I would only get one chance to get this right. "Mike, the Canadian Press is investigating a story that certain firms, with which Mr. Rioux formerly had some involvement, benefited from certain initiatives announced in the Budget," I said. "And ..."

"There's nothing inappropriate about some firms benefiting from a Budget," he snapped. "That can happen quite legitimately, can't it?"

"Yes it can," I said. "But you didn't give me a chance to finish my question. It's inappropriate if those firms benefit when they were given advance notification of what would be in the Budget. It's inappropriate if Budget secrecy was violated to benefit those firms, right?"

"Is that what you plan to write?" he hissed.

"More or less," I said.

"That is preposterous and, what's more, it's libellous," he said. "If you print that, I can assure you that Mr. Rioux will be reviewing the matter with his lawyers."

"Can I quote you on that?"

"You can quote me on the record as saying that the allegations are false, libellous and politically motivated," he said. I could almost hear him gritting his teeth. "Off the record, you can go and fuck yourself, you slimy piece of shit." He slammed the phone down.

Joey got approximately the same response from the Prince Group. Kevin Ritchie had decided that Joey should call the lobbying firm, in light of my encounter with Dick Thorsell, et al. When Mark Petryk finally deigned to return Joey's calls, on the same afternoon I spoke to Mahoney, Joey, too, was informed that the matter was libellous, and that the Canadian Press would be hearing from the Prince Group's lawyers.

As Joey and I were discussing Petryk's threat, a call came in for me. It was Walt Hume, the PMO's director of communications. I guess Mike Mahoney had briefed him about our story.

In the first few days following news of Bobby Laurier's heart attack, Hume's political stock had taken a precipitous nose-dive around town. His apparent attempt to cover up the details surrounding Laurier's condition — details which were so obviously, and properly, within the public domain — had left a lot of reporters highly unimpressed. For the life of me, I couldn't figure out why he had been so tight-lipped. The net effect of his stonewalling had been to destabilize Laurier's leadership, and to traumatize a lot of average Canadians. It had also resulted in Jean Rioux openly declaring — in the Liberal caucus meeting I had witnessed — his desire to capitalize on Laurier's illness, and that hadn't particularly helped Rioux, either.

To offset the political damage, Hume had fired off a volley of "talking points." These documents, for which Hume possessed a great enthusiasm, were typically one or two pages long. They concerned whatever the hot political issue might be on a particular day — the flip-flop on the VAT, or the good news in the first Grit Budget. The "talking points" were generally faxed out to Liberal members of Parliament as well as a select group of other pro-Liberal folks likely to be contacted by the media for comment. Generally, these documents ensured that loose-lipped MPs didn't stray too far from the party line. Hume had not invented talking points, but he liked to tell everyone he had. His primary contribution to the talking-points concept had been the introduction of tiny pointing hands where "bullets" — those big black dots found at the start of each paragraph — used to be found.

Hume was an odd fellow. He certainly had a likable personality, and he could small-talk about popular culture better than anyone I had ever met (he had ten years' worth of *Flintstones* episodes on video, for example, and he had one of the biggest collections of Pez candy dispensers in the known universe). He was gregarious and bright. But his lingering associations with the more partisan members of Jean Rioux's gang had hurt him with some of the Laurier people. They didn't trust him as far as they could throw his chubby body. And, by phoning me to protect Rioux's hide, he was simply ensuring that they never would.

After I had tolerated Hume's patented zippity-doo-dah patter, he came to the point: "Chris-baby, this story you guys are working on," he said. "I can set you up for background briefings with some bureaucrats, to show you why it's impossible for someone to know what is in the Budget. The security measures they take, all that kinda stuff."

"Walt, I appreciate the offer, but we've got taped interviews with bureaucrats in a half-dozen departments, telling us that Budget secrecy *was* violated," I replied. "And we've got securities people, and forensic accountants, who have looked at the performance of the stocks belonging to these various firms. And they are saying that there is no way these people could have benefited so dramatically from the Budget — not unless they knew in advance what was going to be in it. Or helped to write it."

"Forensic accountants, eh? You guys have really gone to town on this one," he said, sounding concerned.

"We've invested a lot of time on it, that's true," I responded.

Hume made a few more halfhearted attempts to dissuade us from writing the story. But I rebuffed each one, and we ended the conversation. A few minutes later, Joey and I sat in Kevin's office, discussing the calls. Were Mahoney and Petryk serious — or were they simply trying to use the threat of a libel action to scare us away? "Petryk sounded rather serious to me," Joey said. He was still nervous.

"Well, at least he didn't call you a slimy piece of shit," I countered, trying to generate a laugh. "I've never been called that one before."

Neither Kevin nor Joey was laughing. I wanted to get the story out quickly. I knew it was solid, but I didn't know if Igor would become impatient with us, and try to market the story to some other news organization. As I was preparing to replay my tape of the brief Mike Mahoney interview, Luc Bergeron knocked on Kevin's door. "Thought you might want to see this," he said, handing a few sheets of paper to Kevin. "It just came over the fax machine."

I knew what it was without even seeing it. The Prince Group, I figured, had retained a big corporate law firm to fire off a letter threatening a libel action if we went ahead and printed the story. I said as much to Kevin. "You're a psychic," Kevin said, without smiling. He kept reading the fax.

After Joey and I had been given a chance to read it ourselves, Kevin stood up to fax the letter to our own lawyers. "I think we'd better sleep on this one, fellas," he said, as he made his way to the fax machine. "We're not where we need to be, yet."

*　　*　　*

My beloved father aside, lawyers are gutless. Our lawyers didn't associate any benefit with the Canadian Press breaking a major story. They didn't know, or care, how methodically we had documented everything in the story. Instead, they simply wanted to ensure that we didn't get sued by anyone, even if we would ultimately win the case. So our lawyers said what lawyers always say: "Don't take the chance. Don't print it."

Kevin, to my astonishment, took their advice. As he stood by my desk, sombrely informing us of his decision, I was crestfallen. It was the first time he hadn't backed me on a story. That, I think, hurt even more than the actual decision to spike the Prince Group exposé. My exhaustion magnified my sense of hurt. "Is that your final decision?" I asked him, furious. My Irish temper, having been dormant for some time, was now getting fully exercised.

"Yes it is, Chris," he said. Joey, at his own desk, was shaking his head a little, trying to get me to calm down. He, too, was worried about publishing. He also seemed to be worried about my saying something I might regret.

"I see," I said. "So, it won't ever see the light of day?"

"Never is a long time," he said. "But the way it is at the moment, no, I can't let it go. I'm sorry, Chris."

"No problem," I said, grabbing a copy of the story and throwing on my raincoat. Moving as quickly as I could — so that Joey could not catch up to me if he followed — I dashed out of the national bureau and across Wellington Street. For about an hour, I walked along the sidewalk behind the Centre Block, looking at Hull and the Ottawa River. From where I was standing, I could spot the Hotel Claret, where I had spent my first night in Ottawa, more than three long years ago.

Finally, my mind made up, I headed towards the office of Nils Andersen, member of Parliament.

※　　　※　　　※

The way in which a member of Parliament prepares for Question Period is fascinating. With the notable exception of the Reform Party, all of the parties — the Liberals, the Tories, the NDP, even the Blockheads — take QP, as it is known, very seriously. In the television age, QP has become all that people generally see of their federal government. It is loud and dramatic and adversarial — and frequently puerile nonsense. But it is also, in the view of the Opposition parties, forty-five minutes out of every day in which the government does not control the agenda. The Opposition gets to ask the questions, and the government has to answer them. To an Opposition party seeking to form a government one day, a solid Question Period performance is absolutely vital. For a government seeking to remain the government, the same is true.

The Reformers didn't understand that. Because they loved to style themselves as "populists" — whatever that is — they had always been highly critical of QP. As a result, they didn't spend any time preparing their members for it, and it showed. Their QP approach was unfocused and disorganized, so the TV media seldom covered them. And they started to dip in the polls as a result.

Back when they were in Opposition, John Derbyshire and Mary Kennedy had allowed me to spend an entire day watching how they prepare for QP. It had made for a great news feature.

When the House was in session, every day would start at about 8:30 A.M., in the Opposition Leader's boardroom on the fourth floor of the Centre Block. About twenty or so Opposition MPs would assemble around a large wooden table, flipping through the morning's press clippings, drinking coffee, sharing gossip. Bobby Laurier, I was told, seldom, if ever, attended these meetings — "so that members won't feel intimidated about speaking up," Mary Kennedy had explained. The members, she said, were there to represent their various regional caucuses (Atlantic, Quebec, Ontario, the West) or to represent certain policy committees (economic, foreign affairs, social policy, and so on). The vast majority of those present were male, I noted. Mary Kennedy didn't disagree.

At this meeting — called "QP Prep" — Kennedy and her assistants would take notes, while MPs went around the table, offering their advice as to which questions should be asked. There were usually about eight slots available — each slot representing one opening question, and one supplementary. (Bobby Laurier, as leader and the first questioner, would get to ask three in his slot.) Most of the time, I was told by Mary Kennedy, the top four or five slots go to issues then dominating the headlines. And, more often than not, the questions would be posed by some of the party's better communicators, such as John Derbyshire. If there wasn't a lot going on, Kennedy would turn to a list her staff maintained of proposed questions by various MPs; these questions were generally "quite dull," Kennedy admitted off the record. They would typically be saved for the end of the list, or for a Friday, when Question Period is watched by maybe forty people, and attended by even fewer.

Once the lineup was developed by Kennedy, her staff would notify the various members who were expected to ask questions. Some, like Derbyshire, would be able to throw together a show-stopper of a query in about as much time as it takes to brush one's teeth. Other members, however, would take up most of the morning preparing for their forty-five seconds of fame. They would harangue staffers to develop pithy comebacks, and sweat about anticipated Tory ministerial responses, and time themselves endlessly with a stopwatch. (Questions exceeding one minute were *verboten*.)

At one o'clock or so, the eight MPs who had been asked to prepare questions would return to the boardroom beside Bobby Laurier's office. There, they would stand at a podium, while Kennedy and some of the party's better elected and unelected communicators — Derbyshire was always invited, I was told, but seldom showed — would coach them on tightening the question up. Kennedy would time each attempt. If she felt that the question was too long, or not as interesting as it had sounded when it had been proposed at the QP Prep meeting, she would strike it off the list. This almost always resulted in a lot of hurt feelings, but Question Period was showbiz. And showbiz was about who, and what, could do the best box office.

Jean Rioux, surprisingly, was usually thrown into a tailspin when Kennedy asked him to pose a question. He was very nervous about his questioning ability, it seemed. As a result, he would spend the entire morning with Mahoney, going over the question a few dozen times, practising in front of a full-length mirror. There were many mirrors in his office, apparently.

Bobby Laurier, on the other hand, hated Question Period, and it showed. He was used to being on the government side. Answering questions was what he usually liked to do, not asking them. So, whenever he was absent from QP, and whenever we would ask where he was, we would invariably be told that Bobby Laurier was in some important meeting somewhere. Which meant that he was up at the Royal Ottawa, perfecting his chip shot.

The Conservatives and New Democrats, whenever they were in Opposition — in the case of the Tories, that was every few years or so; in the case of the Dippers, that was all the time — would adopt more or less the same approach. For most of the political parties, Question Period was a big deal.

It certainly was to Nils Andersen. Nils, of course, was the NDP MP who had greeted me at the airport when I moved here to work for the Canadian Press, more than three years ago. Over the course of my time in Ottawa, we had maintained a good relationship. Even though the NDP was not my assigned beat, we talked on the phone every once in a while. A couple of times a year, we would have lunch together. He was an amiable, non-ideological sort of fellow, which made him immediately suspect to many of his NDP colleagues. A goodly number of them were hemp-growing, Birkenstocked sixties Marxist retreads — or storm-the-barricades union class warriors, also of the Marxist variety. Nils, with his excellent wardrobe and friends in all parties, was seen as a silver-spoon socialist, which I suppose he was. But I liked him.

I showed up at his Confederation Block office unannounced and unexpected. His long-time secretary, Jeannie Something, knew me and invited me in. She said that Nils was meeting with a couple of mayors from his B.C. riding, but would be finished at any moment. I sat on the House of Commons couch — all the couches on the Hill were actually made and upholstered, at great expense, in the basement of the Wellington Building, if you can believe it — and stared at Andersen's padded office door. All of the MPs had padded doors so as to prevent anyone on one side of the door from hearing the conversation taking place on the other side.

Soon enough, as Jeannie had said, Andersen appeared to escort the two elderly mayors out. He brightened noticeably when he saw me sitting on his couch, but he didn't introduce me to the mayors, who looked like a couple of ancient Rotarians. Once he had escorted the pair to the elevators, Andersen jogged back to the office to shake my hand. "Hey, Chris!" he said. "To what do I owe this pleasure?" MPs love reporters, as I said. Most of them, anyway.

Nils led me into his office and shut the padded door. We chatted about B.C. politics for a while — always a source of much amusement — and then I pulled out the tearsheet of the Prince Group "Gang of Nine" story I had written with Joey's help. Nils eyed the folded piece of paper as if it were a scrap of the Dead Sea Scrolls.

"Nils, I'm pretty mad at my employers right now," I said, "and I may be doing something that will get me fired. But I'm holding a story I've been working on for weeks, and my bosses have decided not to run it."

"I see," he said, stroking his impressive jaw line. "Is it about the Prince Group, by any chance?"

"Yes," I said. "How did you know?"

"The whole town knows you have been working on that story," he said. "It's a story that needs to be told." He paused. "Can I also ask why you are going to let me see it?"

"CP is worried about getting sued if we run the story," I said, bitterly. "We probably *will* get sued if we run it — even though the last time I checked, truth is a defence to a libel action."

"But if the matter gets raised in the House, perhaps, there's no way anyone can get sued. Because MPs can't be sued for libel for what they say in the House of Commons," Nils said. "Right?"

"Right," I said. "Are you interested?"

He thought about that for a minute. "Not if it gets you fired, Chris," he said.

"I appreciate that," I said. "Maybe I exaggerated. I doubt they'd fire me. They'll be plenty pissed off when they find out. But I'm prepared to live with the consequences."

"Okay," Nils said, leaning forward. "Let's see it."

*   *   *

Getting recognized is not normally a problem for Nils Andersen. Not from what I had observed in the past, anyway.

With his movie-star looks, and his thick blond hair, Nils was probably one of the best-recognized members on Parliament Hill. Wherever he went, heads would turn, usually heads belonging to women. But getting recognized in the House of Commons was a different issue.

After the pummelling they took in the general election, the New Democratic Party slipped below the number of MPs required to be officially recognized by the Speaker of the House of Commons. With party status came the right to ask a fixed number of questions — about eight for the Blocheads, and about six for the Reformers. But the New Democrat MPs, tucked away in a distant corner of the Opposition benches, needed to bob and weave like a gang of punch-drunk professional boxers if they were ever to catch the Speaker's attention.

After a number of attempts — and five days after I had provided him with a copy of the Prince Group story — Nils Andersen was finally recognized by the Speaker late in a Tuesday-afternoon Question Period. Nobody else knew what was coming, when Nils stood to ask his question, of course. Joey and I were sitting in the media section of the gallery, overlooking the chamber of the House. Joey, who had been eyeing me carefully for the past few Question Periods we had attended together, suspected something was about to happen. "Christopher, my boy," he whispered, leaning closer, "you haven't done what I think you have done, have you?"

I kept staring at Nils Andersen. "I have done exactly what you think I have done," I whispered back. "And I'm prepared to take whatever the consequences are."

"I don't think there'll be too many for you," Joey hissed. "For Mr. Rioux, however, I'm not so sure."

"Mr. Speaker," Nils said, looking very serious, holding a piece of paper I already knew contained the names of the companies on Igor's list. "My question is for the Minister of Finance. Specifically, I wish to know whether the minister is aware of any companies which may have improperly benefited from changes announced in the last Budget."

On the government side, nobody was paying much attention to Nils's query — except for Jean Rioux, that is. Apart from him, all of the members and cabinet ministers present were gathering up their papers, getting ready to leave. Some were chatting among themselves. Rioux, however, looked very uncomfortable. He flipped nervously through a big binder of paper — his House of Commons answer book, something all ministers maintained on the newsworthy issues in their respective departments — frantically looking for something. Unable to find it, he stood up.

"Mr. Speaker, the honourable member will of course know that this government went to extraordinary lengths to ensure that the principle of Budget secrecy was not violated," he said, twirling his earpiece in one hand. "If the honourable member has evidence to suggest otherwise, he should table it in the House forthwith." Rioux sat down, watching Nils closely.

I leaned towards Joey. "That was a big mistake," I whispered.

Nils stood again, buttoned his jacket and smoothed his hair. His supplementary question, he knew, was likely to get him on the national news tonight. He cleared his throat. He took a sip of water. "Mr. Speaker," he finally said. "I would like to table a list of companies with the Clerk. This list names companies that enriched themselves through the improper release of Budget information — in advance of the release of the Budget."

All of the MPs and cabinet ministers who had been preparing to leave, or chatting, suddenly fell silent. They scrambled back to their seats, and watched as a page retrieved the list of companies from Nils Andersen.

"My supplementary question is also for the Minister of Finance, Mr. Speaker," Nils said. He had everyone's attention, now. Rioux looked scared shitless.

"Can the minister confirm to the House whether his staff, or his officials — deliberately or inadvertently — provided secret Budget information to lobbyists at the Prince Group, which in turn then passed on that information to the companies named on the list I have just tabled in the House? And, if so, Mr. Speaker, is the minister prepared to immediately submit his resignation for this shocking breach of Budget secrecy?"

Nils sat down. Rioux gulped for air. And the House erupted in shouting, in both official languages. Joey turned to me, grinning.

"You naughty, naughty boy," he said. "You naughty, clever boy."

CHAPTER TWELVE

After Kevin Ritchie had finished bawling me out, and after Joey Myers had stopped giggling, and after Walt Hume had faxed out a half-dozen talking points defending Jean Rioux and the Budget process, and after Nils Andersen had given the biggest scrum I have ever seen in the House of Commons lobby, and after I had filed my story on the whole mess, I decided to walk west, towards Sandy Hill. It was around six o'clock, and the smell of spring was everywhere. After Ottawa's long, bitter winters, it is always encouraging to smell the earth again. I missed Victoria.

Nils Andersen's bomb planted in Question Period had gone off exactly as he had planned it. And nobody could sue anyone. The Rioux people would know that I passed on my story to Andersen, of course, but there was nothing they could do about it. One of the cardinal principles of a parliamentary democracy is that all elected members should be able to speak their mind in the legislature, without fear of defamation actions designed to shut them up. As long as Nils was careful to make his allegations only in the chamber of the

House of Commons, no lawyer in the world could lay a finger on him. The words he uttered there were completely privileged.

In the huge scrum that surrounded him in the lobby outside the chamber, after QP, Nils had been a little bit more circumspect. He didn't specifically allege anything. He merely asked a lot of questions, most of them rhetorical. The reporters, he knew, would do the rest. Most of them already believed Andersen was on to something, anyway: a good number had seen the Finance minister's facial expression when Nils asked his questions. And they had all noted that Rioux had used the back door of the chamber, to avoid any reporters wanting to question him. In Ottawa, where there is parliamentary smoke, there is usually fire.

Stan Silversides and Sherry Bickle, suspecting that I knew a lot about how this drama was unfolding, started looking for me. They left messages all over the place. I had become part of the story, unfortunately, and Stan and Sherry suspected as much: it was time to make myself scarce. As I sped out of the Centre Block, I spotted Mac Lee, his rosy cheeks aglow, a microphone in hand. He was in his element, exposing a nasty Liberal scandal. Patrick Stone, meanwhile, was hurtling up to Ottawa on the CBC corporate jet, a sure sign that this was a big event.

Kevin had been furious with me. I had admitted to him, right away, that I had given our Prince Group story to Nils Andersen. He told me, gravely, that he regarded my actions as a serious mistake, and that he intended to place a letter of warning in my personal file. I didn't say anything about that, because I didn't much care anymore. In the days since Kevin had spiked my story, Joey had learned the *real* reason why the Canadian Press had refused to print it. According to him, on the day I spoke to Mike Mahoney, Jean Rioux had called the new proprietor of Southam News, Carswell Spence III. Jean and Carswell were old pals and — more significantly — Carswell's Southam chain was the biggest subscriber to the services of the Canadian Press. When the number-crunchers at CP in Toronto were informed of the long friendship between Spence and Rioux, a diktat went out without even consulting Spence: CP management did not approve of the Chris O'Reilly story. So, CP's heroes of journalism chose not to support their own employee — namely, me. Whether Kevin Ritchie was party to this disgusting spectacle, I knew not. But I did know, as I walked along Wellington Street, that I was a lot less enthusiastic about my association with CP than I once was.

Nils Andersen was the Man of the Hour. Every political journalist in the nation wanted to interview him. Between open-enders with the CBC's Ralph Nearing and CTV's Charlie Burke, Nils called me at the office, minutes after I had filed my story on the exchange in the House. Nils hurriedly and profusely thanked me for the tip, then asked how things were going at the office. "Not so hot," I said.

"Is there anything I can do, Chris?" he asked.

"Do you know anyone at the *Toronto Star*?" I asked him, more than half-serious. The *Star* was the only major daily left in the country that Carswell Spence III did not control.

"I do, and I will get back to you on that," he said, then dashed off to his CTV interview.

Bobby Laurier, meanwhile, was still recuperating at 24 Sussex, so he couldn't be reached for comment on the Jean Rioux controversy. But the response of his PMO had been rather odd considering that one of the government's most senior ministers was under a serious cloud of suspicion, the markets closed low, and the dollar was starting to slide. In the two hours following QP, communications guru Walt Hume, as mentioned, did all that he could to defend Jean Rioux. And then, abruptly, silence descended upon the Prime Minister's minions. Reporters calling his office were offered no more than a cryptic "no comment," then referred to Jean Rioux's office. "It sounds to me as if Bobby Laurier has decided to let his Finance minister sink or swim all on his own," Joey mused, before I left the national bureau for the day. "If Laurier wanted to protect Rioux, he could. But he's not protecting him. My, my, the plot thickens."

I said goodnight to Joey, but no one else, as I left CP. I needed to see France. In the days leading up to, and following, Bobby Laurier's triumphant return to Canada, she had been working eighteen-hour days. I, meanwhile, had been tied up with my doomed Prince Group story. We had not seen each other much.

I reached her apartment building on Wilbrod just as it was getting dark. I didn't have the key she'd given me, so I rang the buzzer and, a few seconds later, heard her voice. "Hello?"

"Hi, it's Christopher," I said. "Can I come up?"

"Christopher!" She sounded surprised. "Um, can you hold on a minute?"

"Sure," I said, just as surprised that she didn't just buzz me in, as she always did.

A half-minute later, I heard her voice again. "I'll come down right away, okay?"

My heart sank. There was someone else in the apartment with her, and she didn't want me to know. She was going to dump me. I was about to dash away, when France suddenly appeared at the security door. She looked as beautiful as ever, but slightly distracted.

"Hi," she said, stepping outside. She didn't try to kiss me.

"Hi," I responded. "Is there something wrong?"

She couldn't look at me, because she knew that I knew, I guess. "No, nothing," she said. "Do you, um, think something is wrong?"

"Don't jerk me around, France," I barked, feeling a flash of anger. I decided to leave before I said something stupid. "I think it was a bad idea for me to come by like this, okay? I'll see you around."

I had walked down the steps when she called to me. "Chris," she said, still clinging to the door. "I think the two of you should meet. Then maybe you'll see how juvenile you are being."

I didn't look at her. "Fine," I replied. "Give him my number. I'm listed in the yellow pages, under 'suckers,' okay?"

I started the long walk home.

*　　*　　*

In Ottawa, bureaucrats — and, after they've spent enough time with the bureaucrats, politicians, too — like to use certain words. They chatter endlessly about *streamlining* things, or *restructuring* them. They prattle on and on about reducing costs through the elimination of *overruns,* and — a big favourite — *waste and duplication.* They talk in a language most of the rest of us do not understand, declaring that they were planning to do things like *recalibrate the regulatory network.* I actually heard one of Ross Hamilton's ministers say that, once.

The two words bureaucrats and governing politicians most adore, however, are these: *top secret.* They love to stamp documents, no matter how inconsequential, no matter how bland, TOP SECRET. When something was stamped TOP SECRET, you see, it could not be disclosed to the great unwashed. It became what was called a "cabinet confidence," which was the most confidential of the confidential documents known to Canadian governance. Anyone who attempted to obtain one of these documents under Freedom of Information legislation would be waiting a very long time — and, if he or she ever received it, it would be censored to the point of absurdity.

But there I was, sitting at my kitchen table, looking at a document stamped TOP SECRET. It was a single page, written on Minister of Finance letterhead. ADVICE TO THE MINISTER, it was entitled. The document was dated the day I spoke to Mike Mahoney on the phone. There was another document, too. It was a handwritten memorandum dated almost three years ago, on green, environmentally friendly House of Commons letterhead. Paperclipped to the handwritten memo was a small interoffice message slip from Roger Fournier, the murdered Montreal lawyer, to Maryse Boivin, his secretary. The message slip was in French, so I wasn't too sure what it said. Something about filing in a safety deposit box, I think. But the handwritten memo — which was clearly an original, and not a copy — began with a salutation to Fournier, and ended with two initials: *J.R. Jean Rioux?*

Igor had given the two documents to me, naturally. I hadn't been the slightest bit surprised when he showed up at my door, around ten o'clock. He was still wearing his wide-brimmed hat, but the overcoat and dark glasses were gone. I invited him in, but he declined.

"There will be time for that, perhaps," he said. He gave me a thin smile.

I took the envelope containing the Finance Department memo from his extended hand, but I didn't return his smile. "I'm not so sure about that," I said. "I may be unemployed very soon. I may move elsewhere."

Igor eyed me for a moment. For lack of a better word, I would say that he almost looked fatherly. "You should be more self-confident, Mr. O'Reilly," he said. He nodded at the envelope in my hands. "The contents of that envelope will ensure that you are employed in your chosen field for a long time."

"Carswell Spence may ensure otherwise," I said.

Igor laughed at that one. It was a dry, humourless laugh. "Mr. Spence's power does not extend nearly as far as he probably thinks that it does, or as far as you apparently think it does," Igor said. "Even a man like Mr. Spence cannot stop the truth, ultimately."

"*Your* truth, you mean," I said, bitterly. "The only difference between your side, and the other side, is that your side invented someone like you first."

"Ah, well, Mr. O'Reilly, I'm sorry you feel that way," he said, shrugging. He looked away. "But you are wrong, as you journalists so often are. I am indeed someone's employee, as are you. Many years ago, my employer assisted someone who is very close to me in escaping from a dictatorship."

"Where?"

"China, but that does not matter," he said impatiently. "As I told you at our first meeting, I am fundamentally a democrat. I will not serve a tyrant."

And, with that, Igor walked down my building's hallway, and into the dark.

*   *   *

I was exhausted. I read and reread the Finance Department memo, as well as the handwritten note, at least three dozen times. I knew I had to write the story — and it was truly an explosive, incredible story — revealed in the two documents. But how? My future employment status at the Canadian Press was in considerable doubt. And Carswell Spence III had effectively placed my career on death row, from what I could see. How could I get the story printed?

I had been screening my calls most of the night. There had been a call from a desperate-sounding France, begging me to pick up the phone, but I didn't. I felt bad about that, sort of. There had also been calls from Stan Silversides, Sherry Bickle and some other friends, but I hadn't answered those, either. Only when Joey phoned did I pick up the receiver.

"Christopher, my boy, how are you?" he said, sounding as if he had decided to cheer me up. "Jean Rioux was calling you at the office all evening, you rascally pup, trying to get you to take his job offer. You should call him back, you know. It's only common courtesy."

"Ha ha, very funny," I said. "What did happen at the office, after I left? Have they cleaned out my desk, yet?"

"Uh, no, but you certainly are the talk of the town this evening," he said. "Some are hailing you as a champion of journalism. And others ... well, let's not talk about the others, shall we?"

"What is Kevin saying?" I asked.

"Do you really wish to know?"

"No, I asked you because I really *don't* want to know," I said. "Tell me, okay? And don't lie, because you're a terrible liar."

"That's what my beloved spouse tells me," he said. He sighed. "Kevin was fielding calls all evening from Toronto, I believe, calling for your termination and the immediate termination of my contract."

"They're after you, too? You didn't leak anything to Nils Andersen!"

"Carswell Spence's reach is a long one, dear boy," he said, sounding very sad. "You shouldn't be surprised. Journalism — truly free journalism — disappeared in this country long ago. That is what happens when one or two men control most of the media organizations in Canada."

"So what is Kevin going to do to us? Are we going to get fired?"

"I don't think so," Joey said. "He's a good man, you know, Christopher. I know you are annoyed with him at the moment. But I also know he is fighting hard for you and me. The whole news room knows that he is."

I thought about that for a while. It was time to let Joey in on my little secret — and to show him the documents Igor had given to me. I told him that he should come over right away. "I have something to show you," I said.

"I thought you would never ask," he said. "I'll be there in a jiffy."

*   *   *

I approached the door to the national bureau at about 8:00 A.M., my usual time. I was beyond exhaustion. Joey and I had been up most of the night, writing the outlines of the story contained in Igor's documents. He had finally fallen asleep on my couch at around 5:00 A.M. I snatched a couple of hours of rest, then left a note and a key on top of Joey's car keys. I headed towards the office. As I approached the front door to CP's bureau, I saw her: tall, gorgeous, miserable. It was France. Her eyes were bloodshot, as if she had been crying. She spoke first.

"Why didn't you return my calls, you asshole? What is going on with you?" She seemed as if she was ready to belt me, right there in the middle of the sidewalk on O'Connor Street.

"I'm sorry I didn't call you back," I mumbled. "I was being a jerk. But I guess I was sick of being used ..."

"*Used?* Are you saying that *I* used *you*? Was I *using* you when we were in bed, you stupid jerk? Did I *use* you when you got that information out of me?" She looked as if she was ready to cry again. A couple of heads turned our way. Not wanting to get us into the next issue of *Hank* magazine — its sources were littered throughout the Press Gallery — I quietly suggested we talk later in the day.

"*No!* I want to talk about this right now! I love you, and I want you to tell me what's going on, right now!"

"France, I love you, too, okay? But I have to go in right now and talk to my boss, because there's apparently a push on to get me fired," I said, holding her arms. "But I want to get something printed before they fire me, okay? After they fire me, you will have me around twenty-four hours a day, because you'll be supporting both of us. That is, if you still want me."

She wasn't amused by my feeble attempt at humour. "Fire you? Who wants to fire you?" she asked, then realized. "Rioux! He's the one, isn't he, that bastard ..."

"France, we took on some very powerful, very wealthy people, okay? We shouldn't be surprised by any of this," I said. I gave her a long hug. "Look, I have to go. Let's talk later, okay? Okay?"

Reluctantly, she agreed. We kissed, and she started walking down Wellington Street towards the Langevin Block. I watched her for a minute, really loving her, and then dashed into the bureau.

Kevin was there at his desk, as I had known he would be. He was sombre and alone, scanning the morning's papers, most of which carried front-page accounts of the exchange in the House of Commons between Jean Rioux and Nils Andersen. I knew that one paper, the *Star*, had done a quick story on the Prince Group. An anonymous source there — probably Avie Fleischmann — had confirmed that the controversy surrounding the lobbying and communications firm had started to drive away some clients. Avie, Joey had heard, had decided to quit the place. Good for him. He was always too honest to belong in a dump like that.

Kevin looked up at me before I could knock at his door. "You look terrible," he said. "Are you all right?"

"I'm fine," I said. "Do you have some time? We need to talk about something."

"Have a seat," he replied, pointing at a chair. "And close the door behind you."

I did so, then reached into my inner jacket pocket and pulled out Igor's envelope and handed it to him.

TOP SECRET
MEMORANDUM TO THE MINISTER OF FINANCE

Surveillance conducted on behalf of the office of the Minister by the investigative firm of Fournier LaBelle Ltée of Montreal, in which Roger Fournier maintained a controlling interest, has confirmed that Christopher O'Reilly of the Canadian Press has been contacted by an unknown source or sources having access to the files of Mr. Fournier. Telephonic and visual surveillance of O'Reilly strongly suggests that this individual is [*here the memorandum, likely authored by Mike Mahoney, gave what I now suspected was Igor's real name*]. In light of this, Fournier LaBelle were immediately retained, as per instructions, to destroy any and all evidence contained in Roger Fournier's files relating to Plan 829.

Following our libel warning sent to the Canadian Press, as discussed, we did not expect O'Reilly to leak a version of his own news story to the NDP. This was ultimately unavoidable, but the P.G. is prepared to sue Nils Andersen should he continue to pursue the matter outside the privileged forum of the House. Walt Hume is aware.

All relevant memoranda, documents, etc. were located and destroyed by Fournier LaBelle, save and except those which formed the basis of O'Reilly's story published prior to Christmas. Still missing from the documentary inventory, however, is the original copy of the draft memorandum written in 1991. A representative of Fournier LaBelle attended at the location of Roger Fournier's private safety deposit box in Place Ville Marie on yesterday's date with Maryse Boivin, but found it empty. Mrs. Boivin speculated that the safety deposit box had already been emptied by the Montreal police.

Fournier LaBelle have informed us that Mrs. Boivin's brother-in-law is Montreal police Inspector Etienne Cadieux.

The top secret memorandum ended there. Inspector Cadieux, I suspected, was a Bobby Laurier fan. When the Montreal cops determined that the document was unrelated to Roger Fournier's murder, they passed it along to someone else — probably the RCMP. The handwritten 1991 memo, meanwhile — the one presumably referred to in Mahoney's own memorandum — opened with a salutation that read: *"Cher ———."* No name had been filled in.

> In recent weeks, I have received calls and correspondence from many of you. You have told me of your growing frustration with the current leadership. It is a frustration I certainly share. Unless we deal with this situation quickly and decisively, Canada's future generations will be immeasurably poorer.
>
> We must act. We must do all that we can, selflessly, to ensure that leadership is returned to Canadian public life.
>
> To do so, your help is urgently required. Along with any financial assistance you can offer — and such assistance is always needed — a number of other concrete steps are being planned. These include:
>
> 1. Exposure in the media of the shortcomings of various Opposition loyalists;
>
> 2. Cultivation of key media contacts;
>
> 3. Establishment of a communications/lobbying agency to assist us in getting our key messages disseminated;
>
> 4. Targeted fundraising with key corporations, secured through their involvement in policy development;
>
> 5. And other measures we deem necessary.

The memorandum went on from there, overflowing with lots of language about the divine mission of the 829 Club, and then concluded with what could only be Jean Rioux's initials. Significantly, points one through five had each been covered with a large red X. But they were still readable. From what I could tell, the memo seemed to have been some sort of a funds solicitation that Rioux's office never sent out — but, stupidly, incredibly, gave to his lawyer Roger Fournier for safekeeping. I watched Kevin Ritchie read the memos, his eyes widening behind his wire-rims.

"Jesus Christ," he said. Kevin, who looked pale, almost never used profanity. He stared at the two memos. "This is extraordinary. I have never seen anything like this. I can't believe Rioux would be idiotic enough to put this kind of thing on paper! Are these real?" He paused. "Maybe the person who gave them to you faked them, Chris. Maybe we're being used here."

"Believe me, the thought has occurred to me," I said. "But I'm almost certain they're genuine." I waited. "So what do we do, Kevin? Then again, maybe I should first ask whether I'm still employed here."

He glared at me. "Of course you are," he said. "What are you talking about?"

"Never mind," I said. I was tired. "Joey, who is still probably asleep on my couch, stayed up all night with me writing a story about all of this. All it requires is comment from the PMO and Rioux's office." I handed the story, written on my laptop at home, over to him. "Will you print it? Or will our lawyers let it be printed? Or, more appropriately, will the CP brass permit it to be printed?"

"Christopher," Kevin said, annoyed, looking me in the eye. "One of my own reporters has apparently been under illegal surveillance by a minister of the Crown. That alone is news, and certainly grounds for his dismissal from cabinet. If this checks out, you should know that I will print it, whether our lawyers approve or not. And I can say that I certainly don't appreciate your insinuation that I am Carswell Spence's property."

"I apologize, then," I responded. "That's not what I meant."

"Apology accepted," he said, scanning our story. "Now, once you and your sleeping friend get this story completed, I think it would be proper for us to supply copies of these documents to the Prime Minister's Office. The RCMP will be coming after us with a search warrant for them, anyway. What do you think?"

I stood up to call Joey. "Oh, I don't think you have to worry about notifying Bobby Laurier about this stuff," I said, wearily rubbing my eyes. "Something tells me that he already knows about it."

*   *   *

Our story was placed on the wire by Kevin Ritchie, personally, while Question Period was under way. Kevin had edited the story himself. Only Joey's byline was used, because I had become the subject of the story.

Finance minister ordered illegal
surveillance of Canadian Press reporter
By Joey Myers, the Canadian Press

OTTAWA — The office of Finance minister Jean Rioux, already under a cloud of suspicion for alleged budget leaks and links to a shadowy lobbying firm, is reeling this after-noon after disclosure of a document stating that he or his officials ordered an illegal wiretap on the phone line of a Canadian Press reporter.

The top secret document, obtained by the Canadian Press, also states that Canadian Press reporter Christopher O'Reilly, who has been probing Rioux's links to the Prince Group lobbying firm, has been the target of "visual surveil-lance" by a Montreal detective agency.

The Montreal detective agency, Fournier LaBelle Ltée, refused any comment on the matter. But Mike Mahoney, a senior Rioux aide, said only "Oh my God" when reached for comment. He hung up and no Rioux officials would return repeated Canadian Press calls this afternoon ...

Before we placed the story on the wire, Kevin gave me permission to send a ten-minute advance warning to Nils Andersen. I reached a House of Commons page, and urgently requested that she tell him Chris O'Reilly was on the line. Thirty seconds later, Nils was on the phone in the Opposition Lobby, out of breath. He was getting ready to ask someone on the government side — Rioux was still absent, as was Bobby Laurier — for a judicial inquiry into the Budget leak story. He would probably get one, too, if parliamentary tradition meant anything, anymore. I briefly summarized the contents of our story for him, as well as the two Igor documents. Nils scribbled down notes, asking me to repeat one or two points. "Holy shit, Chris," he whispered, not wanting to be overheard by a nosy Tory or Bloc aide. "This is fucking amazing. They had you under surveillance?"

"That's what we lead the story with, Nils," I said. "Can you use it?"

"Can I use it? Can I use it?" He laughed uproariously. "I'd give my left nut to use this one!"

"Well, give them hell, Nils," I said.

Joey, Kevin and I watched QP along with a few other reporters and editors present in the office. I knew I was about to see something historic — if Nils Andersen caught the attention of the Speaker, that is — but I was so tired, I wasn't excited. Just tired, and a little disillusioned. Ottawa: once a happy little lumber town, now the centre of evil in the known universe.

Joey clapped enthusiastically. He was wearing one of my clean dress shirts, which was stretched dangerously at his belly. "Nils got recognized by the Speaker! Here we go, fellas!"

Nils stood, buttoned his jacket, smoothed his hair, sipped at his water glass. Unlike yesterday, there was no need for him to wait for quiet. The place was so silent, all we could hear was the hiss of the television.

"Mr. Speaker, I am holding a story just placed on the Canadian Press news wire," Nils finally intoned. He certainly sounded convincing. "This story states, Mr. Speaker, that the Minister of Finance or his officials approved of an illegal wiretap on the phone of a Canadian Press reporter — because that reporter was getting too close to the truth about the ministry's relationship with the Prince Group, and the lack of Budget secrecy ..."

A rumble went through the House. Around Nils, members of the NDP, Conservatives and Reform Party stared at him, mouths agape. He continued, a flush growing in his cheeks: "Mr. Speaker, why in the name of *God* is the minister not here to answer my question?"

The Speaker cut him off; it was against the rules to point out that a member of Parliament was absent. But the damage had been done. The

House erupted with a massive, animal roar; parliamentary decorum went out the window. It didn't matter whether Nils asked anything else.

Kevin shook my hand, then Joey's. "Gentlemen, good work," he said. "My bet is that Mr. Rioux won't last twenty-four hours."

Joey looked happier than I had ever seen him. "My own educated guess is six hours," he retorted, giggling.

"Whatever," Kevin said, smiling. "I think the two of you should get ready for some interview requests. Especially you, Chris."

I shrugged, looking down at the pink message slip in my hands. "There's someone I have to see first," I replied. "I'll be back in an hour."

*   *   *

Charles Lafontaine, who had left the message for me, had said the navy Buick would be waiting for me in the alleyway that bisected the Langevin Block, and it was. Without a word, the driver — an RCMP officer in plainclothes, I guessed — closed the door behind me and we drove along Wellington, past the Château Laurier, and turned up Sussex Drive.

I had never been inside the fence at 24 Sussex Drive, nor had I ever been in a chauffeured government car. Today was a day for firsts.

Charles Lafontaine greeted me warmly at the door to the Prime Minister's residence. He was tall, with white hair, a friendly smile and an almost regal bearing. "Mr. O'Reilly," he said, shaking my hand. "How nice to meet you. It is good of you to come on such short notice."

I didn't know what to say. I was nervous, so I just shrugged.

He ushered me in through the salmon-coloured vestibule. Ahead, there was some sort of a sunroom. To the right, another room; to the left, the PM's study, where Lafontaine led me. He knocked on the door, gave me a friendly smile, then walked away. I opened the door, slowly. I was terrified. Why had I been summoned to the Prime Minister's residence?

I walked into the room, my heart in my mouth. I felt faint. Sitting on an overstuffed armchair was Bobby Laurier, looking better than he had at the airport. A few feet past the chair, near a wall of books and watching me intently, was Igor. Bobby Laurier stood to shake my hand.

"Chris," he said, smiling broadly. "Tanks for coming. I tink you know Mr. Lajoie, eh?" He gestured over his shoulder at Roland Lajoie, France's father. Briefly, I recalled the photo of the three of them wearing cowboy hats, at the leadership convention in Calgary. The photo had been on France's mantelpiece the first time I visited her apartment, of course; after "Igor" contacted me, it had disappeared. France, I suddenly thought, must have been in on all of this. I didn't shake hands with "Igor," and he didn't try to shake hands with me. We just looked at each other.

Bobby Laurier steered me towards a chair and I sat down. He offered me some coffee. Normally, I didn't drink much of the stuff. But I thought the caffeine might help me keep a clear head.

Before I could say a word, there was a knock on the door I had used. The door opened slowly — and France stepped through. We all stood as she looked around, her eyes wide.

"Daddy? Chris? What ..."

From the expression on her face, it was clear that France had not been expecting a meeting with her employer, her father and her boyfriend. Laurier walked over to her and led her into the room. She embraced her father, then looked at me. She still appeared bewildered. "France, I asked for you an' Chris to come 'ere to explain a couple o' tings," Laurier said, gently. "Have a seat, hokay?"

Quietly, France slid onto the couch beside me; her father continued standing in the corner, watching us, sipping at a cup of coffee. Laurier returned to his chair.

"So, dis is all off de record, right, Chris?" he said, still smiling, but his eyes clear.

"Yes," I replied. "Nobody would ever believe it, anyway."

Laurier laughed and looked at his watch. "So Jean Rioux wants to meet wit' me in a little while. What do you tink it is about?"

"My guess is he plans to offer you his resignation," I said, feeling a return of the anger that had been with me ever since my last meeting with Roland Lajoie at Lansdowne Park, on the football field. It was on that evening that I had started to finally realize that *I* had been *used*. It wasn't my skill as a journalist that had been responsible for the amazing scoops that had come my way; rather, every bit of information I had received had been almost literally dropped in my lap — because someone, somewhere, knew I was gullible enough to use it. Bobby Laurier, I suspected, was that someone. Some investigative reporter *I* am. "I suppose that was the plan all along, wasn't it, Mr. Laurier? To get Jean Rioux out of the way."

"No, no, no, Chris, not at all," he said, looking wounded. "Jean had a big power base in de party, you know. Lots of big companies who make donations, lots of powerful people. He kept in touch wit dat power base — although, unfortunately for him, he kept in touch in writing on one occasion." Laurier looked over at his old friend Roland Lajoie and grinned; Lajoie smiled thinly and looked away.

"You see, Chris," Laurier said, continuing, "I don't like Jean very much, dat's true. But, even as Prime Minister, I don't have de power to just get rid of him. A big fight between us would've destroyed de party, an' de Tories would've won de election, an' so on. The Liberal Party only survives if it keeps all its parts togedder, you know. Dat's politics."

"That's what my father used to say."

"Your father was a good man, and a good friend to me," Laurier said. He paused for a minute. "Jean is de author of his own ... what do you call it?"

"Misfortune," France responded.

"Yeah, misfortune," he said. "He screwed himself. Canadians don' like it when a guy gets too ambitious, you know? And dey don' like it when he tries to steal a guy's job, when dat guy is in a hospital bed."

Nobody said anything for a while. I watched Laurier refill his coffee cup, marvelling at him. I, like every other opponent he had ever faced — including my father, at a moot-court contest, many years before — had seriously underestimated him. All of this time, I had assumed he was just the nice old guy of Canadian politics — one who had achieved the prime-ministerial post through luck, and persistence, more than anything else. A nice old guy who was more interested in his golf game than in affairs of state; a regular guy. But I had not ever imagined he could be the man I now saw before me: a canny, cunning operator who had laid a trap for Jean Rioux, and me, and everyone else, and snared us all. *Boom.* Just like that. Niccolò Machiavelli had nothing on this guy.

The fact remained, however: I had been used. I had been used by Bobby Laurier, and his spook pal Igor, and — possibly — by France. I reflected for a quick moment, remembering that *I* had used France, too. Everybody used everybody else, which was the Ottawa way of doing things, I guess. As I sat on the couch, I forced myself not to look at her.

Bobby Laurier, sensing this, spoke. "France didn't know anyting about most of dis stuff, Chris," Laurier said. "Her father isn't the kind of guy to let dat happen. She was sent to the Prince Group party to get information for us, but not on you. And dat's the truth."

"So who gave her the document on the contracting between the Prince Group and Rioux's office, then?" I asked, making sure not to look at France. I didn't want to lose my nerve.

"I told Charles Lafontaine, my chief of staff, to give it to France," he said. "I did dat when CSIS told us dat Jean had a bunch of private detectives following you around, tapping your phone, stuff like dat. Dat made me mad. Dat, and what dey did to Annie Frosini. Dey knew what you were doing, so I figured you deserved to know what dey were doing."

"I see," I said, my mind racing. "Should I ask you how you got documents from Fournier's office, the things that were supposed to be in police possession?"

He laughed. "Hey, Chris, I'm de Prime Minister, you know? You get to know certain tings in dis job. Especially when one of your cabinet ministers is up to his ass in bad stuff."

I laughed then, too. France slipped her hand into mine and I gave it a little squeeze. "Do we know who killed Roger Fournier, then?"

Laurier shrugged. "Yeah, dat was a bad ting. The police tink it was a mafia ting. Fournier was mixed up with some bad people. Lots of gambling debts, stuff like dat. Who knows?" I doubted this explanation, but I didn't argue. It was far too neat.

"What about Annie Frosini? Will she get her job back?"

Laurier looked at his watch again. "Well, I tink dere's gonna be a cabinet shuffle pretty damn soon. So maybe it's a good time to bring her back, eh?"

"What about Walt Hume, your communications director?"

"Boy, you are filled wit' questions, you reporters," he said, rising to his feet. "Walt is going back to a job in Toronto or someting. Sudden career opportunity came up dere." He laughed.

"How about Flash Feiffer?"

"Oh, he got a little too close to de Rioux guys, I guess. But he's always been loyal to me. I'll keep him around," he said. He sounded as if he were discussing a pet.

Bobby Laurier was clearly preparing to go and meet with Jean Rioux, so I rose to my feet, too. There was only one question left. Perhaps it was a dumb question, but I had to ask it.

"Mr. Laurier," I said. "Maybe it's because I'm tired, or maybe it's because I'm naive, but don't you ever feel politics is just ... a lot of bullshit?"

He looked at me with surprise for the first time. Everything else I had said, or asked him about, had been anticipated. This hadn't been. Bobby Laurier regarded me for a few moments, his famous features revealing nothing, evidently trying to determine if I had just fallen off the proverbial turnip truck or not. Finally, he said: "Chris, let me give you some advice before I go meet wit' poor old Jean Rioux, hokay? Number one, you should marry dat girl holdin' your hand, right now, 'cause she loves you. Number two, you should get to know my friend Rollie, over dere, because he's probably gonna be your father-in-law. And number three, don't expect any big wedding presents from me, hokay?"

Everyone laughed. What a politician this guy was.

"No, you asked me a serious question, an' I should answer it," he said, gazing at the ceiling. "To me, politics is de greatest game dere is. But to other people, it's ..."

"Bullshit?" I said.

He shrugged, escorting France and me to the door. "Well, don't quote me, hokay? But I guess you could say it was a lot of bullshit. Lots of people say dat, dese days. But, to me it's the greatest game dere is. And it's important, too." He trailed off for a moment, staring into the middle distance. Abruptly, he smiled and patted me on the back. "Now, you kids go an' have some fun, hokay? I got some work to do."

*   *   *

Ottawa is an unhappy, unpleasant little place, where a lot gets said and little gets done. Although it aspires to be much more, it isn't ever going to be more than that: a former lumber town, packed with hundreds of megalomaniacs essentially lacking in souls.

Ring.

It was a cold spring day, and the sky was a flat, metallic grey. I was sitting alone on a bench in a park near Rideau Hall, overlooking the Ottawa River, thinking about my father, when my cell phone rang. I didn't answer it.

The meeting with Bobby Laurier had presumably been designed to tie up some loose ends, and make France and me feel better. But it hadn't. The day after, a morose France told me she was taking the train up to Montreal to see her mother. "I feel as if my own father used me," she told me. "I need some time off."

Ring ring. The cell phone continued to sound, and I continued to not answer it.

Mike Mahoney and Walt Hume were gone, and a parliamentary committee had pledged to look into the conduct of the Prince Group. But Jean Rioux, incredibly, was still in the cabinet. Following the meeting with Laurier, the Finance minister had gone into hiding, and no amount of complaining by the Press Gallery or the Opposition would flush him out. Bobby Laurier, meanwhile, wasn't commenting on the matter. The House was on a scheduled week-long break, so that helped him, I suppose.

It was still possible, of course, that Jean Rioux was not long for political life, and had been given a few days to pack his bags, prior to a return to the anonymity of corporate law in Montreal. But it had surprised and disappointed me that Laurier had not taken swift, decisive action, and booted Rioux out. Joey and I had discussed it on the evening France returned to Montreal. In his view, Laurier was smart enough to know that it was better to keep a wounded Rioux inside the government, with the Prime Minister's control over the Finance minister now absolute. If Rioux left Ottawa, Joey suggested, he would be better able to launch openly a jihad against his long-time rival. My view was that Rioux would be offered the Annie Frosini option: to resign, clear his name if he could and return.

At the moment, I didn't much care. The wreckage of the past few days still loomed large, to me. The ease with which unseen forces had used me, and abused me, had left me feeling like a rank amateur. A kid.

I had come to Ottawa with the belief that the good guys and the bad guys were readily distinguishable, and that my job would be to chronicle the achievements of the former, and the misdeeds of the latter. But it hadn't worked out that way. The demands of public office, I had learned, required that good guys occasionally — and sometimes more than occasionally — adopt the methods of the bad guys. Certainly that had been the conclusion reached by my father, about halfway through his tenure on Parliament's backbenches.

Bobby Laurier wasn't all saint, and Jean Rioux probably wasn't all villain. They were, however, political men, prepared to cut ethical corners to satisfy the demands of ego and ambition. In that regard, I knew, I was a little like them, too. In my headlong pursuit of The Big Story, I hadn't looked upwards long enough to notice that someone was pulling my strings.

Ring ring ring. The phone had stopped for a while, and now it had started chirping anew. Who was it? I guessed that it was either Joey, to tell me Rioux's fate; or France, to tell me she was staying in Montreal for good, or that she was coming back; or my mother to see whether I was all right.

I answered the phone. It wasn't any of those. It was Kevin Ritchie, my boss. "How are you, Chris?"

"Fine, Kevin," I said. "Thanks for giving me the day off."

"Well," he replied, "I'm about to withdraw the offer, I'm afraid. I'm short-staffed, and I've got a story that needs writing. Are you interested?"

To my surprise — to my amazement — I was. "As long as it isn't about Jean Rioux, or secretive lobbying firms, or Liberal Party fratricide, I'm there," I said.

Kevin laughed. "It's about none of those," he responded.

"Then I'll see you within the hour," I said, and he hung up. I sat on the bench for another minute or two, watching the river. Then I stood up and began the long walk back to Parliament Hill.